**NIGHTINGALE'S S**

Celia gasped.

She really had not considered marriage
—had not dreamed that this fascinating and
wonderful young man who was her father's
trusted and brilliant partner—would ever want
to *marry* her. She was dumbfounded. She had
never before received a proposal of marriage.
She was used to hovering in the background,
watching some more attractive girl-friend enjoy
being the focus of attention. With Philippe's kiss
still hot on her lips, she felt that she had been
transported into realms she had never before
entered. She could not easily accustom herself
to them. The pace had been too swift and the
dawning of her own susceptibilities and
sensuous enjoyment too sudden and startling.

**Also by the same author,
and available in Coronet Books:**

# Nightingale's Song

---

# Denise Robins

**CORONET BOOKS**
Hodder and Stoughton

Copyright © 1963 by Denise Robins

First published in Great Britain by
Hodder and Stoughton 1963

Coronet Edition 1966
Second impression 1969
Third impression 1976

Printed and bound in Great Britain for
Coronet Books, Hodder and Stoughton, London
by Richard Clay (The Chaucer Press), Ltd,
Bungay Suffolk

ISBN 0 340 01437 7

FOR MY DELIGHTFUL COUSIN
FELICITY JEWELL

# ONE

THE moment that Celia came down to breakfast, her aunt, Miss Cotland, who had just finished scrambling the eggs, knew that the girl had had a bad night.

Miss Cotland loved Celia dearly and was grieved for her. She knew quite well that Celia had been sleeping badly. She was worrying; she was going through a bad phase. She was completely unsure of herself. And although Miss Cotland had little use for ultra-modern psychology, she had to agree there *was* such a thing as an 'inferiority complex'. Celia had one! However, Miss Cotland's way of coping with the niece who lived with her, was to be tolerant and good-humoured.

'Good morning, my pet,' she said cheerfully. 'How nice you look! I like that suit. Is it new?'

Celia Frayne flushed and gave a brief resentful glance at herself in the mirror that hung at that end of the kitchen which they called their 'dinette'. She said:

'Aunt Tiny—*really*, you know it isn't new. And it doesn't fit anywhere—like me. *I* don't fit anywhere.'

Miss Cotland turned to the stove to hide the consternation in her eyes. Shrewd, kindly eyes behind horn-rimmed glasses. Celia *was* in a mood this morning. Poor child! She had been out to a party last night. Something must have happened to upset her.

'Well, you fit in beautifully in Flat 1, Dendham Court, Battersea, S.W.,' she said, with gay emphasis on the address of the little home which they shared. It had belonged to Miss Cotland before the war and was still at a low rent. But enough for her slender purse. All that Miss Cotland had was the small amount of money she had inherited from her father who had been a doctor in this very part of London. She took in a little dressmaking to swell the exchequer. Celia, whom she had adopted when her mother died, fourteen years ago, earned good money as a shorthand-typist with a firm of insurance brokers.

A deep affection existed between aunt and niece. Celia, stirring her tea, felt slightly better just at the sight of this dear, friendly aunt, who at fifty was angular and too tall, with shortish grey hair, and a face already wrinkled. She stooped a little

7

because of her height. It was a family joke that she had been christened 'Tiny'. The name had stuck to her despite the fact that she had grown to six feet tall. But in her case her character and personal charm triumphed over lack of looks. Behind her plain exterior she had a warm generosity and kindliness which endeared her to all her friends—and particularly to her niece.

This morning especially, Celia wondered what she would do without Aunt Tiny. She began to confide her reasons for her extra depression.

'I wish I had never gone to that party,' she said.

'Ah!' said Miss Cotland. 'But why? You looked so attractive in your yellow taffeta.'

Celia choked over a mouthful of toast and gulped down her tea. This was where she could never be quite frank with Aunt Tiny. She made all Celia's clothes, but they were never quite right. They lacked *chic*; Celia knew it. She never lacked boyfriends but they seemed to want to *talk* rather than make love to her. That wasn't much fun! She knew she was intelligent. She could be witty and amusing when she tried. But that didn't seem to be what the boys wanted. They preferred you to be *glamorous* and to suggest 'sex'. Celia didn't suggest it. She didn't talk about it. She didn't appear to want it.

She began to tell Aunt Tiny about one boy who, after dancing with her, discussed her with another girl and Celia overheard.

'Did you see what I got in the Paul Jones just now? That one in yellow. Celia Something-or-other. She had nice eyes and attractive hair, but what a *grim* dress. Awkward kind of kid.'

Not very flattering but the girl's reply had been even more crushing.

'*I think it's desperate shyness that's against Celia. She lives with an elderly aunt who doesn't seem to have the know-how, so poor Celia hasn't got it either. Personally I think she is attractive but . . .*'

That was all that Celia had waited to hear. She had felt sick and rushed away. She went home. She meant to tell them at the office this morning that it was because she had not felt well. She told the story to Aunt Tiny—with reservations. Not for the world would she let dear Aunt Tiny think that her yellow dress had been criticised.

Her aunt tried to comfort her.

'Don't believe a word anybody says. You looked sweet and one day you will meet a boy who thinks you're the cat's whiskers—like I do.'

Miss Cotland meant it. She was certain that Celia had possibilities. How right, for instance, that boy had been about Celia's hair. It was thick and wavy and looked like polished copper. And those wide-set eyes which were smoky-grey—they were beautiful. How could anybody say that Celia wasn't pretty? Miss Cotland couldn't think why things always went wrong for Celia. But Celia knew. It hadn't needed last night's disaster to tell her. She dressed badly. Her hair wasn't well cut. She walked badly. She was not good at parties. Yet Mr. Flack, to whom she was personal secretary, was always telling her that she was the perfect secretary.

Gloomily Celia looked at Aunt Tiny. Dear, darling Aunty T. as she sometimes called her—she was no advertisement for her own dressmaking. She would wear knitted twin-sets that had gone out of shape, and skirts almost to her ankles which make her look so elongated. No man had ever proposed to Tiny Cotland. She admitted it. But she said cheerfully that she didn't care. She liked being an old maid. Celia didn't believe it. She knew that *she*, herself, *did* want to get married. She had all the capacity for love.

A knock on the door brought Aunt Tiny to her feet.

She returned from the hall with a circular and a letter bearing a French stamp.

'Here's something to cheer you up, very foreign-looking. Have you a friend in France, duckie?'

'No,' said Celia and took the envelope and blinked at it.

*Monaco.* For a moment she stared at it, remembering how often she and Aunt Tiny had looked at their neighbour's television and seen Prince Rainier and beautiful Princess Grace and Monte Carlo harbour. All that splendour, that glamour— the incarnation of any woman's secret dreams.

Feeling suddenly thrilled, Celia slit the envelope so as not to tear the stamp.

She read only a few words, flushed scarlet, turned over the thin foreign-looking sheets of paper and blinked dazedly at the signature. Then she gave a cry.

'Oh! Aunt *Tiny*, this is from my *father*! I can't *believe* it!'

Miss Cotland, most placid of women, confessed to her own heart missing a beat.

'My goodness gracious me—*no*!'

Celia sprang up, went round to her aunt and spread the letter out on the table.

'Let's read it together.'

'So he's still alive!' exclaimed Miss Cotland, adjusting her horn-rims. 'How on earth has he traced you after all these years?'

'Goodness knows!' breathed Celia.

Her black mood had passed. Yesterday's frustrations and miseries were forgotten. It was as though a miracle had taken place in the little flat in Battersea this bright April morning.

Celia could not remember her father. He had walked out of her mother's life, and hers—when she was only two. Of course she had seen a photograph of him; the one taken with her mother on their wedding day. That had been two years before the Second World War. He looked rather a sulky young man with thick curly hair and intense eyes. All that she had ever heard about him from Mummy was that he had been 'too much for her'.

Poor Mummy was a bit like me, Celia often thought; too shy and reserved. She had found it difficult to express herself. She and Daddy just couldn't get on. But Mummy had admitted that Daddy had a flame of genius in him. An engineer by profession, he had possessed a quick inventive mind. In a good job, with a big firm, but always pressed for time, always frustrated. Always bringing home new gadgets of his own making. When they moved to London he got a better-paid job but still found no scope for his real ambitions, his unusual brilliance. Then one day he vanished. Celia's mother had never seen him again. Three years later, a letter came from Nat Frayne—from Chicago—asking Mary to divorce him for desertion. Typical of the hard ruthless man he was, he avoided sentiment, told her nothing except that he had at last found his *milieu* in America, and he would never return to her. Aunt Tiny once mentioned to Celia that 'poor Mary had never had the spirit to be malicious'. In her negative timorous fashion she gave him a divorce. Afterwards all she ever knew about her strange husband was that he paid her alimony regularly into her bank. Once she died, the money stopped. Aunt Tiny adopted Celia. All these years, like her aunt, Celia had believed that she would never see her father again. But now he appeared to be very much alive, and living in France. What could be more exciting, she asked herself?

Miss Cotland began to read the letter aloud:

'*My dear Celia,*

'*I am a man of few words so wish to be brief. I have traced you through a detective agency, being at last mindful of the fact that I have a daughter in the world.*

'*I was sorry to leave you, but I had either to live my life in my own way or remain at home and be crushed by domesticity. Rightly or wrongly I quit and broke every tie that bound me.*

'*I know it was wrong. A young girl like you will probably hate me for having abandoned you and your mother, but I had something to offer the world and I met an American who gave me my chance. I went with him to the States. The first invention we put on the market succeeded beyond my wildest dreams. I became a wealthy man overnight. Today I own huge factories in several capitals.*

'*During the war I played my part in France, but a tricky heart put me out of action, and I went to America to make munitions. Now I am retired, virtually a millionaire. I live here in Monte Carlo in a villa overlooking the harbour.*

'*In a roundabout way I heard of your mother's death and was told that my sister-in-law adopted you, so I knew you were all right. Until now I had no wish to be involved with a daughter, so I never got in touch with you.*

'*I married again—a young and lovely French girl. I suppose I centred all my affections on her, but the full circle turned. She died in childbirth. It was a fearful blow to me and one which I imagine you will think I deserve. Now I, myself, am ill and old. My doctors tell me my heart is really bad nowadays. I may live a few years—or only a few days longer.*

'*A few weeks ago, I suddenly felt a nostalgic longing for my one and only daughter. I have no heir. I am surrounded by friends, but who is to know whether they are not sycophants or fortune-hunters? I want to leave my money to somebody who has a right to it and upon whose honesty of purpose I could rely. So I had you traced. I discovered that you were earning your living as a typist.*

'*What exactly you are like I can only guess, but you must have something of me in you—that part of me that the British always call "guts". Your poor mother had none, but you are mine as well as hers.*

'*I want you to come to Monaco to live with me at Villa Psyche. If you go to the Midland Bank (head branch in London) you will find that I have opened an account for you and paid five hundred pounds into it. Buy yourself what clothes you need, your air ticket, etc., and come to me as soon as you can. Perhaps I haven't long in which to make amends.*

'*You have much to forgive and I thank God that I can prove to you that I wish to become what I have in the past failed to be.*
*Your father,*
*Nathaniel Frayne*'

There was a P.S. to this letter:

'*Upon thinking things over I have decided that for the moment I wish to let it be thought that you are my niece. I am sure it will not be difficult for you to call me "Uncle Nat". I have seen too many wealthy young women pursued and married for their money. I intend to see that does not happen to you. Later I will publish the fact that you are my daughter—and heiress.*'

Miss Cotland finished reading and looked up.

'Did you ever! Nat Frayne alive and a millionaire. Well, he always swore he'd invent a world-shaker, and he's done it . . .'

'And he wants me to join him in Monte Carlo!' Celia gasped.

Aunt Tiny stood up. She had to admit that she was shaken. But she said:

'I couldn't be more glad for you, duckie.'

'But I don't think I shall go. He left my mother and me. I despise him.'

Miss Cotland smiled at the flushed passionate young face. Ironically she thought that it took a cyclone to infuse this brilliance into Celia. The pale sulky young girl who had come into breakfast was transformed.

'Don't judge him too harshly, child. Nat was always a bit cracked and unreliable. Morally, nobody could excuse his actions. But your poor mother was a weak timid girl and Nat just could never take weakness. He and I, as a matter of fact, were quite friendly. In a way I understood him, sorry though I was for poor Mary.'

'I couldn't like him,' persisted Celia.

'You will. Everybody adored Nat. As a matter of fact, you've got quite a lot of him in you, Celia. You're physically brave. You're intelligent. And you'll soon blossom out once you start leading a new life with him in a place like Monte Carlo.'

'No—I heard the truth last night!' said Celia, biting her lips. 'I know I'm too ordinary for my father. I'd disappoint him.'

'No—I know Nat. He'll infuse you with some of his own

supreme self-confidence. Look child—there's £500 waiting for you in the bank. We'll buy you a trousseau, and fly you over to Monte Carlo, looking as the daughter of a tycoon should.'

'But what about this business of being called his niece?'

'Nat was always a wise one. I can see his point. He doesn't want the men to make a rush because they think you're an heiress.'

'I admit I'd hate to be married for money,' muttered Celia.

She was in a daze. This letter from Monte Carlo seemed to have dropped from the skies. In one way it terrified her, in another it excited and thrilled her because of its staggering possibilities. She was critical of her father's past behaviour; but as Aunty T. said, who was she to judge him too hastily. And if he wanted to make up for it all now, how could she deny him? Besides what right had she to deny *herself* the chance he offered.

She caught her aunt by the hand.

'But how can I leave *you* all alone, Aunty T?'

Miss Cotland turned to the sink and made a great to-do by swooshing hot water over the dirty crockery. Not for worlds would she let Celia see there were tears in her eyes, or guess that she dreaded the very thought of being left here, alone. Celia was as dear to her as her own daughter. She had always been such an affectionate little thing—such a real home-girl. They had shared their good times and their bad. The day's hard sewing and cooking for Miss Cotland had always seemed worthwhile because Celia was coming back at night.

Miss Cotland sniffed.

'I'm not so sure I shall miss you, my girl. I shall be free to find myself a nice boy-friend, and make whoopee at last,' she said gruffly. 'You sit down and write to your father and tell him you're on your way.'

# TWO

'Is there anything more that I can do for you, sir?'

Nathaniel Frayne leaned back in his chair, glanced at a pile of papers on his desk and took a cigar from a cedar-wood box open before him. He sniffed it, then rolled it against his ear, listening to the crackle of the dry leaves.

'Not another thing. I'm through for today, boy.'

'Then I think I ought to be off, sir. I've arranged for the car to take me to Nice at half past four.'

Nat Frayne lit his cigar and puffed at it for a moment without speaking. He knew that he oughtn't to be smoking. He had been warned neither to smoke nor drink alcohol, nor indulge in the rich food that he liked too well. He could feel his tired heart pumping too fast, but he refused to take any notice. To hell with doctors and gloomy prophecies of sudden death. He was fifty-five tomorrow. Queer . . . his very own daughter would be here for his birthday. She wouldn't even know that it *was* his birthday.

He glanced at the secretary who was putting some papers into a brief-case. Nice chap, Geoffrey More; what the French called *charmant garçon*. Good brain and a tireless worker. He was twenty-five and had been personal assistant to Nat for the last four years. His father, Ted More, had, like Nat, been in the engineering world and assisted Nat through some difficult times long years ago. When Ted and his wife died in an air crash, leaving the boy more or less alone in the world, Nat had offered him a home. Geoff had just come down from Oxford. He knew nothing about engineering. He had taken a degree in economics, which made him invaluable in business to Nat. He also had a love of art and literature, and these two things were Nat's passions now that he had put work behind him.

When Nat settled in the villa down here on the Riviera he started to collect paintings and antiques. For amusement he opened a splendid shop in Nice. As usual, whatever Nat Frayne touched turned to gold. *Frayne et Cie* was now a flourishing concern; the salon was visited by some of the most famous dealers in Europe. There followed branches in Paris, London and New York. Geoffrey took care of Nat's enormous correspondence when he was at home and attended to all his private business.

Power and money—those things used to be Nat Frayne's personal gods. But now he felt the need for something more. He had felt it when he married poor Marie-Thérèse, but he had lost her. He was positively excited by the idea of seeing his daughter today.

What would she be like? He hadn't even seen a photograph of her.

When Marie-Thérèse died he had learned what it was to suffer, for he had loved her. Now he was a tired sad old man. He wanted the one thing left in the world that was his own— *Celia*.

Geoffrey said:

'Weather's brilliant. Your niece should be having a perfect flight.'

Nat blinked. His niece! Yes, of course, that was how he had wanted Celia to be known.

'Okay, Geoff, cut along to the airport,' he said, and chewed on the butt of his cigar.

Geoffrey More closed the door of the study behind him. A magnificent book-lined room, air-conditioned, and with every luxury, like all the other rooms in the Villa Psyche.

Geoffrey did not always approve of Nat Frayne's ruthlessness. The young man was, himself, first and foremost a humanitarian with a sympathy for all living creatures, including animals. It amused Nat because Geoffrey was always befriending some overworked horse or neglected dog. When Nat wanted to pull his leg he called the boy 'a vet'.

Nevertheless Geoffrey—like most of his staff—was devoted to the Chief and served him with an abiding loyalty. And perhaps Geoffrey, who was so closely associated with Nat in his work, knew how lonely the great man had been since his second wife died. Geoffrey had been a little surprised to learn that Nat had 'a niece' in England and that he had sent for her. But he thought it not a bad idea. He hoped the girl would be the right sort, and look after the old man a little, and he hoped, too, that she wasn't a self-centred 'glamour-girl' like so many of them here in the golden warmth of the south. Geoffrey couldn't stand seeing them spending the whole day sunning their brown bodies on the beach, drinking endless aperitifs, wasting time and money at night in the Casinos.

He looked at his watch. Miss Frayne's plane was due in

about an hour. He would have time to bath and change before he went to the airport. He had been invited to a dinner party which the Chief was giving for his niece this evening. He was not particularly glad about that. Formal parties bored Geoffrey. And he would have preferred to spend the evening exercising the mongrel which was his own particular pet.

Geoffrey occupied a ground-floor room in an apartment house at the back of Monte Carlo, where he had lived for several years. Well looked after by *Madame* Pavette, the amusing, sharp-tongued old creature who allowed him the use of her back-garden for his animals. (Even while she made it plain that his love of animals was, to her way of thinking, *fou*. Crazy!)

In particular, Geoffrey wished that he had not got to meet Philippe Clermont . . . or the *Comtesse* Nadine de Sachelles.

Geoffrey was by nature gregarious and good-humoured, but if there was one man in the world he could not stand, it was Clermont—Nat's right-hand man and adviser in the fine arts business. Philippe looked after *Frayne's* in Nice, and sometimes accompanied Nat on a buying expedition when there was a private sale of treasures. Philippe was a nephew of the late Duc de Froganard, whose money and estates had been dissipated long before his death. Philippe had inherited nothing from him except the old Duc's exquisite taste. Nobody, even Geoffrey, who could not stand the fellow, could deny that Philippe had a flair for laying a finger on the right thing. He rarely made a mistake and he had been clever enough to teach Nat without appearing to do so. He was a master of subtlety and wit. Women adored him. Nat found him indispensable, more particularly because he was a blood relative of Marie-Thérèse, who had also been a Clermont.

Geoffrey had no jealousy in his disposition, but somehow he could not like or trust Philippe. The temperaments of the two men clashed. Geoffrey was essentially English. Philippe so smoothly, charmingly French. There were times when Geoffrey wondered whether Nat knew all there was to know about Philippe's private life, facts that Geoffrey himself was aware of. For instance, that Philippe had an old blind uncle living up in the mountains above Grasse, whom he totally ignored; and that he had been responsible for the death of a young Yugoslav girl whom he had left with an illegitimate child and completely abandoned.

Geoffrey More had found during his four years in Villa

Psyche that it was difficult not to become a cynic. One broken heart or so mattered so little to Philippe (or many other people who surrounded Nat). But to Nat, the artistic delightful Frenchman was his 'cher Philippe'. The touch of diablerie about him found, perhaps, an echo in the older man's heart—an echo of his own past.

Then there was the Comtesse, Nadine de Sachelles, who was also coming to dinner tonight. If it was irksome for Geoffrey to have to make himself agreeable to Philippe, it was even more so where Nadine was concerned.

She was a young and beautiful widow whose husband, twice her age, had died in an accident two years ago. Her father used to be one of Nat's many friends on the Riviera. Nadine was persona grata at Villa Psyche (nobody quite knew whether she came so often to see old Nat, or Philippe—or Geoffrey). Philippe was crazy about her. Everybody knew that. What they didn't know was that Geoffrey More persistently refused to number himself among her admirers.

In his opinion she was a dangerous woman. She was wonderful to look at but she was greedy. Geoffrey hated greedy women. But Nat admired her and indulged her. Queer, how the brilliant Nat managed to surround himself with the wrong friends. The late Comte de Sachelles used to be a close friend of his. And he had been a gambler—a fool who had lost most of his money at 'the Tables'. To Geoffrey, Nadine was just another of the lovely acquisitive girls who flew around the flame of Nat Frayne's wealth and position like hungry moths. He also had a shrewd suspicion that she was playing with Philippe. Nat wouldn't like that, if he knew. But it was none of Geoffrey's business.

He had been invited to the family dinner and he had to accept her. Just as he had to meet Celia Frayne—bored though he was by the prospect.

Half an hour later Geoffrey was driving in Nat's fabulous white Cadillac down the Corniche Road that wound along the spectacular coast between Monte Carlo and Nice.

The Comet bringing Celia to Nice touched down dead on time. The young girl looked to Geoffrey a trifle dazed when she finally got through the Customs and appeared in the beautiful clean French airport, and stood for a moment looking around her, doubtfully; wondering if the father whom she did not remember would recognise her after all these years. She had supposed he would meet her. All that she had received in answer to her letter, giving him the date of her arrival, was a wire which said:

'*Good. Looking forward to seeing you.*

*Uncle Nat*'

Celia had wrinkled her nose a bit over that signature and Aunt Tiny had laughed.

'Just like him. *He*'ll play the part properly, you'll see.'

But Celia saw nobody among the crowds of passengers who even faintly resembled the Nathaniel Frayne of that early photograph. She only knew that this was the first time she had set foot on French soil; that she had had a wonderful flight and that it was so warm that she could hardly bear the light summer coat she was wearing. She did so hope that she had brought the right clothes.

Then she saw a tall loose-limbed young man with a rather rough head of light brown hair and very blue eyes set in a bronzed earnest face. He was striding towards her. Not exactly handsome, she decided, his features were too irregular and his mouth too big, but he was nice-looking, what Aunt Tiny would call a 'likeable type'. He wore a thin light suit that might be called Continental, and a very English-looking tie.

Face to face with her, he said:

'Are you by any chance Miss Frayne?'

'Yes,' said Celia breathlessly.

His furrowed brow cleared.

'Good. I was wondering if I had missed you. I'm Geoffrey More—your uncle's private secretary.'

She understood now. 'Uncle Nat' had sent this young man to meet her.

'What about your luggage?' added Geoffrey.

She pointed to the two brand new suitcases lying on the ground beside her. (What a thrill it had been buying them with Aunt Tiny.) Geoffrey looked surprised. Unusual for a fashionable female not to have a lot more luggage than this, he would have thought. But he supposed that the Chief's niece could hardly be called fashionable. *Au contraire.* She was rather nondescript and young-looking. She had a small innocent face, and *grâce à Dieu*, thought Geoffrey, she bore no resemblance to any of the glamorous young things he was used to seeing down here on the Riviera. *Mediocre English tourist* was written all over Celia Frayne. Printed silk dress with matching navy blue coat. White cloche hat, white bag, floral silk scarf—it gave

Geoffrey a bit of a shock to find a niece of Nat Frayne's looking so *ordinary*. She seemed shy, too. She bent to pick up a case. He bent to take it from her. Their heads knocked together.

'Oh, I say—frightfully sorry! Did I hurt you?' from Geoffrey, his face red.

'It was my fault,' from Celia, equally red.

Then they looked into each other's eyes. Celia felt more nervous and stupid than usual, but Geoffrey More decided suddenly that Celia Frayne was not so ordinary after all. She had lovely grey eyes, and with his intuitive compassion for the timid, the forlorn, the *difficult* people in this world, he was drawn to her.

'Poor little thing,' he thought, 'she's the type that just can't cope . . . immature, I'd say. Nat isn't going to be impressed.'

Quickly he led the way into the sunlight. When Celia saw the white and silver gleaming Cadillac she gasped:

'Is *that* my . . . my uncle's car?' (It was still not coming easily to call her own father by that name.)

'That's only one of 'em,' said Geoffrey cheerfully.

'He must be terribly rich,' Celia sighed and settled back against the pale blue leather cushions luxuriously.

'Right first time,' laughed Geoffrey, 'he *is*.'

'How *awful*!' said Celia, and now she too laughed and the young man thought that it was a pretty unaffected laugh, and that when this girl smiled, she had charm.

'Do you think it's so awful to be rich?'

'Well, I never have been, so I don't know.'

'Same here.'

'I'm just a shorthand-typist,' she confided.

He liked the simple directness of that confidence.

'I'm one of the world's workers, too,' he grinned. 'But make no mistake, your uncle has had to work mighty hard to get where *he's* got, and from the bottom, he told me. He's terrific.'

'I've never seen him. This will be the first time,' said Celia. 'He—he left England when I was nearly three.'

'Oh, well,' said Geoffrey, 'life in the Villa Psyche will be an eye-opener for you, Miss Frayne.'

'It terrifies me,' she admitted.

Geoffrey thought: 'It will terrify her still more after she has had dinner tonight with Nadine de Sachelles and Philippe Clermont. They'll seem to her like people from another world. Poor little shorthand-typist from London! It won't be fair.

She'll be flummoxed. But I suppose this is the Chief's idea of giving his niece a holiday.'

Now Celia gazed dumbfounded at the passing scenery. The Cadillac rolled smoothly along the lower Corniche Road which led from Nice to Mentone. Never in her life had Celia seen such green palm trees, vivid flowers and elegant, shuttered villas. And once away from the crowded town it all seemed even more glorious. Her eyes were dazzled by the blueness of the sea; the sparkle of the hot sun upon the beaches and rocks below; the palatial hotels and the famous white Casino.

She kept uttering little cries of delight.

'Oh, look at that marvellous creeper all over the walls.'

'*Bougainvillaea*,' said Geoffrey a little astonished by her ignorance, but wishing he had her capacity for enjoying what was to him a monotonous sight. He had long since grown tired of the glitter of the *Côte d'Azur*.

'All this is very artificial really,' he added, 'but before your holiday ends you'll have to go up to the hills—see the real Midi. The olive groves, the fields of carnations, the lemon-tree plantations, etc. I think you'll like those better than this hot-house orchid-like cultivation down on the coast.'

Celia hardly heard him. She was still fascinated by the scenery. When they reached the little principality of Monaco which had become so famous she could hardly believe that she was really seeing it at last. She only caught a glimpse of Prince Rainier's palace high on the cliffs, and the beautiful gardens of the Casino, then the Cadillac climbed up a winding road, through some wrought-iron gates and came to the villa which was her father's home.

She was overwhelmed. It was superb—too much to take in at a glance. A low white building built in Spanish style round a patio. There were pale blue shutters, scarlet-tiled roof and a wide terrace; a fine swimming pool and a well-watered garden full of ilex trees, multi-coloured carnations and scarlet salvias. Blue and white striped awnings shielded the windows from the hot sun. An air of tranquil beauty lay upon the Villa Psyche. The white statue of the marble nymph, which had given the place its name, stood in the middle of a fountain, her lovely limbs constantly moistened by the falling water as it splashed into a deep stone basin.

Geoffrey glanced sideways at Celia's rapt face.

'Poor kid, she can't have ever seen anything like it in her life. She's in a whirl,' he thought.

Then he handed her over to a smartly-dressed maid.

'Annette—take *Mademoiselle* to her uncle's study,' he said.

'Oh—are you going?' asked Celia, blinking at Geoffrey through her lashes.

'Yes, I must. See you tonight at dinner,' he said and vanished.

She looked after him. He had been awfully nice and kind and attentive. She liked him. But now she was all agog to meet the man who owned all this magnificence; the father whom she did not know whether she would love or hate.

As soon as she saw him, she knew that it must be the former. She was to recall and understand Aunt Tiny's words: 'Everybody adored Nat.'

In the big cool library Nathaniel Frayne waited to greet his daughter, a half-smoked cigar in one hand, a glass of iced lemon and water in the other. He put down both as Annette ushered Celia into the room. To her, he looked old for his years. He was dressed informally in a tussore suit, no tie, and open-necked blue shirt. He wore sandals. She stood dumbly staring at him for a moment. His face was old, yes, but she had never looked into such deep, dark, attractive eyes—young eyes still, in the brown ageing face. Then she stuttered:

'I . . . oh, hullo . . . I'm Celia!'

Nat stared back. He had the capacity of being able to sum up a person at a single glance. He prided himself on that. He knew at once that his daughter was just a simple unsophisticated child. She might have been sixteen instead of twenty-one. Like her mother, he thought a trifle grimly. Mary had never grown up. (But that was why she had bored him.)

Frankly he was disappointed by his first glimpse of his daughter. Nice little girl, but how had she spent his five hundred pounds? That uninspiring two-piece must have come off the peg in a cheap store, and as for her *hat* . . . why wear one? Her hair was more attractive.

He held out both hands to her.

'Give us a kiss,' he said gruffly.

She had only to receive the invitation and she was in his arms. Something seemed to well up inside her and flow over . . . a torrent of longing for the father she had never had. She clung to him. Gently he pulled off her hat and threw it on the floor (where it belonged he thought). He ran his long bony fingers through her thick coppery hair. That was better. Beautiful hair—just like his own had been when he was a boy.

21

Naturally wavy, glossy as a chestnut. Feeling her tear-wet cheek against his, he was moved as Nat Frayne had not been since his young French wife was buried.

'Welcome to Villa Psyche, honey. Glad you've come.'

'I'm glad, too,' she said, fumbled for a handkerchief and blew her nose.

Immediately Nat drew back into his shell. He hated people who blew their noses, and with him, moments of sentiment passed as swiftly as they came. In an abrupt way which scared Celia, he motioned her to a cane-backed settee with yellow leather cushions which stood at right-angles to windows opening on to the broad terrace.

They sat there side by side under a striped blue-and-white awning. Nat put on sun glasses. Celia sat blinking at the hot Mediterranean sky trying to remember where she had put her own smoked glasses. She was always losing things. But she wouldn't like her father to know that or to realise how difficult everything in life seemed to her. Mr. Flack, her employer, had found her an efficient secretary, but once away from the office, she seemed to become a different person.

She had hoped to feel very close to her father and to be comforted and reassured, but all he did was to puff at a cigar and bark out a few words about the past—with obvious reluctance.

After a few preliminaries, he said:

'Don't let's delve too deeply into what is dead and gone. Let's face up to the present. I daresay you think I behaved very badly. We'll leave it at that.'

'Oh, I—I expect you had your side of the story,' stammered Celia.

'I have adhered to every contract I have ever made except the one of marriage,' he said grimly. 'But I'd have gone mad if I'd stayed with your poor mother and I wouldn't be where I am today.'

'I hope it's made you h-happy,' Celia stammered again.

'Is that a crack at me?' he asked grimly, his lined face looking still more lined and suddenly formidable to her.

She shrank back and whispered:

'Oh, no, no, of course not.'

'There, there, don't look so terrified. I'm not going to bite your head off really.' Now Nat grinned in the friendly way he could summon up at a moment's notice, and which made people forgive his hostilities. He thought:

'Poor brat—she's scared out of her wits. She knows nothing and I bet Tiny Cotland chose those clothes. I remember old Tiny's own appalling garments.'

But he'd soon change all *that*. He wasn't going to have a gauche suburban daughter. Nadine would put her right. He'd already had a talk with the *soignée* French woman whom he knew to be short of money, and willing to take the 'job'. Well, in London, penniless· ladies of high degree often accepted a fat cheque to present a débutante at Court. He'd promised a few very nice emeralds to Nadine if she would 'put his niece' through her paces.

'My dear Celia,' he said aloud, 'tonight you are going to meet one of the most beautiful and polished young women in Monte Carlo. Just emulate her example. She'll help you. She'll take you to places where you'll be taught how to walk and talk and learn French, and so on. We're going to streamline you into taking your place as my heiress—not that Nadine knows *that*,' he added with a chuckle.

Now with sudden indignation Celia spoke up:

'Surely I don't need more clothes. Aunt Tiny and I bought heaps which I've brought out with me. I spent quite a hundred out of that money you sent me. Isn't that enough?'

Nat got up and walked a little away from her.

'You've got to stop thinking along cheeseparing lines, my child. Get it into your head that money's no object. That one day you'll be one of the richest girls in France.'

A little sullen and red-faced, Celia stared at her father's eloquent back and sighed:

'It's all so—so new to me. It doesn't seem real. It's like a fairy tale.'

'With me as the chief ogre,' he said with a dry laugh. 'Oh, well, the really important thing is for me to find you a suitable Prince Charming. But that's another story. And not a soul is to know you are my daughter. I've got to be sure that you're being married for love and not for my fortune. That's become a fetish with me, Celia. I'll pack you up and send you back where you came from, if you ever let out the truth to a soul down here.'

'I shan't let it out if you ask me not to—Uncle Nat,' she said, and with a sudden impish grin (like his), added: 'But maybe *I* shan't like it here. Maybe *I'll* decide to take myself back whence I came. You don't really know me, but I'm afraid you'll find I've got a mind of my own.'

Nat looked at the flushed young face and noted for the first time the beauty of her eyes, and suddenly laughed aloud.

'Bravo—you've got a bit of my spirit in you after all. I'm delighted. But just keep our little secret. One day we'll break the news to the wondering world. And until that day . . .' he thumped his chest . . . 'this old heart of mine has got to go on beating.'

'Oh, it's got to, *it's got to,*' exclaimed Celia, and knew that suddenly, wonderfully, she wanted to love and to cherish this extraordinary, fascinating, newly found father.

'Now,' said Nat, 'go and see your room and have a rest and change for dinner. Brought a really pretty frock with you?'

'Yes, a lovely one!' she said breathlessly.

'If it was chosen by that aunt of hers, I doubt it,' thought Nat with his tongue in his cheek.

He piloted his 'niece' through the big palatial hall of the villa to the foot of the stairs where Annette waited to take *Mademoiselle* to her room.

'Come down when you are ready,' Nat smiled at Celia.

'*Par ici, Mademoiselle,*' said the maid, tripping up the stairs. Celia noted the beauty of the pure white marble steps and the delicate wrought-iron tracery of the fine banisters. She had never seen a more glorious home than this. It was full of art treasures, antique furniture, famous paintings, wonderful bronzes and sculptures. She spent the next hour, not resting as she had been bidden to do, but unpacking and writing to dear Aunt Tiny. Just to say that she had arrived, to describe the sensational villa and to announce that she *was* going to like her father after all! She did not forget to mention Geoffrey More who had brought her here and been so nice and kind.

'*My bedroom,*' she wrote, '*is fantastic. Like a film star's, all light panelled wood and blue satin draperies, and I've got a huge gilt bed with a blue satin spread covered with the most exquisite lace, and lovely blue taffeta curtains. There are thick white rugs on the polished floor. The windows have shutters and open out on to a balcony from which I can see the whole of Monte Carlo stretching down to the sea. It's terribly hot after London, but I'll get used to it. I adore the heat! My own bathroom leads out of here and is gorgeous—all black marble with water running from a silver lion's mouth, and mirrored walls and big fleecy blue towels. Uncle Nat, as he wants to be called, seems to have thought of everything for me including great bottles of perfume and bath lotion, and of course, bowls of carnations everywhere—huge scarlet and pink carnations which seem to grow down here like daisies.*

'*Oh, Aunt Tiny, I wish you were with me. I'm more than a bit confused and like a fish out of water. All this magnificence rather scares me . . .*'

But she was too fond of Aunt Tiny to add that it was perfectly obvious that Uncle Nat didn't like her clothes. He had actually trodden on her new white hat and ruined it (was it only an accident?) and told her that he'd send her out in the morning with a French *Comtesse*—a widow and friend of his—who would help Celia choose a dozen new models straight from Paris.

Oh, yes, she could see she had a lot to learn. And she was a bundle of nerves about tonight's dinner party.

Later she took a bath and tried the exciting shower; after it she felt rather more hot than she had done before. Then she examined her new trousseau. She and Aunt Tiny had bought two dinner dresses. One a pink taffeta; one, coffee-coloured lace.

She decided to wear the lace and the new brown satin shoes that went with it. She also decided that now she was in Monte Carlo she ought to use more make-up. She had bought some eye-shadow and a new pink lipstick and a foundation recommended by the girl in the cosmetic department of the stores where she and her aunt had done nearly all the shopping. She took a long time 'doing' her face and wasn't at all sure she liked the result. It looked too *much*. On the other hand, she supposed it was appropriate, for a dinner party in a place like this. She had had her hair cut, shampooed and set in London, but it was that springy sort of hair that went back to its own wave and shape. And it seemed to her tonight to be too 'schoolgirly'. But at last she had to be content, and went downstairs feeling rather warm and flustered, holding tightly on to her bag—a new satin one with a diamanté clip which she and Aunt Tiny had thought a great extravagance.

The villa seemed deserted. It was seven o'clock. She wondered whatever time they dined here. Feeling more than a little homesick, she pictured dear Aunt Tiny sitting down to her lonely supper at home. She sighed and decided to take a walk through the grounds, and get some fresh air before the ordeal of the dinner started. As she opened the front door a young man rushed in and almost knocked her over. He apologised and stepped back. He was slimly built with smooth hair

25

like black satin, and very dark eyes, almond-shaped, attractively set in a pale face with rather high cheek bones. A fascinating face. The owner of it stared back at Celia and muttered another apology, in French.

Celia said:

'Oh, please, it doesn't matter . . .'

Philippe Clermont drew a carefully folded silk handkerchief from his pocket and dabbed his lips.

He was not in a good mood. He had spent a fiendishly hot day in Paris and missed the early plane he had wanted to catch. Who on earth, he wondered, was this girl? He had never seen such a frightful dress. As for her make-up—it was pathetic. Then suddenly he realised—this must be the old man's English niece.

'You are Miss Frayne?' he asked.

'Yes.'

Philippe bowed.

'How do you do? Let me introduce myself—Philippe Clermont. I work with your uncle.'

'Oh yes,' said Celia.

'I hope you'll have a delightful holiday here,' said Philippe politely. '*Au revoir, Mademoiselle*. We shall meet at dinner.'

He took her right hand and touched it with his lips in true French fashion (but he spoke marvellous English, she decided).

In all her life Celia's heart had never fluttered as it did at that single salute from this young man's lips. Such a warm *intime* expression lay in those handsome sloe-dark eyes. Philippe was adept at flattering all women, young, old, plain or beautiful.

'Until tonight,' he murmured and departed.

'What a heart-throb,' she thought, and hoped, childishly, that she would sit next to him at dinner. Truly, the evening was beginning to shape, and an excitement that she had never before experienced flowed through her veins.

In Nat Frayne's deserted study, Philippe put a telephone call through to *Madame la Comtesse* de Sachelles at her apartment in Menton. Philippe said:

'Yes, I'm back, *ma chère*. I can't wait to see you at dinner. Yes . . . I've just met *her*. You never saw such a sight. No, she isn't exactly *plain*; quite a nice little figure, and so on; but such ghastly clothes and make-up. Next to you she'll look like a duck beside a swan.'

A low laugh from the other end of the wires. Nadine could

do with any number of compliments. Philippe was mad about her. They had had their 'moments' together—moments that Nat Frayne wouldn't have liked at all if he had known about them. But Philippe had no money and that was what Nadine needed. A pity because physically they were well matched and enjoyed each other's kisses. But the *Comte* had left her almost penniless. *Dieu!* How Philippe wished that he were Nat Frayne, instead of a distant cousin. He answered another question from Nadine.

'Yes, Geoffrey will be at the dinner party. More is the pity. He irritates me. Don't be too nice to him or I shall be jealous. *À-bientôt, mon ange.*'

Now Philippe walked out on to the terrace and looked at the garden, which in this deep golden light of the late afternoon was as beautiful as a dream. He caught sight of Celia Frayne walking alone. He groaned. He did not envy the part that had been assigned to him helping to entertain this dowdy English girl. Maybe Nadine could do something with her, but he doubted it.

To be rich was Philippe's burning ambition. He was obsessed by it. Only a rich man would ever get Nadine.

The little figure in the coffee-coloured lace dress vanished from sight. Shrugging his wide, Egyptian shoulders Philippe moved back into the study. He was never angry or frustrated for long. He had a mercurial disposition and infinite charm. At times he charmed himself. He forgot Celia Frayne and began to dwell on the thought of how Nadine would look at the dinner party this evening. He did not really worry about Nat's secretary. How could an impecunious employee, no matter how handsome or basically sound and English and dependable, make a real mark upon the life of a woman as alluring, as glorious as the *Comtesse* de Sachelles.

Philippe's almond-dark eyes glanced at his reflection in a gilt-framed mirror in the wide hall as he passed through it. He gave himself one of his gay Southern smiles, showing splendid teeth. He was going to flirt madly with Nadine right under Geoffrey's nose. He would pay only as much attention to Nat's dull, dowdy little niece as courtesy demanded. (Philippe was always impeccably courteous.)

Then he drove himself in his black, elegant Mercedes to his apartment in a block of flats facing the sea. He needed an hour's rest and a bath after his long tiring day in Paris, where he had been buying a new sculpture that Nat wanted.

# THREE

To Celia, the dinner party was a long-drawn-out torture. She wished passionately that she did not so completely lack confidence. She longed to make conversation, to joke and laugh and be at her ease like these other people, but she seemed incapable of it. Yet it all should have been so wonderful.

She was seated (as she had hoped) beside the handsome and charming Philippe. He looked more than ever attractive, she thought, in his white monkey jacket, with red cummerbund that gave him the air of a slender Spanish bull-fighter. Whenever Celia timidly addressed him, he turned the warmth of his bright dark fascinating eyes upon her and talked to her engagingly. But she felt that she made no headway with him. It was all too obvious that he had eyes and ears only for the lovely young woman who sat opposite them. Without envy, with a simple admiration, Celia could understand why men were attracted by the *Comtesse*. Oh, how poised Nadine was and how exquisitely she moved her long slim fingers and flashed her expressive, honey-coloured eyes, first at one man, then the other. And how did one learn to be dressed with such simplicity and yet such chic? Nadine's tall slim body looked as though it had been poured into that black chiffon dress she was wearing. Celia had put on necklace, earrings and bracelets, and pinned flowers on her shoulder. Nadine de Sachelles wore only large gold and ruby earrings, and bracelets. No other jewellery to spoil the severe line of that wonderful dress and those camellia-pale shoulders.

Humbly Celia told herself that she must try to model herself on Nadine. Now, miserably, she realised that the coffee-lace which Aunt Tiny had thought so pretty was all wrong. Too frilly, too insipid. This evening, when Celia first met her father in the *salon*, she had noticed with her usual painful sensitivity, the dismay in his quick critical gaze. Obviously her dress had displeased him. He had growled.

'Oh, my poor girl, you must get yourself an entirely new trousseau. I'll send you over to Cannes tomorrow. A few hours on the *Croisette* with Nadine should work wonders.'

He had meant well but his very words had started the evening off badly for Celia.

28

Geoffrey More glanced at her from the far end of the table. He observed the fact that she was gradually growing more silent and subdued.

'Poor little thing,' he thought, 'the great Nat and Nadine between them are getting her down.'

He wished he had been put beside her. He might have talked to her and helped a little. As a boy he had known the agonies of shyness. With the years he had conquered it. Now he was completely at ease in this gilded kingdom over which Nat reigned. But Celia . . . he watched the shadows flit across her face, her pathetic struggles to give the right answers. He wondered, with his usual mistrust of the *Comtesse* if it were not on purpose that she said to Celia:

'Are these *scampis* not delicious? Your uncle's chef is the finest in France.'

Celia's reply was frank and unthinking:

'It's the first time I have ever eaten this sort of thing.'

'The first time?' repeated Nadine.

Geoffrey, scowling, watched Nadine shrug her beautiful shoulders. Then Celia, making a valiant attempt to prove that she was not without her own taste in food, went on:

'But I sort of agree with my aunt in London. She always says a kipper's more tasty than anything.'

There was a dead silence. Geoffrey thought:

'*Oh, the poor sweet . . .*'

Nadine gave a low laugh and turned to Nat:

'What is a *kippaire* like, *Monsieur*?'

'It's so long since I've eaten one, I wouldn't know,' growled Nat and fixed one baleful eye on his daughter. Raw material here all right. He hadn't Geoffrey More's capacity for understanding or sympathising with human beings who made exhibitions of themselves. Hastily he engaged Nadine on another subject. Celia was ignored.

Celia thought with a curious sadness—'*I should be very happy tonight, but I am not.*'

She was lost in this huge lofty room with its three windows opening on to the moonlit terrace. How incredible to her was the round table, black marble, laid with delicate porcelain, gilt-handled cutlery, exquisite Venetian glass. In two tall gilt candelabra, a dozen black wax candles burned steadily. Food such as Celia had never eaten before was served by two white-coated menservants. And out there, under huge stars, lay

Monte Carlo, and those twinkling lights all along the *Côte d'Azur*, fringing the purple moon-silvered sea.

It was romantic beyond words. *And one day this would be hers.* She could hardly believe it.

Yet by the end of the long-drawn-out meal, she was more miserable than she had been when it began. She felt that she had made several *faux-pas* and must appear uncivilised and plebeian to this millionaire crowd. She had also failed to attract the slightest attention from Philippe. When Geoffrey More said something nice to her as they walked on to the terrace, she was not much comforted.

In this new glamorous atmosphere in which she found herself, she lacked a most important factor. The vital quality that the *Comtesse* seemed to have. That warm exciting wonderful knowledge that *you are attractive . . . that you are a success.*

Philippe managed to whisper a word into Nadine's ear as they left the *salle à manger*.

'Isn't she pathetic?'

The *Comtesse* smiled but spread out her hands eloquently.

'Yes, maybe, as she is now—*affreuse*. But you might be surprised, once I have worked on her. She has potentialities and a very pretty figure.'

Philippe shrugged his shoulders.

'I find it a bore having to help entertain her, I can tell you. I only wish the job had been assigned solely to Geoffrey.'

Nat, not in the best of moods, looked for his secretary and unable to see him at the moment, called out to the Frenchman:

'Philippe, be a good fellow and nip into the study. You'll see a box of cigars on my desk. Coffee is being served on the terrace. Bring the box out there.'

Philippe sauntered into the study.

As he picked up the box of Havanas, he noticed that the little drawer on the left side of the desk had most unusually been left open. A key dangled from the lock. He had never before seen this drawer open. It was kept locked and Nat had the key always on his own personal chain.

Philippe had never been scrupulous. With half an eye on the door, he slid the drawer further open and took a swift glance inside. He noticed a letter with an English address. He wondered what this letter was about. It was marked '*Strictly private*'. Curiosity was one of Philippe's vices. He glanced swiftly at the 'strictly private' letter. The first paragraph was enough.

'*Bon Dieu!*' said Philippe softly.

Because he thought he heard footsteps, he hastily pushed the letter back into the drawer and shut it. He began to walk on to the terrace with the Chief's cigars in his hand. His olive skin was flushed. His heart beating enormously fast. *Bon Dieu!* The great Nat had slipped up—forgetting to lock that drawer.

He stood there in the warm scented night, staring at Celia's back. Geoffrey had just said something to make her laugh. She turned and looked at the young Frenchman.

He stood still a second, smiling back at her. A long, thoughtful smile. Then he sauntered towards her.

'Friend Geoffrey cannot be allowed entirely to monopolise you, *Mademoiselle*,' he said in his gentle, cream-smooth voice, took the chair from which the secretary had just risen, and seated himself beside Celia

# FOUR

CELIA was surprised, to say the least of it, when Philippe took that chair beside her—and stayed there, talking to her animatedly. She could not fail to be flattered because the young Frenchman was a very handsome and charming boy. She judged him to be about twenty-five or six—perhaps a little older than Geoffrey More although nobody could have been more different in type than these two. Geoffrey so essentially English with his light brown hair, his very blue eyes and that impression of good health and honesty that only a clean-looking, clean-living Englishman can give—particularly when he is abroad among the swarthy Mediterranean types. Celia, who liked to watch people and sum them up in her shy reserved way, was quite sure Geoffrey was very reliable; a one hundred per cent *nice* person. Little wonder her father trusted him and valued him as a personal assistant. But *Philippe*—oh, *Monsieur* Clermont was all sparkle—like champagne with his brilliant laughing almond-shaped eyes, his gay frothy chatter and his expressive hands which he moved so swiftly and often while he talked. Those hands with the thin flexible wrists fascinated Celia. Philippe, himself, fascinated her. And if earlier in the evening she had thought he had eyes only for the *Comtesse* she soon began to think she was wrong because he left Nat to entertain the beautiful Nadine, and seemed to find a great deal to talk about to her, Celia. Why, she just couldn't think but it was certainly flattering.

He drew her out of her shell; asked about her London life, the aunt she lived with, all the things she liked to do. Philippe could be very *sympathique*, as the French put it, and she thought it sweet of him to take such a friendly interest in her because she was sure the life she described must seem very boring to him.

It was. And it completely astounded Philippe. He knew a lot of girls—and had numerous 'amours' quite apart from his secret passion for Nadine. But the sort of girl he was accustomed to—French or American—and some of the English—whom he met on the *Côte d'Azur* knew how to play as well as work—and of course there were few girls who didn't work nowadays. Philippe had friends among actresses, dancers, model girls, and one or two attractive secretaries. Such women worked but filled every instant of their spare time with the sensual pleasures that life offered down here. The sunbathing, the swimming, the aqua-skiing; the hours spent drinking aperitifs or coffee at little tables under striped umbrellas on the beaches or in lovely gardens. The dancing, cheek to cheek to languorous South American music, or the gay 'Twist' at which Philippe was an expert, in the night clubs of Cannes or Monte Carlo.

Philippe himself had to work hard and enjoyed travelling around Europe picking up treasures for Nathaniel's shops. With his special form of cynical wit he often told himself that finding these beautiful rare pieces held much the same excitement as he felt in meeting beautiful rare girls—they were all treasures to be carefully handled and admired (and later disposed of). He was not the faithful type although his frustrated passion for Nadine was lasting longer than most.

Celia was certainly different—quite a novelty. So simple and gauche; completely lacking in experience of the world. Incredible to think that the only thrills she had ever known were annual summer trips to some grim seaside town with her aunt or an occasional mild party with her girl-friends. Philippe asked her during the evening, as he gently probed through her guard of reticence, if she had left a boy-friend in London. She had coloured up until her face was like a rose and stammered:

'Good lord, no, nothing like that.'

By the time Philippe finished with her he had developed almost a benevolent affection for 'la petite' as he called her. Why, poor little thing! Here, indeed, was virgin ground waiting to be cultivated. There was something rather fresh and sweet about Celia. As for her legs—*they* were poems, Philippe decided. Nadine had been right when she said that little Miss Frayne might for the moment look *affreuse* but that like the ugly duckling with the right handling she would turn into a swan.

'Over to you, *ma chère*,' he said to himself, looking reflectively at Nadine. 'This promises to be quite interesting.'

And by the time he had finished amusing Celia who thawed in the sunlight of his personality and laughed freely and frankly at his jokes, Philippe was beginning to consider himself quite a philanthropist. He, too, would help to educate *la petite*. A few weeks of his company and she would soon have learned more about life—in more ways than one. If old Nat knew, he would, perhaps, be grateful to me, reflected Philippe. Oh, *mon Dieu*, but if old Nat knew also that he, Philippe, had read that letter in the secret drawer—it *would* put the fat in the fire. Nat must never know. And Philippe must keep his mouth shut and play his own private game no matter how madly he wished he could tell Nadine about it. She was usually the recipient of his confidences but *this* he could not tell her. Nobody but himself—and that went also for the secretary, Mr. Geoffrey More, whom Philippe frankly detested. Nat didn't want anybody to know that Celia was *his daughter*.

Philippe drew in his breath as he smiled and looked at Celia's delicate profile. What a break, getting to know about this. And what an odd game the old boy was playing—presenting her to the world as his niece in order that she shouldn't be married for her money.

'I shall help "Uncle Nat" keep his secret,' thought Philippe shaking with silent laughter. 'Indeed I shall.'

Nadine de Sachelles, sitting on the other side of the coffee table beside Geoffrey, played her own particular game this evening. She was accustomed to being pursued by men. This Englishman alone seemed to be impervious to her beauty and charm. She could never get anywhere with him. And she found it infuriating. Philippe, who had always been a bit jealous of her admiration for Geoffrey, called him dull and said there was nothing behind his bland exterior. But Nadine didn't believe that. Geoffrey had plenty of character. She was positive there was considerable fire behind the ice.

She adored his height—he was so unusually tall—and the width of his shoulders, and muscular strength of his big brown hands. She knew, too, that he had a good brain. Nat had often commented upon it. In fact Nat had several times observed to Nadine that Geoffrey was wasted as his assistant although he had no intention of parting with the boy. Geoffrey ran the Frayne estate and managed the financial side of his business excellently, and that was a big undertaking. He wasn't just the sort of secretary who took a few letters, bought tickets, and arranged trips. But why, Nadine often asked herself each time she met Geoffrey, was he always so detached? He was courteous—coolly attentive and had partnered her at one or two of the dances Nat had arranged for visitors. But never did he make her feel one inch nearer to him. Never did she seem able to catch him off guard. This fact hit her particularly hard this evening. He made it so plain that the dinner party had bored him, and that he had no intention of going on to the Casino after Nat retired.

'Not even if I ask you very nicely?' Nadine pouted at him.

Geoffrey looked into the *Comtesse's* beautiful eyes (they were fringed with such fabulous lashes) and for the second time regretfully declined the invitation.

'I have a sick dog I've got to get back to.'

'Oh, *là là!*' Nadine shook her head at him in mock horror. 'You and your dogs.'

'But they're such nice dogs,' he smiled.

'The English are crazy about animals to the point of imbecility.'

'It isn't as imbecile as it may seem to you, *Comtesse.* They are very rewarding creatures to be crazy about.'

'Rewarding—how?'

'They are so grateful. They give unstinted love and loyalty and ask for nothing in return.'

'That sounds like a woman,' said Nadine, flicking those long lashes at him.

Geoffrey's wide humorous mouth curved into a somewhat cynical smile.

'Not the sort of women I've met, so far, *Madame la Comtesse.*'

She persisted:

'*Tiens!* But a woman in love can be *very* rewarding—very loyal and loving and also asking for no reward.'

Again Geoffrey's smile was cynical as for a fraction of an instant he let his gaze rest on a huge white square-cut diamond that Nadine was wearing.

'Show me this person and I'll propose to her,' he said lightly.

Nadine compressed her lips. Even she dared not identify herself with *that* particular girl. Oh! he was maddening. Why did he waste his spare time on animals. She knew all about them . . . he had told her often enough. He ran a kind of a home for the lost or the sick that were only too often abandoned by a callous owner. Nat said that he'd saved some dogs even when the veterinary surgeon had despaired of their lives. He would sit up all night with a dog that was gravely ill.

If only he would direct that warmth of heart, that tenderness on *her*, thought Nadine. She glanced angrily at Philippe Clermont. She had had many amusing moments with him and expected to have more in the future. He could rouse her passion and satisfy it, too. But this intriguing English boy who played hard-to-get was beginning to creep under her skin. Possibly because he *was* so hard to get; she could believe that, but it irritated her to think of herself as falling seriously in love with a man who had no money and was more interested in dogs than romance.

Geoffrey turned to his employer. Nat was talking to him about tomorrow morning's programme. He told Geoffrey to order the Cadillac and chauffeur to take Celia to the *Croisette* to meet Nadine for shopping. He could tell the chauffeur to leave them there and then go back for them later.

Nat had just finished his cigar, and thrown away the stump. He glanced at his daughter, surprised to see how animatedly she was talking to Philippe.

'It takes a Frenchman to make an inarticulate English girl talk to him,' he observed to his secretary in an undertone— his lined, monkey-face amused.

'So it would seem, sir,' said Geoffrey stiffly.

'Did you find her hard to talk to, coming from the airport?' asked Nat.

Geoffrey threw a doubtful glance towards Celia.

'No. I thought she had quite a lot to say. I think this must be a great experience for her, sir.'

Nat reflected:

'*I only hope it's going to be a success—bringing Mary's child and mine out to this place.*'

Personally, he had found the dinner and Celia's *gaucherie* trying. He was pleasantly surprised to find Philippe willing to pay so much attention. Or was it that the boy was just sorry for her, and being kind.

Then suddenly Celia turned to Nat and said, breathlessly:

'*Monsieur* Clermont says he is going to teach me to water-ski, Uncle Nat.'

Now both the men—Nathaniel Frayne and Geoffrey— ceased to think that Celia either looked—or was—at all non-descript. Those smoke-grey eyes of hers were enormous—the pupils black, dilated with excitement—lighting up her small pale face. Animated, like this, she had a beauty and vitality which certainly her father had not expected. He barked:

'Can you swim?'

'Yes. In fact I won my school championship,' she said with a laugh. 'Diving and swimming have always been my chief hobby and form of exercise. I go to the local baths at home and I was semi-finalist there last year.'

Nadine, who had heard all this, felt faintly nauseated. She herself didn't swim very well. Her knowledge of the water was mainly *looking* at it from the beach—hoping everybody else was looking at her beautiful sun-browned body.

But Nat was amused and felt faintly nostalgic because he, too, in his youth had been a fine swimmer. Now his 'dicky' heart didn't allow him to pursue the sport.

'So you take after me,' he began, but didn't enlarge on that. He must be careful not to make any silly slips. Still, a niece could inherit something from an uncle. Why not?

Geoffrey also continued to watch Celia with his kindly thoughtful eyes. What a quaint little thing she was. Full of unexpected charm when she smiled and opened those great grey eyes so widely. And who'd have thought she swam so well? She didn't look strong or muscular (thank goodness—he disliked muscular females). But now he came to think of it she was very well built—straight back, small waist, long legs tapering to fine ankles. He could imagine her looking very nice indeed in a swim suit.

But that was as far as Geoffrey allowed himself to think because he had quite frankly had enough of this evening—including the Chief's niece. He wanted to get home. *Madame* Pavette, dear old thing, was keeping a special guard on the mongrel puppy that he had brought in from the streets this morning, dying from exposure and starvation. He must get back at a reasonable hour to allow the old girl to go to bed. She was very good about helping him with the animals when he couldn't be there. He paid for her time, of course. Most of his spare money went on those dogs. A long succession of strays had passed through his hands during the last two or three years. He usually managed to find new owners for them. Only those with incurable diseases or who had been too badly hurt did he take to his good friend André Angelo—a half-French half-Italian vet—to be put to sleep.

Philippe decided that he must not make it over-obvious that he was interested in Celia and rose from his chair and now made a point of turning his charm upon Nadine. In fact, he and Geoffrey exchanged seats so it was Geoffrey who began to talk to little Miss Frayne.

Celia was sorry when Philippe deserted her. She had found him utterly fascinating. She hadn't laughed so much or felt so gay in her life before. However, Geoffrey was very pleasant and friendly and it didn't take him long to get on to his pet subject. Then she was genuinely interested . . . for she, too, had a great feeling for animals.

'Aunt Tiny and I had a Jack Russell that we adored. But he died of hard-pad three months ago. There was never anywhere to exercise him but Battersea Park, and I think all public parks are a menace—alive with germs. So we haven't replaced him. But I love dogs and miss not having one. As a child I always had a pet. Do you look after stray cats as well, Mr. More?'

'Call me Geoffrey, please. Everybody does. No—I don't look after cats. It's too difficult. They just don't get on,' he said with a faint smile. 'And I haven't the time to give them, really. Nobody but my friend *Madame* Pavette helps me.'

'When do you do all this work? Uncle Nat was telling me that you work frightfully hard for him.'

'Oh, I get up very early in the morning and give a couple of hours to my kennels. Then when folk take a siesta after lunch, as they do on this coast, I go back to my kennels and do a bit more work.'

Celia thought this rather admirable. She said shyly:

'I'd like to help you while I'm here. I really do love dogs.'

'It's really immensely good of you. But——' began Geoffrey.

'No, really. I mean it,' she interrupted. 'I'm not in the least afraid of dogs. And I know quite a bit about treating them. Poor Tiggy, our Jack Russell—I nursed him until he died. That hard-pad is such a ghastly thing, isn't it? But he was with us for six years during which time I nursed him through distemper, enteritis and cured his ear canker and so on. And I help my friends who have dogs. Animals seem to take to me.'

'Then you must be a very special person,' said Geoffrey, his heart warming to her. Here was a girl who really did appeal to him. He added: 'I'd love you to come down some time and see my menagerie but I wouldn't dream of asking you to do any work.'

'But I shall!' she exclaimed. 'That is, if you'll let me. I don't want to spend the whole of my time just playing. Monte Carlo is called the "Playground of the Rich" isn't it? Well, thank goodness *I'm* not rich!' And she said those words with another laugh.

Philippe heard them and smiled to himself.

Now Nat Frayne stood up.

'Don't let me break up the party but I'm off to bed.'

The other men stood up too. Geoffrey lay aside the cigar he

had not yet finished. He walked to his employer. He thought Nat had been looking very tired and grey most of the evening.

'Can I do anything, sir?'

'No, no, stay out here and look after the party.'

'If you wouldn't mind, sir, I'd like to get home myself.'

'One of your strays?' Nat smiled faintly.

'Yes, sir. A new arrival.'

'Well, well, get home then. See you in the morning. No doubt my niece will not want to be too late on her first night here.'

'No, I won't—I'm beginning to feel terribly sleepy,' said Celia who had overheard this remark.

'Good night, my dear,' said Nat.

'Let me come in with you,' she said.

'Would *Mademoiselle* like us to take her down to the Casino——?' began Philippe.

'*Pour l'amour de Dieu, non*,' Nadine whispered in his ear in their own language. 'Haven't you had enough of all this for one night?'

Perforce, Philippe said no more. He did not wish to upset or betray himself. So good nights were exchanged and the dinner party was over.

Celia accompanied her father into the Villa. He went up the stairs slowly, holding her arm.

'Are you sure you're all right?' she asked anxiously.

'Fine, fine,' he lied. He had no intention of letting the girl know what poor shape he was in.

Outside his bedroom door, Celia lifted her face in her rather timid childish way for him to kiss her. He looked down at her. He had been annoyed by her lack of *savoir faire* during dinner and irritated by her clothes—he didn't want his daughter (or niece) to look so *bourgeoise*. And when she reminded him of her mother, he retreated—he did not want to remember *that* part of his life too much, either. He didn't come out of it too well. But now he thought if the poor child was a bit *bourgeoise*, whose fault was it but his?—leaving her to be brought up by that old scarecrow, Tiny. Nevertheless he had been agreeably surprised by Celia's success with the two men in the party tonight. There must be a lot more to young Celia than at first met the eye. He had liked that bit about her swimming. Himself, all over again. The child had guts and he liked guts. He kissed her quite affectionately and patted her shoulder.

'Very nice to have you here with me, darling.'

It was the first time he had called her that. She kissed him back gratefully.

'Thanks for everything. I *do* appreciate it. I didn't disgrace you, tonight, did I, Uncle Nat?'

'No, no, of course not. There are things for you to learn but you'll soon learn 'em.'

'I think *Monsieur* Clermont is charming,' she said ingenuously.

Nat smiled wryly down the big shining grey eyes.

'So he is—a very charming fellow. I'm fond of him.'

'Mr. More too—Geoffrey—is awfully nice.'

'Yes. Like his father. The salt of the earth the old chap used to be. My contemporary and one of my great friends. Geoff is his Pa all over again.'

'I've had a really thrilling evening,' sighed Celia.

'Poor little thing,' he thought and said aloud:

'There'll be many more, and better ones. Nadine will fix you up with a trousseau tomorrow.'

Celia nodded. She was ready to praise both Philippe and Geoffrey but she found nothing much to say about *Madame la Comtesse* whose elegance and sophistication rather overawed her. She kissed her father again and went into her own room, not to sleep but to write another long letter to Aunt Tiny describing everything that had happened tonight.

'*I think Philippe is marvellous. He is going to teach me water-skiing. Oh, Aunt Tiny, it's all like a dream——*'

She could have written a lot more than that about Philippe Clermont but decided not to do so. She didn't want to give Aunt Tiny a wrong impression. Or would it be a wrong one, she wondered, her cheeks hot and her heart beating fast, if she gave Aunt Tiny to think that her niece had very nearly, if not quite, fallen in love at first sight with the fascinating Frenchman?

# FIVE

The shopping expedition in Cannes was certainly exciting for Celia. Her 'uncle' appeared to have given Nadine *carte blanche*, backed by a cheque that seemed to the young girl phenomenal —in order to turn his 'duckling' into a swan. It was hard for Celia at first to get used to the wild extravagance of buying exactly what one wanted without regard for the price tags. She had been brought up in a frugal fashion by dear Aunt Tiny and it takes time for anybody to get out of a lifetime habit.

The *Comtesse* was, of course, an expert in the game and under her tuition it was not long before Celia was also throwing caution to the winds and saying, 'I must have that' long before she asked the price. It took a little more time to make her stop feeling guilty afterwards. But the whole of that morning proved a revelation to her which would have been a very pleasant one if it hadn't been for the woman who was her guide and mentor.

However, she found Nadine charming and helpful—she rendered invaluable service to the young girl from Battersea who was so utterly ignorant in this world of wealth and fashion. Nadine was used to moving in 'Café society', and Celia privately envied that cool appraisal of the models they were shown—her sure knowledge of current fashion and, of course, the easy way in which she talked to those who ran *haute couture salons*, hat shops, and the others. Celia felt that she was a kind of puppet being pulled on a string—she undressed and dressed so many times that she could not count them. Nadine just pulled the strings with apparent pleasure but, Celia suspected, a certain degree of malice. Under the veneer of courtesy and the interest the *Comtesse* displayed in transforming the little English 'Miss'—lay an obvious disdain for her ignorance, what Nadine called her English suburban dowdiness.

One or two of the most famous houses in Paris, with branches in the *Croisette* in Cannes, displayed their latest fashions to the visitors from Villa Psyche. Designers and tailors who had hitherto been only names to Celia. Balmain— Balenciaga—Ricci—Lanvin. The luxurious, gilded, thick-carpeted, flower-decorated *salons* were all here. Tall, thin, impossibly beautiful, languorous model girls drifted in and out,

41

wearing the new season's creations, dazzling and dazing Celia. She wanted desperately to learn, and not to be thought so stupid. All that was feminine in her wanted also to match Nadine de Sachelles at her own game; but of course, to begin with, she couldn't, and once or twice when she timidly pointed out a dress or suit that she thought suitable, her choice was received with a chorus of disapproval both from the *Comtesse* and *vendeuse*.

'It was the wrong colour for *Mademoiselle* . . . she couldn't possibly wear *that* . . . she was too small . . . or her complexion was not right for *this* . . .'

Celia argued with Nadine once out in the sunlit street again.

'Why couldn't I have that blue and gold kid belt?'

'Because it was wrong for you.'

'I can't see why.'

'You will learn,' said the *Comtesse* pityingly, 'once your judgment is developed. Believe me, it was that vivid cyclamen pink that suited you so well, and gave you colour—life.'

'But I've never worn pink before——' began Celia.

'My dear,' interrupted Nadine, her blue-lidded black-lashed eyes sparkling half with amusement, half with scorn, 'when you follow the trend of fashion, you try everything—especially the new shades. You just don't stick to old colours.'

'I've always thought one should wear what suited one, and rather quiet colours at that,' said Celia gloomily, as she remembered how Aunt Tiny disliked the vivid hues that the younger generation fancied today. She used to say to Celia:

'*You* always look so ladylike—so nicely turned out.'

That was a description which, Celia soon learned from Nadine, one must not breathe. It would have made her writhe. One mustn't be 'nicely turned out' when one was a smart woman of the *Côte d'Azur*, or in London, Paris or New York. One was just *chic*. Nadine told Celia frankly that what she lacked was *chic*, and it was *chic* she must acquire.

'Didn't you like that coffee-coloured lace I wore for dinner last night?' asked the unhappy Celia.

'My dear,' said the *Comtesse*, 'I do not wish to hurt your feelings, but I am asked by your uncle to help train your eye, so I must be honest. That lace dress was an abomination. It was dated and much, much too old for you. It did nothing for you. You must always wear clothes, my dear, that flatter your personality and enhance the colouring that God gave you.'

Then, with a little artificial laugh, she went on to tell Celia that it was also time she altered (or subtly improved) Nature's colouring with a few of the fashionable modern aids. Her thick chestnut hair must be properly cut and set (oh! those waves and curls produced by the Battersea hairdresser!).

With her heart-shaped face, the new Egyptian style, rather straight-cut, brushed-back, bouffant from the forehead, pulled down in a sculptured way over both ears, would suit Celia. There were rinses to bring out that chestnut hue—enhance the red lights. Her skin looked dry. She must use sun-tan oil out here, and have a course of 'facials' and hair-do's from Antoine, the hair stylist who the *Comtesse*, herself, visited regularly.

She found herself having to get used to designs that she and Aunt Tiny had never dreamed about—narrow shoulders, silk evening coats with rolled over collars in shades of buttercup yellow or fuchsia pink, exquisite linens (one she particularly liked and bought was pale grey, flecked with white, and a long copper-coloured tunic over a straight skirt which seemed to match Celia's hair). If she had been a little taller she would have looked like one of those model girls, she thought, with sudden new pride in herself. She wasn't Aunt Tiny's niece any more. She was a creation of *Madame la Comtesse*.

On to the next salon, and the purchase of a cocktail dress. Not the nice 'grey' that attracted Celia, but a seemingly innocuous plain midnight-blue satin, cut very low at the back and high in front. When Celia put it on, it made her look quite startlingly different. That word *chic* sprang at her from the very mirror that reflected her. Then the *Comtesse* seized two huge ropes of pearls which were on display, wound them dramatically round Celia's throat, stood back and joined with the *vendeuse* in little cries of admiration.

'*Ah, ça c'est quelque chose . . . étonnante! . . . ravissante . . .*'

The blue dress was only a little matter of eighty pounds (doing a little mental arithmetic Celia hurriedly transferred the sum from francs to her own currency). *Heavens!* it seemed stupendous.

But the Dior full evening dress that Nadine finally chose for her, made her gasp even more. *One hundred and fifty pounds*. It seemed really a dreadful price, although it was a gorgeous thing—white satin, the tight bodice embroidered with little aquamarine stones that glittered as she moved; a bell-shaped skirt hung just below the knees. And when the *vendeuse* threw a pair of white Icelandic foxes over Celia's bare shoulders the

*Comtesse* nodded and drew a satisfied breath of the Russian cigarette she was smoking. She was never really bored by looking at, or talking about clothes. They were a passion with her, and it was quite interesting to try and *make something* out of the English girl. As Nadine herself had prophesied to Philippe, Celia had such good bone structure and colouring, she could certainly be turned into a 'smash hit'.

By the end of that morning, however, Nadine felt just a teeny-weeny bit envious of the extreme youth and innocence, the dewy freshness that sat upon Celia which she, Nadine, had long since lost.

None of the men who had been at the Villa last night was present during lunch. This was served on a table under a large tree in the garden where it was so green and cool after the noontide heat. Philippe and Geoffrey were both out, presumably at work. Nat was not yet up. He had had a bad night and sent a message to say that he would join Celia and the others for tea. An English custom which they preserved at the Villa Psyche.

There was a brief hour in which to rest, then at three o'clock, Celia was dragged out for more, feeling very much at the mercy of the *Comtesse*—and of her father's wishes. Lovely clothes were all very well, but surely, there was a limit and what *was* she going to do with the trousseau that she and dear Aunt Tiny had bought. Those things which had seemed so exciting, backed by Aunt Tiny's taste. Now Nadine had made them seem worthless. She had even suggested that Celia should take the whole lot and hand them over to Annette, the maid, to distribute among the staff who had their poor relations.

This annoyed Celia.

'I'm not a socialist, and I want to be glamorous and please Uncle Nat,' she had thought at the time, 'but I really do think that people like the *Comtesse* and these Ritzy friends of hers waste far too much time and money on appearance. They're incredibly snobbish!'

With some conflict of feeling, she watched Annette unpack the boxes that the chauffeur had brought in from the Cadillac. Some of the morning's purchases. Of course, she did like those narrow Italian slacks—to be worn with beautifully-cut, sleeveless tops. And what Nadine called the 'casuals' were divine—the shorts, the wide skirts in gorgeous colour, with tight silky jerseys to make amusing little jackets with huge gilt buttons; the slenderness of the waist accentuated by enormously wide belts, pulled so tightly that it made Celia's hips swing as she walked.

There were new shoes, with high heels, 'flatties', gorgeous sandals, Dior nylons, new lingerie. Not the nylon slips from cheap London stores which she had always worn, but exquisite things of gossamer cobwebby material, edged with the finest lace, and costing a fortune.

'But what do I *want* all these things for?' she cried to Nadine at the end of the exhausting expedition—looking forward to a rest at the hairdresser's.

The *Comtesse*, who was really less exhausted than Celia because she was more used to it, twisted her lips into a pitying smile.

'My dear, why does any girl want beautiful clothes? To make other women jealous and to attract men, putting the thing in right order . . .' and she smiled again at her own wit.

'I don't particularly want to make other women jealous,' said Celia, 'and . . .' her colour deepened . . . 'there's no particular man I want to attract,' although even as she said it, the memory of Philippe leapt to her mind and she thought rather pleasurably that she might wear that glorious blue satin tonight. *He* might like it more than the coffee lace. She heard Nadine's shocked voice.

'*Mon Dieu!* You amaze me, Celia. Surely, it is in all women to wish to attract men, and the right sort of man, even if he has no idea of the cost of a dress or who made it, recognises the fact that it is beautiful, and that the wearer is a *soignée* woman.'

'Yes, I suppose M. Clermont would know,' said Celia with a naïve candour.

Nadine put her tongue in her cheek.

'*Oh, là, là,* so that is the way the wind is blowing,' she thought with some irony. 'Dear Philippe is very quick to attract even Nat's schoolgirl of a niece.'

But she found not so much the schoolgirl later that afternoon when Nadine presented her to Nat on the terrace for tea at half past five; Geoffrey had also joined them. Nat liked good strong English tea, and Geoffrey fully approved. Let Nadine and the others enjoy their pale yellow China liquid with a slice of lemon if they wanted.

Nat stared at his daughter. His lined face creased into a grimace that might have been half pleasure, half surprise. He even gave a wolf-whistle.

'What have we here?'

'I've been working very hard on her,' said Nadine with that metallic laugh which Geoffrey More disliked—he found it so utterly humourless. It was the sort of laughter that suggested no real joy. And now he, too, stared at Celia. A transformation all right.

As suggested by Nadine, Celia had changed into a pair of her new Italian tight slacks—vivid turquoise with matching sleeveless top, an outfit which showed every slender, graceful curve. Her hair had been done at Antoine's. The straight Egyptian style chosen by Nadine, with most of the wave taken out and a bunching curve over both ears. The grey eyes had been outlined with black pencil and shaded with silver blue, the lashes darkened. Her lips were a bright pink and she had sun-tan make-up which did away with the London pallor and gave promise of what Celia might look like after a few weeks of the sun out here.

'By Jingo,' thought Nat. 'My kid *is* a beauty. I feel proud of her. I shall double Nadine's cheque. That young woman's got taste even if she is a bit of a witch at times.'

'Bravo Celia, and bravo Nadine,' he said aloud.

Starry-eyed, Celia basked in her father's praise.

'I'm glad you approve,' she said, and felt now that the wearing, anxious hours had been worth while. She thought so even more later on, when Philippe Clermont turned up and kissed her hand, and added his flattery in no uncertain terms.

'But, *Mademoiselle*, you look *exquisite. Mais, c'est formidable!*'

Nadine twisted her lips and shrugged. She was beginning to wonder if Nat's cheque was going to be worth all this. She had done her work rather too well, perhaps, but it would not amuse her if the men turned their attention from her to this silly girl. She decided to put in her spoke.

'Lift the head—hold back the shoulders—you are slouching, *chérie*,' she addressed Celia spitefully.

Celia coloured, but with that show of Frayne spirit that her father was beginning to recognise and approve.

'Honestly, *Madame la Comtesse*, I can't learn everything at once. After all, I'm only a new girl in your *école de haute couture*.'

'What an accent,' muttered the *Comtesse* disagreeably.

Geoffrey listened and watched silently. Suddenly, Celia was

made aware that he, alone, hadn't praised her. She was intrigued. She went so far as to joke about it with him.

'Do I look awful to you? You've got such a funny, disapproving expression in your eyes.'

His very blue eyes twinkled.

'On the contrary, you look absolutely the cat's whiskers, and I think the *Comtesse* has an apt pupil.'

'That still sounds as though you don't like the change in me,' pouted Celia, with truly feminine vanity.

Geoffrey stuck a pipe between his teeth.

'As if my opinion mattered.'

She probed a little deeper.

'You don't really *like* a lot of make-up, do you?'

He was embarrassed now.

'I really know nothing about such things, but I thought you looked awfully nice before. I don't know why a girl like you wants to bother with make-up, etc. You've got such a nice complexion of your own. Oh, but that's what Nadine and the others would call "stuffy". Afraid I don't belong to the *chic* set,' he added with a laugh.

Now Celia spoke with what he thought was touching candour. She was the most frank, uncomplicated girl he had ever met. Even her little display of vanity just now was without guile or deliberate intent to make an assault on his physical senses. She was just a naïve, charming child. She lacked conceit. It struck him all of a sudden that it would be a pity if Uncle Nat tried to turn her into a vain and empty-headed creature like Nadine.

She was saying, 'Do you know, I rather agree with you, but my uncle seems to want me to take the *Comtesse's* advice. I'm doing it to please him, really.'

'Well, the result is stunning,' murmured Geoffrey, 'so don't worry.'

Celia gave the unaffected and delicious laugh which he liked so much.

'What you really mean is those dogs of yours wouldn't care whether I was using a new season's lipstick—or none at all.'

He laughed with her.

'Sure thing. But I don't suppose you were meant to dress for my dogs.'

'Maybe I'd rather,' she said, with a sudden sigh, 'and when can I come down to the kennels and see the darlings?'

'Whenever you want, but please don't wear those beautiful

pale blue slacks. The beasts will all jump on you and annihilate your fashionable purchases.'

'I'll come along in an old cotton frock,' she nodded.

They agreed that one morning just before twelve might be a good time. By then, Nat would have stopped dictating any letters to his P.A. or giving orders. Tomorrow Celia had only two appointments—one early in the morning with the tailor who was making a summer-weight coat for her in that shade of petunia pink which Nadine called 'her colour', and the other with a furrier in Monte Carlo where Nat said that his niece should be fitted out with what she needed. (Goodbye to the little squirrel cape so gallantly bought by Aunt Tiny who had saved up for it.) Nat insisted that his 'niece' be properly decked out. She must have a short sapphire blue mink jacket for chilly evenings, and white Icelandic foxes because they had suited her so well when she tried them on this morning.

That night, during dinner, Celia said to her father:

'I feel sort of that you—oughtn't—well, oughtn't to be spending such a fortune on me.'

He grinned at her amicably.

'Who else should I be spending it on, my dear? Don't worry your head about finances.'

'It's rather difficult for me to remember sometimes, that I'm living with a millionaire.'

'No doubt—you've been too long in the company of that cheeseparing old aunt of yours.'

Celia bristled.

'You can't call Aunt Tiny that. She's terribly generous, but we've never had money to waste. We've had to be careful.'

Nat laughed. He enjoyed her defiance.

'There, there, I didn't mean to be nasty. Afraid you'll find I've got rather a nasty tongue and temper, my dear. Being a millionaire doesn't necessarily sweeten one.'

Celia, who had resented aspersion flung on her beloved aunt, softened.

She and her father were dining *à deux* tonight. No party for his birthday. He preferred to be alone with his daughter. She liked this *tête-à-tête*, because it meant she could get to know her father more intimately. (He looked shockingly ill, she thought.) And Annette, while running the bath for Celia this evening, had mentioned the fact that *Monsieur* was *très fatigué*. Already last week, a German professor had flown from Frankfurt to see him. That was a bad sign because *Monsieur* did not like Germans but this one had special knowledge of his particular trouble, so he had sent for him. To Celia this father of hers was virtually a stranger, but he *was* her father, and she could not bear to think that anybody still as young and vital as Nat, should be in danger of his life. For that was what Annette had hinted.

Celia said:

'I think it's a shame you don't really enjoy your life, Uncle Nat—that you don't find it over sweet.'

He shut one eye and looked at her with the other, which was a trifle bloodshot and cynical, yet not without tenderness tonight. By jingo, Nadine had done her stuff. The little girl looked really as he had wanted, in that blue dress. What she needed now were some lovely clips. He'd tell Philippe to go and choose some from Van Hoffman tomorrow. Aquamarines would suit her—set in diamonds with a few rubies thrown in, perhaps—bracelet and earrings to match. Her mother used to be fond of aquamarines, but he could not afford jewellery when Mary was alive. Nat squirmed uncomfortably at the thought of his first dead wife. He grunted:

'Seem strange to you to call me "Uncle"? Or are you getting used to it?'

'Used to it,' she nodded. 'After all, I've never had to call you anything else.'

'True. Now returning to your wish that I should enjoy my money and find life sweet—first of all, you've got to be fit and then you've got to believe in your fellow creatures. I've got rotten health and I don't believe in anybody.'

Celia blushed.

'That sounds horrible,' she whispered.

Nat waited until Jean, the white-coated manservant, had placed the iced pudding made with kirsch in front of his daughter. He himself had eaten little but he sipped the excellent *Coteaux du Layon* which was his favourite white wine. He was going to try and teach the little girl about wines. He had been pleased when she said she liked his choice tonight. He had almost expected her to ask for a Coca-Cola.

Once Jean had departed, followed by the pretty French parlourmaid who wore a dark green uniform, with coffee-coloured lace apron, and a coquettish bow in her hair, he commented on his daughter's last statement.

'Maybe it *is* horrible, my dear, but life does these things to you. You're very, very young. Your experience of life is so narrow that it almost scares me. It makes me afraid for you—these are so many damned pitfalls for you to fall into.'

'I can take care of myself,' began Celia, warmed by the conversation and the good wine.

'I doubt that. However, I would suggest you don't go around too starry-eyed, honey. It's miserable to be disillusioned. Better to start out that way, and then be agreeably surprised.'

'I can't agree,' said Celia, biting her lower lip, 'I think it awful not to trust people.'

'So you approve of the English law—innocent until you are proved guilty, rather than the French system—guilty until you are proved innocent.'

'Yes, I think one should start out by having faith in one's fellow creatures.'

He shrugged.

'We must all lead our lives as we want, I suppose. But it still makes me afraid for you.'

'Should I then start out by suspecting you for having brought me out here for purely selfish reasons?'

Nat gave his short, barking laugh.

'Honey, you'd certainly be right to suspect me of being selfish. I am. The most egotistical old so-and-so the world has ever known. But I sent for you because I wanted you to share my money and success and the good living, and most of all I wanted to square my own conscience and make up for neglecting you so abominably in the past—you and your mother,' he added in a reluctant voice. 'Though I'd be a hypocrite to say I've ever regretted going. You see what an old basket I am.'

'I wish you wouldn't say things like that,' Celia sighed and shook her head at him. 'You seem to *want* me to think you horrid.'

'Okay, honey—start out by thinking I am then find out I'm nice. Pleasant surprise.'

'You *are* funny!' she grinned back now, and felt a sudden flow of sympathy towards him. There was something strangely endearing about her father—in fact he was irresistible. She began to understand why her poor mother had adored Nat and, according to Aunt Tiny, refused ever to speak ill of him.

'Don't let's delve too far into the past, honey. Let's anticipate a better time ahead for the pair of us. And I hope it won't mean this "uncle and niece" relationship for too long. But you see, once more, I prove myself a suspicious devil. I'm scared some fellow will approach my pretty heiress with an eye on her fortune, as well as her beauty.'

'That's isn't very complimentary to me. Oh, I know I'm not madly attractive but——'

'Nonsense,' he broke in. 'Don't belittle yourself. I can't stand mock modesty. But no, it isn't "mock" in your case,' he added more kindly, 'you really are unaware of your own potentialities. You've never had a chance to exploit them, of course—counting the pennies, sitting at a typewriter all day and so on. But if you could see how very attractive you look tonight, my little Celia, you'd realise that a lot of men *will* fall for you in the future. Only I want it to be only for *you*. Underneath this thick hide of mine there lies quite a sentimental streak. I didn't hit it off with your poor mother but my second wife, poor little Marie-Thérèse, I adored, and her death broke me. I haven't been the same chap since. I'd like you to be as happy as I was when she was alive.'

'I'm terribly sorry,' said Celia gently, 'that you lost her.'

'No more of this. Let's go on talking about you. And to swell your ego—let me tell you our young Philippe finds you very attractive. You're cutting the *Comtesse* right out, which affords me a certain malicious amusement.'

Now Celia went bright pink and, to cover her confusion, took an extra gulp of wine.

'Oh, I'm sure that's not true.'

'It would amuse me if you ended up by cutting all the other females out,' chuckled Nat. 'That wide-eyed innocence can be very fetching, especially when it's accompanied by a drop of the devilish Frayne blood. And you're not nearly as meek and mild as you appear, my little Celia. I'm beginning to see that. They were all a fiery, spirited lot, the Fraynes.'

'You're getting me confused. I really don't know what I am,' she said.

Her mind was on Philippe Clermont. How wonderful, if it were true that he admired her. Certainly, no man she had ever met looked at her in quite so exciting a way as Philippe.

'By the way,' went on Nat, 'if I feel up to it I want to take you, myself, down to our *salon* tomorrow, and show you a few of my treasures. We've just got a pair of chairs in from a client in Paris who wants to sell them—Louis XIVth—quite lovely. And a Ming vase I had been after for a long time. Superb colour, and perfect. A real collector's piece. You'll soon learn a bit about antiques as well as clothes. You've got a brisk mind.'

She blinked.

'I certainly feel as though I've come to school—there's so much to learn.'

'Well, Nadine makes a damn' good headmistress,' said Nat, and roared with laughter at his own rather *risqué* jest, then apologised, remembering who he was with tonight. What did this daughter of his really know about life? Absolutely nothing. In the society in which Tiny Cotland had brought her up, one was just 'nice' or 'not nice'; a girl of Celia's age eventually married and lived in a soul-destroying flat in a huge block or one of those damn' bungalows that were wrecking the face of England. Honeymooned, probably, in one of those still more damnable caravans that had found a home on the lovely *Côte d'Azur*, took a holiday in one of those so-and-so camps, followed a routine existence on a meagre income, brought up the children, and finally pulled out pension and insurances, and then died. By jingo, what a different life Nathaniel Frayne had led from the time he got himself out of that first hideous rut. Wasn't it rather pleasant to look back and remember all his adventures—the real thrill of living dangerously at times— of gambling, watching the gamble come off—amassing money —then being able to spend it either on wife or mistress? A dying man he might be—and he didn't give tuppence for this old heart of his—but he'd had a good time in the past. And that was what life was for—*one must enjoy it*.

Then Nat Frayne looked again at this young daughter who had everything yet to learn, and the whole of her life before her. Something in her extreme purity (and he was sure that not all modern girls were pure), something in her essential goodness, her honesty of purpose, disturbed him strangely. Who was to say that she and that blasted old aunt of hers weren't right, and that he was wrong? He could remember the quarrels he had had with Tiny years and years ago, during that other half-forgotten life. The young Nat stormed about the place, bellowing at his young wife and his sister-in-law who was staying with them, when they disapproved of his peccadilloes.

'God preserve me from such a pious pair,' he had shouted. 'You can't go through life being so damned perfect.'

Mary had looked sad and remained speechless as usual. Tiny, at least, had the guts to bellow back at him (the big hulking creature).

'Nobody expects anyone to be perfect, Nathaniel Frayne,

but we've all got to try and live a decent life to the best of our ability. You don't seem to have one scruple. And people without scruples aren't going to get anywhere in the next life, even if they prosper in this. As for saying "God preserve you", I don't really see why He should.'

They had always quarrelled bitterly. Tonight in the midst of the gilded splendid world he had built for himself, and with the shadow of the end drawing near, Nat was not so absolutely sure that he *had* been right. (What about the next life—did he believe in it? If there was one, he certainly wouldn't get anywhere near the Throne.) He'd done a lot of things that Mary and her sister wouldn't think right. Yet he had been a man of his word (except when he left Mary)—in business, always straight, integral. He had been absolutely faithful to Marie-Thérèse too, and now he wanted to be a good father to his child. He wasn't so bad (he hoped), but he felt suddenly (most unusual for him) a weariness of spirit as well as of body. A need for comfort. Not the comfort that Nadine Sachelles and her kind were willing to offer—sensuous delight, passion, the oblivion that follows satiety. But comfort of the heart. Yes, that was what one needed when one was growing older and was sick. And this young, fearless, very nice daughter of his might possibly be the one person in the world who could give it to him.

He reached out a hand. Celia placed hers in it confidingly.

'Celia,' he said abruptly, 'do you believe in God?'

'But of course,' she said in a shocked voice.

'In heaven—in hell? All the old tenets and dogmas that our fathers and forefathers have clung to for hundreds of years?'

'Of course,' she said again, without hesitation.

'A lot of people *don't*. Look at the Communist countries.'

'And look at the result—the effect of Godlessness has had on them,' she said promptly. 'They are evil, and one has to have religion and faith in order to conquer evil. Without it, no country could prosper in the long run, even though they may seem to do so to begin with. It's like Germany in the war—look how Godless those Nazis were, and they all sank. The whole country was wrecked and divided.'

'It soon came out on top again,' he argued.

'Because in West Germany, anyhow, the churches are open again,' she said triumphantly.

He sighed, drew his hand away from hers, and pulled a cigar out of his pocket.

'By jingo, you're very sure of yourself.'

'No, I'm not, only sure about God . . . and what comes after,' she said, slightly pink and embarrassed.

'I wish I were you,' said her father in a low voice, and dug a hole in the end of his cigar. '*By jingo*, I wish I were you, Celia!'

But the cynic in him prevailed and he thought,

'I wonder if the first man she really falls for will break through those defences. She's my daughter, she'll be capable of passion. By jingo! We shall see.'

When they said good night, Celia lifted a shy face and said:

'I know you don't celebrate birthdays much but I am going to buy you a present when I see something I think you would like.'

'I forbid you to spend your money on me—just give me a kiss,' he said.

She gave it with all the warmth of a newly-awakened devotion. He had not thought it possible to feel so touched or so content.

# SIX

ONE morning about two weeks later, Celia went down to *Madame* Pavette's house, just before noon. She found a very different Geoffrey from the well-dressed, serious young man who was Nat's personal assistant. The little stout French-woman who wore sombre black, like so many widows of her race, although her husband had been dead nearly twenty years, led Celia into the back garden, talking in rapid French which Celia could not understand. She inferred, however, from the many gestures and rollings of eye, that there was a crisis on. A *'crise'* *Madame* called it. The paved 'garden' had no flowers except a few scarlet geraniums in stone pots. It was almost entirely taken up by a wooden shed which, Celia learned, had been built by Geoffrey himself, in his spare time; with the help of *Madame* Pavette's old brother, who was long past seventy, but still a good carpenter.

Attached to the shed was a wire run, shaded from the sun by one large tree. In this run, Celia saw three dogs lying con-tentedly—the breeds unrecognisable. One, a shaggy type of collie, had a bandaged paw. One, a spaniel type, lay patheti-cally with both legs in splints, but wagged joyfully at Celia when she spoke to it. The other, which might have a touch of Labrador, seemed to be almost well. This, then, was Geoffrey's hospital *'Pour les Chiens—les invalides'*—as *Madame* ex-plained. In the shed there was a new arrival.

Geoffrey, wearing shorts and no shirt, and perspiring pro-fusely, stood over a large wooden table, on which he had just strapped down a small unconscious animal which looked to Celia to be a cross between a poodle and a Cairn terrier.

Geoffrey glanced over his shoulder, saw Celia and wiped the sweat out of his eyes with the back of his hand.

'Hello there! If you really meant what you said about help-ing, would you like to give me a hand now?' he asked.

'But of course,' she answered. She noticed the strong odour of anaesthetic in the air. He glanced quickly at her cotton frock.

'I've just put the poor little nipper out. I think the right hind-leg is broken. I've got to set it. If you could just do as I say, and hand me a few things——'

55

'Of course,' repeated Celia.

'But your dress——?'

'I've come as you told me, in an old cotton thing. I'm sorry I've been given no time to come along before,' she added.

'Ask *Madame* Pavette for an apron.'

'I don't need one,' Celia said impatiently. 'This dress will wash. Let's get on with the job.'

He threw her a grateful look. Now he gave her his orders. She found him very efficient. He worked briskly and smoothly. She was amazed at the professional way in which he handled the dog's injured leg.

She stood giving him the instruments he asked for, holding a bowl of antiseptic and cotton wool. He explained the type of pads and splints, and the bandages he needed, and told her where to find them. The place was scrupulously clean. Bottles and instruments were kept in a glass-fronted hanging case.

'It's like a proper vet's surgery,' said Celia.

'I took lessons in a veterinary surgery from a friend of mine who makes it his career—a delightful Frenchman you'll probably meet down here one day. He thinks I'm a bit crazy to take in all these half-dead or dying mongrels, but he humours me and gives me advice if the job's too difficult for me. Now this is a simple fracture and I know how to set it."

Celia laid a gentle hand on the dog's little head and noted the dust and grime on its coat. An uncared-for skinny little mongrel.

'Poor sweet—where did you find it?'

'Accident happened in front of my eyes as I drove home. A dazzling blonde, driving like a maniac down that hill just below Villa Psyche.'

'I know. But I'm sorry it was a woman driver,' said Celia, with a twist of the lips and looking at him out of the corner of her eyes.

He returned the look, grinning.

'I didn't say it was a *woman*. I said a dazzling blonde. That might mean anything.'

'Honestly, you sound as though you've got a thing against my sex.'

Now he straightened, untied the straps on the still insensible patient, and lifted the little body into his arms.

'Of course I haven't. Follow me. I'm going to carry her to what I call my casualty ward. Clean straw and a cool place where I keep a fan going. The little brute will take some feeding-up now, and keeping quiet. With luck she ought to be on all four paws again quite shortly.'

'Well, I'm glad to see you are nice to her sort of woman,' Celia nodded, smiling.

'They are the nicest females of all,' said Geoffrey. 'The word "bitch" should never have become synonymous with something so unattractive.'

'I agree,' she nodded, smiling again.

She followed Geoffrey, who walked to the other end of the shed and placed his patient gently down on a straw bed, then shut the little gate. Those big muscular hands of his could be extraordinarily kind and tender, she thought. His passionate love for animals endeared him to her.

Now he insisted on her sitting in one of the wrought-iron chairs at a rusty old iron table, in the middle of the *patio*, where he brought her an iced drink. While he smoked his pipe and sipped his own aperitif, he told her about his small collection of patients.

The Labrador, if it could be called so in truth, was Rastus; a cousin of *Madame* Pavette's was going to take Rastus home tomorrow. The little creature with the wounded paw had been offered a home with the small daughter of a waiter who often served Geoffrey at a nearby restaurant. Geoffrey was waiting to find somebody who would take the other, more seriously injured dog.

'I've christened him "Solo" because he seems so very much alone. Now I must find a name for my new, queer patient of this morning.'

'I'll be her godmother and pay for her future treatment, meat and biscuits,' said Celia promptly.

'Thanks. A very delightful idea,' said Geoffrey. 'And the name——?'

'Gigi,' said Celia—'It was my favourite film.'

'Gigi she shall be.'

'Do their owners never claim them?'

'Rarely. I make a point of informing the police who are only too glad to let me look after the weak and suffering. They have them put down almost immediately if they come across them, unless they happen to be priceless poodles or spoiled darlings of high degree whose owners pay handsomely to get them back. But Gigi, I confess, is a comic-looking customer and I am sure she'll never be claimed.'

'Well, I think she looks not only comic, but pathetic, and

in need of love and as her godmother, I'll love her, and if you don't find a new owner I'll take her home myself.'

'I doubt if Nathaniel Frayne would appreciate such a mongrel—or any dog at all—in his beautiful home,' said Geoffrey drily.

'I think he would if I asked him,' said Celia.

Geoffrey puffed at his pipe and looked thoughtfully at the girl. She was gaining in assurance, he thought, even after such a brief spell at Villa Psyche. She was nothing like as shy or diffident as she had been when he first met her at Nice Airport. She had been magnificent this morning—sensible and helpful. He liked her enormously.

'How's the shopping getting on?' he asked.

She grimaced.

'Oh, I'm being turned into ever such a smart young thing!' she said mockingly. 'My aunt whom I lived with in London just won't know me when she sees me again. I shall soon be the complete product of *Madame la Comtesse's* sensational taste.'

Before he could restrain himself, Geoffrey blurted out: 'Don't let her change you too entirely.'

'You said that before,' she laughed. 'It sounds like the old song which was all the rage in Aunt Tiny's day—"*Stay as sweet as you are—Don't let a thing ever change you*". Those were the words. But you see I'm not very sweet, and I do need to change, according to Uncle Nat and Nadine.'

'Nevertheless, I stick to what I said.'

She thought that very nice of him and flattering too. Then she became aware that it was past one o'clock.

'I must get back. I'd completely forgotten—Uncle Nat's chauffeur has been waiting outside all this time. You are rather a long way from the Villa, so I took the car.'

Geoffrey followed her out to the waiting Cadillac.

'It's the first time *Madame* Pavette has ever had such a splendid vehicle standing outside her little residence.'

'Say goodbye to *Madame* for me. Well, I'll be seeing you later,' said Celia, 'and you must tell me how Gigi seems when she recovers consciousness.'

'It is extremely nice of you to take such an interest in my waifs and strays,' he said gratefully.

As she drove back to the Villa, Celia found herself thinking yet again how nice Geoffrey was. But soon her thoughts drifted away from him and his dogs. She began to think about Philippe

Clermont. A delicious tremor went through her at the very memory of those brilliant, almond eyes, which looked at her so disturbingly; and the touch of his lips when he kissed her hand. No two men could be more different, she reflected, than Geoffrey and Philippe. They were both attractive in their way. 'Uncle Nat' gathered charming people about him. But the Frenchman, in Celia's estimation, just made everybody else seem dull by comparison. He was almost wickedly fascinating. She had seen him nearly every day since she arrived here.

She was quite disappointed to hear from Annette that she would be lunching alone. *Monsieur* was not getting up until later. He had had another bad night. But there was to be a dinner party tonight—an American connoisseur of the fine arts and his wife were guests of honour—with two Italians— also antique specialists, man and wife, *Monsieur* Clermont, of course, and the inevitable *Comtesse*.

Celia was not anxious to see Nadine, but she was relieved and happy to know that Philippe would be in the party again this evening.

Later on, she went down to the sea to swim and do some sun-bathing. She returned to laze over a book and later, re-varnish her nails, cream her face and start to think about what she was going to wear tonight. This was when Celia began to feel that she really was learning her lesson from Nadine. She was beginning to pay attention to details. It was quite a thrill also to be able to decide which dress one was going to wear, and have the right shoes and bag to go with it.

Writing to Aunt Tiny that afternoon, Celia found herself rather mixed up mentally. She was no longer the complete *ingénue* that she had been when she left London a fortnight ago. But she was still not yet wholly sophisticated. She felt something between the two. She had enjoyed helping Geoffrey down there with the dogs this morning. She would enjoy (perhaps much more so) flirting with the handsome Philippe tonight.

'This is fascinating,' she thought. 'I feel like two people.'

Of the two, she did not think that darling Aunt Tiny would appreciate the new fashionable product of the *Côte d'Azur*. And when Annette brought her a letter from Aunt Tiny by the late post, and she read it, Celia felt almost guilty. To begin with, poor Aunt Tiny was missing her—that was obvious— although all she said was:

'*I expect you are being far too gay and busy to think much about the old life . . . By the way, I hope, my dear, that your coffee-lace was a great success. I must look out for something else to bring you when I come out for that holiday in a month or two's time . . .*'

It was those last two lines that distressed Celia. She *knew* now that the coffee-lace had been awful. Nobody had liked it. Nat had said so. So had Nadine. And it would be awful if Aunt Tiny chose something equally awful and brought it out to her and she couldn't wear it. She must write to her aunt at once and say something tactful about having been given so much by Nat, she wouldn't want any more clothes.

Celia thought of Geoffrey, begging her not to change.

'Oh dear,' she thought, 'I don't really *want* to change as a person. I must be careful.'

But when she faced Philippe Clermont in the *salon* that evening in all the glory of one of her new beautiful evening dresses, she forgot what Geoffrey had said and also what Aunt Tiny had written. She was a radiant, glowing symbol of sheer feminine attraction—and awakening desire—thinking of nothing but the look in the Frenchman's eyes as he bent over her hand, and whispered:

'But, *M'mselle* Celia, you look *quite* enchanting tonight.'

Celia felt well rewarded for the pains she had taken. The short, backless white crêpe dress fitted her like a glove. She had already achieved a slight natural tan which, in combination with her new make-up, suited her well. The beauticians had taught her how to enlarge her eyes by outlining them with black pencil, and the touch of emerald eye-shadow lent her eyes a mysterious beauty.

'They look more green than grey tonight,' Philippe told her.

'Really!' Celia gave her unaffected laugh. 'I am beginning to be so beauty-conscious, it isn't true!'

'I also, am beginning to be conscious of your beauty!' said Philippe, meaningly.

Her pulse fluttered, like her lashes, with nervous excitement. Philippe looked rather splendid tonight, she thought, in his white dinner jacket with the red cummerbund.

She was fascinated by the quick movement of his long, brown fingers as he rolled a cigarette between them.

Nadine watched them jealously. Even Nat's cheque could not console her for the fact that Philippe hardly turned his gaze in her direction these days. On the way in to dinner she spoke to him in a fierce whisper.

'You are making a fool of yourself, *mon cher*, trying to turn the head of Nat's stupid niece.'

'Now, now, Nadine,' he reproved her, with his brilliant smile.

'I mean it,' she said. 'What good can Nat's penniless niece be to you?'

'My dear, your shopping expeditions have been so successful, you have made her look quite charming,' said Philippe not daring to rate Celia's attractions any higher, with Nadine in such a mood.

'Then I've been a fool,' she said, furiously.

'Why all this sudden interest in me, *chérie*?' he asked. 'You have always played "hard to get" until now. Is it just because you see me trying to make the simple shy little English girl, shall we say, happy?'

Nadine gave a hard laugh.

'You men are all the same—easily taken in. Celia isn't all that shy or simple. I really cannot see why you waste your time with her.'

Philippe looked at his nails and lifted his eyebrows. Naturally, *Madame la Comtesse* did not know just how intriguing Celia had become to him. Her fresh, untouched beauty was not so considerable, but the glow of extreme youth and innocence made her physically irresistible to a man of his type.

Philippe also knew about her other attraction. He chuckled to himself, wondering what Nadine would say if she were to be told that the penniless niece was, in reality, daughter and heiress to Nathaniel Frayne.

But he had no wish to fall out with the sparkling clever Frenchwoman whom he had been close to for so long. He took one of her hands and pressed it.

'You know how I feel about you, *chère* Nadine. You really need not be annoyed because I am being amiable with little Miss Frayne. Beside you—she is nothing.'

This slightly restored Nadine's *amour-propre*. She returned the pressure of Philippe's fingers. At the same time, she thought about Geoffrey More.

The whole thing was a game of chess, she thought, sardonically . . . all of them were pawns moving across the chequer board of fate. But so far, no move she had ever made had brought her an inch nearer Geoffrey. It was the imperturbable

Englishman whom she really wanted, with all the passion of her perverse, greedy nature. Philippe Clermont was with Nadine a question of *faute de mieux*. But now, it was more than her vanity could bear to see him pursuing Celia.

As usual, she took care to subdue Celia's high spirits and new-found self-confidence, by finding fault with her. With an acid-sweet smile, she touched the necklace that Celia was wearing, and whispered:

'A wrong choice, my dear. You should have worn your turquoise collar and earrings with the white crêpe.'

Celia sighed.

'Oh, I *wish* I could be absolutely right for once without your help.'

'Your taste will improve,' said Nadine in a patronising voice.

Celia's spirits were further dampened during the dinner—a rich, long-drawn-out meal, perfectly prepared by Nat's chef. They were not in the *salle à manger* tonight, but on the terrace. It was warm and still this beautiful Mediterranean evening. The party of eight sat at a round, black, marble-topped table, on which there were gold satin Chinese mats. Six tall golden candles in ebony and gilt candelebra burned like tiny torches in the darkness. A green and white Ming bowl of white roses made a lovely centrepiece. Never had Celia seen such elegance. It was an extraordinary metamorphosis from the little wooden 'bar' table in the kitchen at home, she thought—where she and Aunt Tiny used to sit on their little stools, gossiping over a high tea.

'How my life has changed just in these two short weeks, and yet Geoffrey need not be afraid that anything will ever *completely* alter me. I'd be just as happy—and perhaps happier—who knows?—to find myself eating an egg, or a dish of baked beans, with Aunt Tiny tonight—marvellous though this atmosphere is—delicious though the lobster *Thermidor* was,' she reflected, with some amusement. The crisp pale green and yellow hearts of lettuce with French dressing were *cordon bleu* washed down by Uncle Nat's expensive hock which they drank out of tall fine crystal goblets. She learned that these must be reverenced by virtue of the fact that they were over a hundred years old, and had belonged at one time to a set owned by a Venetian prince. Uncle Nat had so many priceless belongings.

She would never forget her first visit to *Frayne et Cie* in Cannes. She had pleased her father by showing a genuine interest in the treasures he pinpointed for her. It would not be long, he had told her, before she would know a Waterford glass jug when she saw one—or a Chippendale piecrust table—or a piece of Dutch marquetry—or a Queen Anne *escritoire*. She had thought the show-room was arranged in exquisite taste. The antiques were displayed against black or white velvet draperies, the floor was black marble, the ceilings hung with marvellous chandeliers, one or two of which, Nat told her, came from Versailles. The long show-cases were full of small but rare ornaments—bottles, cases, figurines in finest porcelain or ivory; gilded, enamelled, or bejewelled—all fabulously expensive.

In particular, Celia had admired a small gold box encrusted with precious stones. Her father had made her open it, where-upon a tiny, jewelled bird sprang out, moved its tail and warbled like a nightingale.

Nat had been pleased because Celia fell in love with this, and with a quick and careless generosity, which she was beginning to know and appreciate, he had insisted on her taking it away.

'It's a Faberge—he was the greatest craftsman of such bits of expensive frivolity that ever lived. He created most of his masterpieces for the Tsarina of Russia just before the revolution.'

'What a pity everything nowadays is plastic or machine-made,' Celia had ventured, at which her father's wrinkled lean face had puckered into one big grimace.

'Honey! Never mention the word *plastic* to me or anything like it. I know the world is changing and that, for the sake of the masses, we have got to accept mass-produced articles. But to let the great crafts die out is a crime. Once gone, we shall never recover them. The same applies to some of the colouring used in painting by the old masters—and even the best Egyptian dyes—we still don't know the secret of them.'

Celia had argued:

'Yet some of the things made long ago were regarded as rubbish by the people of that time. They may only have be-come valuable because of their rarity.'

'So you think that a thousand years from now a plastic cup and saucer or a piece of formica might be worth a king's ran-som, when dug up!'

Nat had roared with laughter over this thought, and driving back to the villa, looked with benevolent affection upon his 'niece'.

63

He had begun to wish, he told her, that he had never started this 'uncle and niece' business. He was becoming so attached to her. He found her sense of humour and ways of reasoning so much in accord with his own.

Across the table, Nadine looked at the younger girl's radiant face and gritted her teeth. She really wished Nat had never brought Celia out here. Even the Italian, Signor Ortelli, whom she had met in the past in Rome, and who had been one of her conquests, whispered to her:

'Nat's niece is angelic.'

'If you saw much of her you would realise how ignorant she is,' Nadine whispered back, spitefully.

'Can it be true?' the Italian had asked, smiling, at this piece of transparent feminine jealousy.

Nadine, who had heard altogether too much about the charm of her protégée tonight, now leaned across the table and addressed Celia:

'Signor Ortelli is very fond of London, *chérie*. He wonders what you think of this restaurant everybody goes to—the Empress. He was dining there last night.'

'I've never been there,' said Celia promptly.

'And what do you think of the Mirabelle?' put in the Italian, feasting his gaze on the young girl's golden-brown face. With its faint flush of health, he romantically likened her complexion to the peaches ripening in the orchards of his beloved Italy.

'I don't know the Mirabelle either,' said Celia, frankly.

'Where would you recommend the Signor to dine then?' Nadine continued her malicious campaign, for she knew perfectly well the humble background from which the girl had come.

Nadine had no wish to annoy Nat, but she could see that he was busily engaged in a conversation with Mamie Anders, the blonde smart wife of the American whom Nat was entertaining. So she could safely taunt Celia and she was delighted when a slight flush now deepened the colour in her victim's cheeks. At last, she had made Celia self-conscious!

Then the young girl said, with her innate honesty:

'I really don't know, Nadine. I've never been to any of the smart London places. My aunt and I couldn't afford it.'

'Oh, you poor darling!' said Nadine, with great affectation of sympathy.

Suddenly, Celia became aware of what the Frenchwoman

was trying to do. She felt a deep scorn, and a desire to defend herself—not in order to impress the Italian, but to uphold the world in which she had always lived, and which she was not going to allow this woman to decry—no matter what the wealthy Signor Ortelli might think.

'I really can't think why I should be pitied!' she said indignantly. 'I think one can have just as good a time in a cheap café in Battersea, or across the bridge in Chelsea, if one is with somebody one loves!'

The others at the table seemed to have stopped talking at this moment and to hear that ringing young voice. They looked at Celia. Nat seemed puzzled, not having heard what had gone before.

'What's all this?' he asked in his brusque way. 'Who likes meals in cheap cafés?'

'I do, Uncle Nat,' she said, throwing back her head, 'so long as I am with the right companion. I repeat—it can be just as much fun then, as dining at the smart places like this Empress or Mirabelle.'

'Well spoken,' said Signor Ortelli. He found Celia adorable, and wished that his wife was not so near, so that he could tell the young girl what he felt. Nadine shrugged her shoulders and dabbed her red lips delicately with her embroidered table napkin. She felt that her shots had misfired. Nat closed one eye in that way he had, and gave his daughter an ironic smile.

'Romantic little soul, aren't you?'

The American woman who was a nice person put in a friendly word.

'Say, I agree with Miss Frayne. Some of the best meals I ever ate in my youth were with the boy-friend in the sort of Help-Yourself joints where we only paid a few dimes for a frankfurter sausage.'

Her husband laughed, and said mockingly to Nat:

'My, my! That must be before I came on the scene. Mamie sure wants the best places in New York these days. Maybe it's this romantic Mediterranean coast that's affecting her tongue.'

'No,' said Mrs. Anders, 'I just wanna uphold Miss Frayne, and say that it's the person you eat with that counts—not the place.'

Nadine, feeling enraged, caught a mocking look from Philippe, who added his shaft.

'It all sounds delicious and I am on Miss Frayne's side.'

Celia's spirits rose again. But looking at Nadine, she felt a trifle worried. She was beginning, even after this short while at Villa Psyche, to feel that she had an implacable enemy rather than a friend in the woman her father had chosen as her teacher.

Celia was no fool. She had often watched the *Comtesse*, and noted that Nadine tried hard to be the centre of attraction both with Philippe and Geoffrey; Geoffrey obviously did not respond. About Philippe, Celia was not so sure. Once, in fact, she had been wandering through the gardens in moonlight, just before going to bed and had seen the two figures—Nadine's and Philippe's—silhouetted against the luminous light in an impassioned embrace. She remembered how, at the time, it had disturbed her. With all her senses roused by the attractive Frenchman, the young girl had found it rather bitter to see him hold and kiss another woman. But of course, she had tried to argue with herself, he and Nadine had known each other for years and perhaps they *had* had an '*affaire*' but not a serious one. Perhaps out here, in this rather intoxicating atmosphere, the men and women in her father's set kissed easily and often, and without real significance. Celia had been quite ashamed to feel distressed by what she had seen. But Philippe had become her *beau ideal*, the romantic figure-head in all her dreams and thoughts. She did not want to have to share him with the *Comtesse*—or have to enter any kind of contest. Attractive though Philippe was—Celia, with her honest and direct simplicity, would not find such a situation agreeable.

# SEVEN

LATER on that evening, Philippe made sure that Nadine was busy—trying to allure Signor Ortelli all over again. Then he led Celia away from the terrace where they were all smoking and talking. He told her that on his recent tour of Italy he had found a new marble statue not unlike the nymph on the water basin in the front garden. It had only been installed in the grounds yesterday. He felt sure that Celia would like to see it. Celia, thrilled by the invitation, walked with him to the grotto. Here, this latest treasure among Nat's acquisitions had been skilfully placed. She was in a kind of grotto—with a natural waterfall sprinkling her with the diamond drops. She knelt on one knee, gazing, with rounded chin on slender hand, at the cascade of water.

Thick vine twisted with purple bougainvillaea made a charming background for the nymph's graceful contours. The moon lit up the beauty of her chiselled face. Celia gave a cry of pleasure as she saw it.

'Oh, how gorgeous!'

'She was shipped from a little village outside Florence, just before you came, but one of her hands was broken and we have just restored it. Nat meant it for a client but he fell in love with it, and told me to have it put here where he could see it. I think her face resembles yours,' he added, turning to look down at Celia.

'That's absurd,' she laughed. 'I'm not in the least like her. She has classic features.'

Philippe narrowed his eyes, critically.

'Nevertheless, in your white dress, you do resemble her tonight, and she has the same style,' he added, laughing.

'Mine is supposed to be Egyptian, not Roman!'

He waved a hand towards the moonlit statue.

'She was excavated with a few other statues, among which might easily have been included one of an Egyptian slave.'

'Well, I'm no slave,' grimaced Celia.

'How factual you are—always so practical,' Philippe said rather regretfully.

'You are laughing at me. Everybody seems to do that——' her eyes twinkled with good humour.

'I don't laugh at you at all. I admire you from the bottom of my heart,' said Philippe, and with his emotional French blood, he meant it at that moment. He almost felt that he could love this slim, cool English girl for herself, and not because she was an heiress.

Celia felt suddenly frightened—of her own turbulent heart. Never had it beaten so fast in her whole life before. She said:

'Hadn't we better get back to the others?'

He slipped an arm through hers.

'Not yet. Stay for a few moments and let us admire your uncle's new acquisition. She is like the Taj Mahal—more beautiful by moonlight than by day.'

Celia stood silent, conscious not so much of the water nymph as of the tall graceful figure of the man close to her, and the fragrance of his cigarette.

She must keep her head, she told herself. She had always prided herself on being the sort of girl who could do so. But there was something quite irresistible about Philippe Clermont on a Mediterranean night—with the perfume of the strange, exotic-looking lilies which grew around this grotto, drifting to her nostrils; and the distant sound of music coming from the Villa where Nat had started to play his favourite record. He had a passion for Spanish music. She could hear the exciting beat of a *flamenco* and later the thrill of a nightingale's song. It was all rather too bewitching and heady for Celia, and she felt a very long way from Aunt Tiny and home, and the old routine. An astonishingly long way.

Once again she tried to be as Philippe had called her—practical.

'I think we really should go in to the party.'

But now the young Frenchman, caught up by the magic of the moment, forgot that he had meant to wait before he spoke one word of love to Nat's daughter.

He reached out an arm—put it around Celia's smooth, bare shoulders and drew her slowly but steadily against him.

'How sweet you are,' he said. 'Celia, Celia, you go to my head like strong wine.'

In the moonlight, her face looked pale and her eyes wide and dark.

'Philippe—please—you mustn't.'

'But I must,' he broke in. 'I must kiss you. You must let me. All the evening I have been crazy with the longing to kiss you. Celia—*adorée*—Celia, *ma très chère*!'

68

She hung back, still half afraid, even though the whole of her young, ardent body felt ready for this new and exquisite delight. She felt, indeed, that she had been waiting for it—for Philippe—waiting the whole of her life.

But she said:

'I can't help being what you call factual and practical. I'm built like that. And I feel I must tell you that I saw you kissing the *Comtesse* the other night.'

Philippe was furious with himself for having been so indiscreet.

He had kissed Nadine so often it had ceased to be of any importance. She was an attractive creature, but impoverished, which made all the difference to Philippe. She also seemed, in his dramatic fancy, to have become rather like a red rose which was drooping a little, whereas this girl, Celia, was as exquisite as a white bud of spring. Yes, really he felt overwhelmed with fervour for Celia tonight. He tightened his hold of her, smoothing back her hair with fingers so sensitive, and a smile so charming, that she was moved to surrender.

'Oh, my little Celia,' he whispered. 'You must not remember that foolish incident. It meant nothing. It was a farewell kiss—the end of the little flirtation between Nadine and myself. It exists no more I assure you. But with you, I am serious. You have put every other woman out of my head.'

'You have only known me two weeks,' Celia protested faintly.

'That is long enough for me to have fallen very much in love. Is it not a little bit the same with you? Or do you need longer in order to learn to love me?'

Now she put both her hands on his shoulders and looked up at him with her large, innocent eyes.

'I think I am a bit in love with you already, Philippe, but really—it is all happening so terribly quickly, I'm a bit confused. I admit it.'

'Don't be confused, just love me,' he said, and his pulses leapt with triumph because he could see that he was not going to have an awful lot of trouble in winning this girl completely and absolutely in the near future.

'*Mon Dieu*, but I love you, Celia,' he began shutting his eyes and now he pressed his lips to hers and kissed her long and passionately.

He stopped. Celia had drawn away from him. Her eyes

were large and supernaturally bright and her breathing fast and uneven. She shook her head.

'No—really. We mustn't—*really*, Philippe—we are being a little too mad——'

'It is the madness of love,' he broke in. 'You have never loved or been loved before, have you, *petite* Celia?'

'No.'

'Does it frighten you?'

'Yes,' she said frankly and with an embarrassed laugh.

'It need not. Love cannot harm you—it can only make you immensely happy,' he said grandly.

She laughed again. It was not a sound that pleased Philippe Clermont. His Latin temperament was fiery and demanded an answering fire. He could not understand these English, he thought irritably; how could Celia giggle nervously in his arms as though the whole thing amused her? Was this typical of the women of her country? No—it was just Celia. Ignorant, inexperienced little girl. (His irritation increased.) He would have a great deal to teach her. However, why worry—with that fortune behind her, and with his strong personality and ability, he could teach her just as well as dear Nadine had done in her sphere. But he wished, in all honesty, that Nat's daughter had the finesse, the subtlety, the sensuousness of the attractive French widow.

He took a cigarette case from his pocket; smoothed back his hair and permitted himself to smile tolerantly at Celia. Her cheeks were crimson. He could see that she was trembling—the hand that pulled a handkerchief from her bag and dabbed her lips showed him that. He was sure she had 'hidden warmth'; her lips had not been so cool or reluctant. They had been astonishingly responsive. He said:

'Forgive me. I lost my head. I admit it.'

Immediately she felt better. She was quite sure she could have lost hers if he had gone on kissing her like that. Her blood was singing—she felt as though she had been lifted into space and was still whirling through it—propelled by the mysterious urgent force of passion. And she was sure she was in love with Philippe. But she was not Nat's daughter for nothing. She had inherited from him her touch of caution and good sense, and, as Philippe divined, she was wholly British in her reactions, not easily to be carried away. She was unprepared for his volcanic passion—it staggered her—and she had certainly not been prepared for his declaration of love.

She said:

'You—you don't need to ask to be forgiven. Good gracious—I—I—it was *me* as well as *you*——' she stumbled rather childishly over the words. She had never felt less poised or capable of dealing with such an attractive man of the world as the young Frenchman. She went on: 'We both lost our heads.'

'*Dieu!*' he thought. 'Such innocence is almost alarming in this day and age. But perhaps I have been wrong in imagining that all modern girls of her age, either in my country or here, lose that innocence while they are still in their early teens. It may be less easy than I have imagined to capture Celia completely but it will be a challenge. Philippe Clermont has never had a failure with a girl *yet*. Celia will be no exception. I must go warily, and respect her lack of sophistication. Later she will change—for *me*. And if she changes as quickly and successfully as she has done since she came here where appearance is concerned, I should find the result enchanting!'

His mood—always volatile—swung to tender charm. He took one of the nervous warm young hands and kissed it.

'*Chérie!* This has been such an enchanting moment. You looked so adorable in the moonlight beside the water-nymph whom you resemble, I was carried away. I repeat—forgive me. But I shall not retract one word I have said. I love you. Remember it. And one day——' he broke off, smiling with deep significance into the large shining eyes raised to his.

'I couldn't possibly ever forget it,' she exclaimed breathlessly. 'I love you, too. But I must wait.'

'Of course. Wait until you are quite sure. I also will do so until both of us are sure,' he said coolly—as collected now as he had been the reverse a few moments ago. 'Just remember, too, when you think of tonight, my adorable little Celia, that there *is* such a thing as love at first sight. It is that way with me—over you.'

'Not possible. I looked ghastly the first night *we* met,' she said, laughing.

He winced. Humour from this factual young girl grated on his sensibilities. He felt a fierce desire to snatch her back in his arms and teach her exactly what passionate love could mean between a man and a woman. He could see he would need a lot of self-control in the immediate future, and that was something *Monsieur* Clermont was not used to exercising when his senses were stirred.

'I've no idea what you wore,' he lied. (He had hated her

dress.) 'I only know that during the fortnight that you've been out here, Nadine has helped to turn you into one of the most beautiful girls in the South of France—and that is saying something—for there are many lovely women around.'

'I can't quite believe it, but I like to hear you say such things,' she admitted.

He looked at the red point of his cigarette. It glowed in the purple darkness. He said:

'Can this be our secret, *chérie*? I don't want anybody to know about—*us*—until you have made up your mind finally that you do love me. Then I shall waste no time—I shall ask your—uncle . . .' he bit on the word (reminding himself that it would be absolutely fatal to make a slip and let Celia or anyone guess that he knew the true relationship). 'Then I shall ask Nat if I may marry you. That is—if *you* wish to marry me, Celia.'

She gasped.

She really had not considered marriage—had not dreamed that this fascinating and wonderful young man who was her father's trusted and brilliant partner—would ever want to *marry* her. She was dumbfounded. She had never before received a proposal of marriage. She was used to hovering in the background, watching some more attractive girl-friend enjoy being the focus of attention. With Philippe's kiss still hot on her lips, she felt that she had been transported into realms she had never before entered. She could not easily accustom herself to them. The pace had been too swift and the dawning of her own susceptibilities and sensuous enjoyment too sudden and startling. She grasped quickly at the refuge Philippe himself had just offered:

'Oh—thank you for being so understanding,' she stammered. 'I—I agree. Don't let's say anything to anybody. I don't want to.'

'I must sort myself out,' she thought. 'I must write to Aunt Tiny and ask her what *she* thinks. Maybe I'm just mad to believe Philippe is being serious. He can't want to marry me. Not without knowing me better. He *can't* . . .'

But he was taking her arm now, cool, comforting, walking her back to the Villa, away from the enchanted grotto, and the nightingale's song. He was so friendly and ordinary that she rapidly recovered her equilibrium and soon felt that everything was normal again.

'We are not going to refer to this until you feel absolutely sure of yourself, dar-r-ling,' he said, using the English endearment with a slight roll of the 'r' which she found most attractive. 'We will be good friends—and we will say not one word to a living soul.'

'Not one word, except I may write and tell my aunt about us. She's so wonderful—my greatest friend and confidante. I tell her everything.'

'Must you——?' he began doubtfully.

'Oh, yes—I never keep anything from Aunt Tiny.'

'Is she likely to write to Nat?'

'Of course not. She never betrays a confidence. I shall make it strictly confidential. It is—just between us, Philippe.'

'For the moment . . .' he nodded and stopped outside the Villa and taking her hand kissed it again very gently and tenderly. 'But don't keep me waiting too long, Celia. I want so much to tell the world how I feel about you.'

She was inarticulate in the face of this renewed declaration of his serious attitude towards her. She felt a wild desire to throw herself into his arms and feel the exhilarating, terrifying, marvellous excitement of his kisses again. But she conquered the wish. It really *was* too soon. They must both make sure . . . she didn't want to marry Philippe or any man until certain that he was the right one. But being a woman, roused to ardour for the first time in her life, Celia had no sooner restored the situation to rational balance than she longed to experience all the delirium and Mediterranean madness all over again. Just for an instant she flung herself into Philippe's ready and willing arms again and lifted her lips to his.

'Philippe—darling Philippe—I do love you. Please don't think I don't. I do!'

He kissed her with sincerity. She was really very lovable and sweet as honey—not as cloying—for she had a determined, practical side that he was beginning to know. It threatened to defeat him. He would have to be clever and patient with her. He released her from his embrace, his handsome eyes smiling warmly down at her flushed young face.

'It is all right, dar-r-ling. I agree. And look here. You are in the Villa—we see each other almost daily. We will soon get to know each other much, much better. I am content to wait until you are quite sure of your feelings for me.'

'I specially don't want Nadine to know,' Celia said, her face hot and pink.

He smiled more broadly but agreed upon this. Nadine was

73

certainly the last person in Monte Carlo he wished to tell. The last who must know until he could go boldly to Nat Frayne and ask for his *soi-disant* niece's hand in marriage.

'But I promise you I am going to feel quite jealous of you from now onward,' he told Celia.

She laughed up at him—delighted.

'You don't need to be, Philippe. There just isn't anyone else. I have no boy-friends.'

'Some man may come along——'

Celia felt warm and flattered, but she shook her head. 'There'll be nobody but you, ever, Philippe.'

'You don't feel attracted by—say—Geoffrey More?'

Wide-eyed she stared.

'Geoffrey? Heavens—no. He's sweet—an awfully nice person—marvellous with animals—I like him tremendously. But——'

'But not too much?'

'Not at all too much,' she assured Philippe.

'I think he is on the dull side,' drawled the Frenchman.

Celia, ever honest, disagreed.

'Not really. He can be quite interesting on his own subjects.'

Philippe shrugged his shoulders. He had in the past been a bit malicious in his thoughts about Nat's P.A. Mainly because he had always had the remote but persistent feeling that Geoffrey did not like *him*; never sought his company, and had on one or two occasions disagreed with Philippe's business tactics. Geoffrey had been backed up at the time by Nat. Philippe hadn't forgiven that. Added to which, during the days when Philippe was rather more involved with Nadine than now, Nadine had not really concealed from Philippe her *penchant* for Geoffrey. Philippe's ego had suffered a blow at the mere idea that Nadine should fall for Geoffrey while she was still playing at the game with *him*. He now felt a spiteful desire to belittle Geoffrey in Celia's estimation. He said (quite casually, of course):

'I know you love animals, *chérie*, and are a very sweet and trusting person, but just don't go down to Geoffrey's place alone too often.'

'Why ever not?' asked Celia in amazement.

Philippe touched her glowing cheek with his forefinger in a caressing way.

'Because, my dar-r-ling, I repeat—I shall be jealous now of any man who looks at you—our dear Geoffrey may act the sporting Britisher who smokes a pipe and encases his emotions solidly behind a wall of convention, but he is not altogether like that.'

Celia felt suddenly worried and even inclined to defend Geoffrey.

'Honestly, Philippe—he is awfully nice,' she declared.

'But not invulnerable, and *you* are too charming.'

'But he isn't *like* that——' she began.

'He doesn't *appear* to be, my dearest angel, but Nadine could tell you——' Philippe broke off and added: 'Oh, never mind. Forget it. It doesn't matter.'

But he knew that what he had said would not be forgotten. It would, perhaps, put Celia off going down to the damned dog hospital too often. Not that Philippe had anything really to be afraid of, where Geoffrey was concerned. Obviously Celia did not find him attractive, except as a friend. But Philippe wanted to make quite sure that the friendship did not develop into anything more, and that Nat's secretary would not be given even the remotest chance to fall in love with Celia.

## EIGHT

'WELL, duckie, you know me—I never form opinions right away. I want to know your M. Clermont a bit better before I tell you what I really think of him.'

Miss Cotland had only been in Villa Psyche for an hour and here she was up in her niece's bedroom, a very hot, perspiring Aunt Tiny (because the temperature of the July day in Monte Carlo was well into the nineties). She sat on the edge of a satin-cushioned, gilded, Louis Seize chair looking rather uncomfortable. She was not one for fragile valuable little chairs. She preferred her own cosy one at home even though it was cheap and ugly. But she admitted that the Villa Psyche was a museum of beauty and little Celia's bedroom quite an astonishing bower of elegance. But all these frills and perfumes and flowers and luxuries were not really down Aunt Tiny's street. Too threatrical for her taste. A good bed with a mat beside it, a chest of drawers and a cupboard. That was enough for Aunt Tiny.

But she could see that Celia was enchanted with her room and all the blue skies and glitter and glory of Monte Carlo. She could see, too, that the girl was in love—rather formidably in love, in Aunt Tiny's estimation, with the fascinating Frenchman.

Miss Cotland had already encountered Philippe. It was he who drove Celia to Nice to meet her. Rather against her will, and because of Celia, Miss Cotland had accepted her one-time brother-in-law's invitation to stay for a fortnight at Villa Psyche. She didn't like him for what he had done to poor Mary. She never would. And she thought this 'Uncle–Niece' business a lot of tommy-rot which couldn't do any good to anyone. It was bound to lead to trouble. All that nonsense about 'someone might marry Celia for her money' indeed! Surely they would see through any fortune-hunters that came along, without resorting to such deception. Aunt Tiny disapproved. But she said nothing. She rarely opened her mouth to criticise anybody and still more rarely did she interfere in other people's lives. She believed in minding her own business. But one thing was certain. She wasn't going to let any harm come to Celia.

They had had a rapturous reunion at the airport. Anybody

would have thought they had been separated for a year instead of two months. When Celia had lifted a flushed excited face and exclaimed: *'Do you think I've changed?'* . . . Aunt Tiny had answered: *'Not at all. You couldn't . . .'*

And, of course, fundamentally that was so. The girl would always be her sweet dear self. But—thought Aunt Tiny, her shrewd little eyes summing up the whole situation in a flash—*there was a change*. Not only outwardly. And it was all to do with the tall dark-haired Frenchman who escorted Celia, looked after Aunt Tiny's suitcase, and drove her to Monte Carlo.

Easy on the eye—oh yes! A most distinguished-looking young man, brown as a berry, charming. But a little too charming for Aunt Tiny. She didn't like 'em so smooth. She always suspected a villain where there was such a show of good manners, such profuse flattery. English to the backbone, with a touch of Scots thrown in, Miss Cotland was not impressed by the hand-kissing Latin types. But she gathered from her niece's enthusiastic letters that Mr. Clermont was as clever as he was good-looking. Nat was fond of him. Oh, yes, dear little Celia had written reams about Philippe. He was so *this* and so *that* . . . They had tremendous fun swimming together. He was a good swimmer—like Celia. He had taught her how to water-ski. He was even teaching her to drive his gorgeous Mercedes Benz. He seemed to be giving Celia a marvellous time.

*But was he genuine?*

That was the burning question that worried Miss Cotland. She couldn't be sure. But she was far too sensible to down Celia's boy-friend at once. She knew that it would have the effect of putting the child's back up and making her all the more determined to go on worshipping Philippe. That was human nature. Besides, Miss Cotland reflected, *she* might be wrong. Philippe *might* be genuine and really in love with Celia. But Aunt Tiny thought the whole thing a bit too rapid. They had only known each other two months.

Celia said that he had no idea that she was Nat's daughter. No one had. It was a deadly secret out here. So he couldn't be after her for her money, she said. She was a darling; but why, Miss Cotland wondered, should a young man of the world—a gay bachelor who must have had dozens of girl-friends—be sincere about little Celia?

'Well, we'll see,' she decided.

She was glad she had come to Monte Carlo. She had felt a bit worried because Celia had plunged into this romance.

It was obviously eating the young girl right up. She couldn't think of, talk of anyone but *Philippe*.

She looked marvellous. Those blue Italian slacks fitted like a dream and impressed Aunt Tiny who considered herself a needlewoman. Of course she wasn't used to that hair-do (like the one she had seen in a photo of Princess Margaret just before she went to Jamaica). It made Celia look a bit older. And gracious! what a lot of stuff she put on her face. All that eye-shadow—that black on the lashes—well no doubt it was the fashion out here.

Celia said:

'I know you'll adore Philippe when you get to know him. He's terribly attractive to all women.'

'I'm sure he is,' said Aunt Tiny drily.

'I could be engaged to him tomorrow if I wanted,' went on Celia with a charming touch of vanity, 'but I want to wait until I think *he* is certain. He is my first love but I know I am not his. Well—I accept the fact. But I want to make *sure* I am going to be his last.'

'Carried unanimously——' Aunt Tiny now nodded her head.

'As I told you in my letters, there is this woman, the *Comtesse* (I call her Nadine now)—she and I are quite friendly but I don't like her and I know she hates me.'

Aunt Tiny fanned herself and smiled at her niece's sun-browned face. Yes, the child had gained in years and wisdom. She could see that. She was far less the little innocent. She had more poise. Not to be wondered at, living in this atmosphere of wealth and sophistication. Not a bad thing.

'Who is this Countess?' she asked.

'You might well ask, Aunt Tiny. Uncle Nat—I'll have to go on calling him that even to you in case I make a slip—so do try to forget he's my father—sometimes, Aunt Tiny, I think that Uncle Nat and Nadine have had an "understanding".'

'I wouldn't put it past him,' sniffed Aunt Tiny, 'and I expect there are a lot of such goings-on in this millionaire world you've been plunged into, my dear.'

Celia laughed and lit a cigarette. A bracelet of gold seals jangled on her wrist. She blew a cloud of smoke into the air.

'My gracious——' thought Miss Cotland, 'Celia smoking as often as I do. I expect she drinks cocktails, too—*and* the rest. They've taught her something, this lot.'

'There aren't any goings-on that I know of, Aunty Tiny,'

said Celia, 'but Nadine is a widow and her husband was a friend of Unce Nat's—older than she, and perhaps they *had* an understanding at one time. But Uncle Nat is a very sick man now, he rarely sees Nadine. And he's grown worse since I've been out here. I think you will see a great change in him,' she added sadly. 'He hasn't even been down to the show-rooms this week. He only gets up for dinner. I don't like it.'

'I'm sorry. Tell me more about your Countess.'

'Well, she really is rather a ghastly woman,' said Celia. 'You won't like her. She's gorgeous to look at and I owe it to her that I've learned how to dress and make up and all that—but there's something underhand about her which I can't bear. I know for a fact that she's had an affair with Philippe.'

'Sounds charming,' said Aunt Tiny sardonically.

'But Philippe doesn't care about her any more,' said Celia proudly.

'Ah! that's a bad situation. The Countess won't like you. She'll be jealous.'

'And she's always dropping hints that Philippe is only amusing himself with me and that I'd better look out and so forth.'

'Maybe she's right,' thought Miss Cotland grimly. 'That's what I'd like to find out.'

'But Philippe tells me not to take any notice of her,' went on Celia, 'he seems to be able to cope with her and I certainly never feel I've taken him away from her. They've known each other for ages. If he'd wanted to marry her he could have done so long ago, after her husband died. He's quite honest about it.'

'M'm,' said Aunt Tiny. 'And in all this whirl, duckie, have you found any other boy-friends?'

'Hundreds,' giggled Celia.

'Well, you look luscious enough to attract thousands. Which reminds me, I've got a surprise for you, in my case. I picked up a treat of a cotton frock—just your colour—in Oxford Street.'

Celia swallowed. She knew it! She had expected and dreaded another of darling Aunt Tiny's dresses. But she made a vow to admire it and *wear* it, no matter what it was like or what the horrid Nadine would say. She could always whisper the truth to Philippe. He would understand that she wouldn't want to hurt Aunt Tiny's feelings.

'Who was that nice-looking boy I saw as we walked through

the hall?' asked Aunt Tiny. 'You introduced me to him but I didn't catch the name.'

'Geoffrey More. Uncle Nat's personal assistant and secretary.'

'I thought he was very nice—just my type,' said Miss Cotland.

'I'm sure you'd think so even more if you knew him,' said Celia and proceeded to tell her about Geoffrey's amateur, yet quite professional work, with his canine waifs and strays.

'Do you see much of him?'

'Every day, on and off. He does all Uncle Nat's paper work.'

Aunt Tiny thought of the bronzed, brown-haired, blue-eyed young man she had met on her arrival. He had a nice English voice, frank gaze and a firm handshake. Yes, *just* her type and she wished he were Celia's. But no doubt he was too quiet and unobtrusive; not as showy as that Frenchman.

'You must take me to see the Dogs' Home,' said Aunt Tiny.

Celia bit her lip. There was one thing she wasn't going to confide in her aunt—that was the slight difficulty she was having in maintaining any kind of friendship with Geoffrey. She liked him very much, and was not one to reverse an opinion without just cause. She had thought highly of Geoffrey when she first met him, and still did. But Philippe was always trying to scotch the friendship. He seemed to be stupidly jealous despite Celia's continued assurances that there was no necessity for him to be. Her feelings towards Geoffrey were so absolutely platonic. He liked her, too. She knew that. He was always most grateful and pleased when she went down there and helped him with one of his sick animals.

But since that night by the moonlit grotto when Philippe had taken her in his arms, Celia had lived on the crest of a wave that seemed to be carrying her out to gigantic seas which she was not altogether sure she could ride. She had not seen over-much of him because a few days ago he had to go to London on business for Nat. Each time they met, they managed to snatch an hour alone and it was always an hour of passionate love-making. His kisses had become sweet and familiar, and Celia responded with all the warmth of her young ardent nature. But she managed to keep her head and Philippe, too, was well controlled. He seemed as anxious as herself to let this be a period of testing—until they could both go to Nat and say *'We are really in love and we want to be married.'*

Physically and mentally, he dominated her life. Now when she was with him she was blissful—when away she missed him and felt utterly lost. And of course there was something very stimulating and exciting about their 'secret affair'. But it also took its toll of Celia. It played havoc with her nerves, and she found herself losing weight she had gained when she first came out here. Even her father had noticed this and told her not to do too much of that damned dieting. She longed to tell him about Philippe and was quite sure it would be all right, but whenever she suggested that they should break the news, Philippe wanted to wait a little longer. So she had told nobody —except Aunt Tiny.

She had even felt at times that she would like to confide in Geoffrey. He always seemed such a substantial, reliable person, and so sympathetic. But Philippe's jealous attitude kept her away from *Madame* Pavette's little house which she would have visited far more often if Philippe hadn't expressed such open dislike of Geoffrey. She had been almost cross with him on one occasion when he had started to repeat his warning against Nat's secretary.

'I'm quite sure you're wrong, Philippe darling. Geoffrey is *not* that kind of person. You're just not to be so jealous. It upsets me. I can't cope.'

He had relaxed and told her to do exactly what she wanted, and that he only wished her to be happy.

So she had forgotten him and tried to accept his ill-feeling towards Geoffrey. After all it was very flattering. He must love her a great deal if he didn't like her even to help Geoffrey with his dogs. Well—everybody had faults—even her wonderful Philippe—and his chief one was jealousy. She wouldn't take too much notice of it.

So on occasions she continued to go down to the dogs' hospital. Then one day Geoffrey asked her to go swimming with him. He had invited her on other occasions. In her frank friendly way, she would have liked to accept but dared not, knowing how Philippe felt. She stammered some excuse and Geoffrey had taken his pipe from his mouth, looked at her out of the corners of his very blue eyes, and said:

'I'm going to give up asking you. I don't think I'm very popular.'

'Oh, but you are——' she had begun to stammer.

'Please—I was only pulling your leg,' he broke in laughing. 'I don't see why you should want to swim with me. You already have a most adequate aqua-sportsman in M. Clermont.'

She had blushed fiery red and been reduced to speechlessness. Then Geoffrey suddenly put a hand on her shoulder and added:

'I had absolutely no right to say that. A girl can choose her own companions. I do apologise. But I'm sorry. I think you're so marvellous and I wish I saw a little more of you other than the odd moments we meet when I am flying in and out of your uncle's study—or when you come down here, which is all too rarely.'

That had made her *think*, not only at the time but long afterwards. There had been a look in Geoffrey's eyes which was both warm and wistful. She had felt awful about turning him down. He had changed the conversation immediately and talked to her about Gigi who had made a complete recovery, and for whom he was still trying to find a home.

Celia had carried out her promises to become Gigi's godmother, and insisted on bringing her presents; a new collar, amusing doggy toys and a special basket with which Geoffrey had always been delighted. But she had not renewed her offer to take Gigi up to Villa Psyche. Deeply involved in her love affair with Philippe Clermont, she cared really only what *he* thought and she was sure he would not approve of her adopting one of Geoffrey's mongrels. She felt rather guilty and ashamed of herself. She also began to think a bit more personally about Geoffrey. Was he really upset because she wouldn't swim with him? Why had he mentioned Philippe? Did he *know* that she was in love with Philippe? Could it be that, he too, was jealous?

Although she had gained so much in self-confidence, she could never be accused of being conceited, and it would not have entered her head that Geoffrey had fallen for her. Yet he had made it obvious that he was sad because she wouldn't go out with him, and he had, after all, said: '*I think you are so marvellous and I wish I saw a little more of you.*'

She rather dreaded meeting him again after that incident, but when they did so he was as cool and friendly as ever, and gave no sign that he even remembered it. She was relieved. She decided that it had been just nothing at all and that she need not worry about Geoffrey.

Nevertheless, Celia was true woman, and deep down she did not forget, either Geoffrey's words or the look in his eyes.

That night—for the first time since Celia came to Villa Psyche—her father did not come down. He kept to his bed. He sent a message to Celia. A scribbled note which, in fact, Geoffrey, himself, brought her. She was sitting out on the terrace with Aunt Tiny. Philippe had just joined them with Nadine. Miss Cotland was feeling very 'go ahead', drinking (most unaccustomedly for her) a Dubonnet. She was admiring the lush beauty of the Villa gardens on this luminous summer night.

Tiny Cotland was resplendent in a long black skirt (which made her look taller than ever)—topped by a black lace blouse with jet trimmings. Her short grey hair was neatly brushed. Her long plain face was powdered too white and because for many years she had scant eyebrows she had pencilled them— and rather badly. The result was grotesque. To Celia, it was the dear, familiar face of Aunt Tiny whom she adored. Of Aunt Tiny's appearance she was uncritical. About herself, she felt a little more badly. She had put on the 'nice little cotton frock' that dear Aunt Tiny had bought in Oxford Street. It was pale blue with pink flowers—a garish pink and to Celia— whose eyes had become trained to *haute couture*—it was 'grim'. It reduced her from the chic young woman to the little Celia who was just 'nobody' again . . . without taste, without polish. But she wore the dress bravely, knowing that it gave Miss Cotland pleasure, and she looked rather boldly into the eyes of the *Comtesse*, even enjoying the slightly shocked disdain that had crossed the Frenchwoman's face when she first saw the new outfit.

Celia said:

'Isn't this delightful, Nadine? My aunt brought it out for me.'

'Charming,' said Nadine coldly, gave a look at Miss Cotland from under her sweeping lashes and shrugged her shoulders. What a height! The old Englishwoman was really *formidable*. And Nat had been once married to *her* sister. What an odd thought! The sisters couldn't have been very much alike.

Then Geoffrey appeared with Nat's note, which Celia opened and read:

'*Sorry dear, not well enough to come down tonight. Give Tiny my salaams, and will see her tomorrow.*'

'Oh! I'm so disappointed!' exclaimed Celia.

'The Chief has been far from well all day,' said Geoffrey.

'What's wrong?' asked Miss Cotland in her blunt way.

Geoffrey, who was also dining with the family tonight, looked grave.

'I wish we knew, Miss Cotland. His heart isn't good, of course, and he has only very recently been sensible about himself. He lives and works at such a pace.'

'Nat Frayne always did,' said Miss Cotland. And remembered rather bitterly those times long ago just after Celia was born, when Nat, still in his thirties, used to race in and out of the little house. Always in breathless haste, always on the brink of some new discovery or invention, always spending money on the wrong things! Or at least then, it had seemed the wrong things. Poor Mary with her infant and life of drudgery, often had to forego her housekeeping money because Nat spent the lot on some treasure he had unearthed in an antique shop. He used to argue that it was worth double and that one day he could sell it for a big profit. Sometimes he did, but more often than not, it was a waiting game which meant that Mary went short. And Nat who could be so charming when he wanted could also be bad-tempered and difficult. How often he had hated his job!

Maybe, Miss Cotland thought, today, here in Nat's magnificent villa with so much evidence of his genius around her, it was because he had been the real square peg in a round hole that had made him a bad husband. That sort of frustration could sour a man's life and wreck his marriage.

Out in America, Nat had found the opportunity to satisfy his craving for big business, and fulfilled all the faith that his wealthy backer had put in him. Tiny had never known the real story until Celia had heard it from her father, then written and told Tiny all about it. A fascinating success tale. Nat had been lucky. But unlucky in love and in marriage. And now, when he had got hold of this fine, young daughter of his, wasn't it too late? It looked very much to Miss Cotland as though millionaire Nat Frayne was a dying man.

Celia did not enjoy the intimate family dinner party that night. She had looked forward to her father and her aunt meeting and becoming friends again. She did not like to see Nat's empty chair at the head of the table. Nadine seemed petulant, and Geoffrey was more silent than usual. It was Philippe who kept the conversation going—making himself

84

utterly charming to Aunt Tiny, unmoved by the remorseless scrutiny with which her small shrewd eyes regarded him over her horn-rimmed glasses. He was not afraid of her or her animosity. He was far too sure of his ability to pull any woman, young or old, over to his side. Now and again, when Celia's aunt snubbed him, he replied with a brilliant smile and compliment. It was not the type of sparring to which Miss Cotland was used and it somewhat floored her. By the end of dinner, she really did not know whether to believe that the handsome young man really liked her and hung on every word she said, or whether he was just playing a clever game.

She watched him like a lynx. He was in love with Celia. Yes, she was sure of that. And she knew all about Celia's feelings, but somehow it gave her a pang to see the young girl look so starry-eyed over M. Clermont. She felt sure that somehow, something, somewhere was wrong.

She might have been a great deal more concerned if she had known what lay in Philippe's mind tonight. He was mildly amused by Celia's elderly aunt. With her powdered face and badly-drawn eyebrows she was a bit of a freak, but someone to be reckoned with, yes. He could see that she had influence with Celia. He must be on his guard. But he was fully determined that once he was married to Celia (which of course he would be very soon now) her dear Aunt Tiny would have to be pushed very gently but firmly out of her life. He couldn't *bear* to see Celia in that ill-fitting cotton dress from a multiple stores in London.

Miss Cotland, unaware of the effect her taste was having on the assembly, actually brought up the subject of Celia's new dress.

She spoke to the *Comtesse*:

'My niece has written such a lot about you, *Madame. Elle a dit que vous êtes très bonne avec les robes,*' she added in execrable French.

'*Madame la Comtesse* speaks beautiful English, Aunt Tiny,' said Celia hurriedly, her cheeks rather warm as she caught the look of horror in Nadine's eyes.

'Well, well,' went on Miss Cotland. 'What do you think of my choice for Celia—the dress she's wearing?'

'You bought it for her, *hein?*' asked Nadine, twirling the long stem of her goblet with slim, nervous fingers, the nails of which were painted a pale orange.

Geoffrey, from his end of the table, listened with a certain ironic amusement. He fancied that he could sense an under-current. Miss Cotland and Nadine were not going to hit it off. Out of sheer mischief he put in his opinion.

'I think it's the nicest dress I've seen this summer, Miss Cotland. It suits Celia down to the ground.'

Philippe glowered at the Englishman then smiled.

'*Tiens!*' he said softly, raising his brows.

'Well,' said Miss Cotland, still fixing Nadine with her eagle eye: 'What does the Countess think? She is the one who knows—my niece thinks most highly of your judgment, *Madame.*'

Nadine was trapped. She was too well-mannered to be openly rude, but all her professional instincts, her expert opinions, were being challenged. She took a drink of iced hock, then wiping her lips, said:

'I'm not exactly fond of cotton frocks, *Madame—M'moiselle*,' she corrected herself somewhat cattily. 'I mean I never wear them myself, and never in the evening.'

'Ah! I'm learning,' said Miss Cotland.

'It is all a question of personal taste,' murmured Nadine.

'There doesn't seem to be any personal taste in your fashions,' said Miss Cotland tartly. 'Women are like a flock of sheep, following each other with one of the big designers as the shepherd.'

At this typical Aunt-Tiny-remark, Celia broke into laughter. Geoffrey said:

'I absolutely agree. I'm all for starting a campaign—more individuality in women's clothes. With the same sort of dresses and hair-do's they all look alike to me.'

'You've hit the nail on the head,' said Aunt Tiny approvingly.

Nadine's eyes sparkled. She felt dangerously bored and she did not like Miss Cotland. Like Philippe, she sensed an enemy. She was compelled to make one of her more spiteful remarks.

'*Chacun à son goût.* Everybody to his taste,' she translated for Miss Cotland with a bitter smile, 'and most of the well-dressed women in the world enjoy following the leaders of fashion, but at the same time I think they preserve their individuality.'

'They may wear different jewellery, or bags, or shoes, but even in those they are much alike,' said Miss Cotland. 'A lot of sheep, I say.'

'Wasn't it the same when you were young?' the *Comtesse* asked her.

'When I was your age, *Madame*, I wasn't concerned with fashions. I wore a uniform. There was a war on.'

'Oh, yes, of course,' said Nadine with a bored air. 'And there couldn't of course have been much individuality in a uniform.'

'None at all,' said Aunt Tiny briskly. 'But looking back a bit further, to my mother's day, for instance—she was an Edwardian—there were no two women alike. The ladies of high fashion had glorious things specially designed for them, and their faces were much as God made them, whereas who's to know what any fashionable woman of today really looks like until the stuff's all scrubbed off?'

Nadine gave an artificial laugh.

'It should never be scrubbed off. I've been teaching dear little Celia about night creams, haven't I, Celia? Soap and water are things of the past, Miss Cotland. And except for tonight, I must say your niece's appearance has improved out of all recognition.'

'Why except for tonight?' said Miss Cotland, pricking up her ears.

'Now Nadine has put her foot in it,' thought Geoffrey, much amused.

'Have some more orange sauce,' said Celia hurriedly. 'Uncle Nat's chef makes such delicious sauce for the duckling, don't you think?'

But Aunt Tiny had fixed her piercing gaze upon the *Comtesse*.

'You don't think my niece looks so attractive tonight, *Madame*? Then it must be because you don't like the dress I brought her.'

Nadine set her teeth. How terrible she was, this old Englishwoman. Nadine looked in despair at Philippe. He was rather enjoying her discomfiture, but with a stubborn wish to ingratiate himself with Celia's aunt for the moment—he put a speedy end to the little combat of words between the two women who were at such opposite ends of the pole.

'I shall not have one word said against the cotton frock with the pink flowers. It is ravishing! And now I am going to suggest, Miss Cotland, that you and Celia allow me to take you down to the Casino after dinner.'

'I don't gamble, young man.'

'No need to—no need at all. But you might be amused to see the *salles de jeux*.'

'Oh yes, do let's all go,' put in Celia, also anxious to restore the good humour of the party. 'After coffee I'll order the car.'

'Allow me,' said Geoffrey.

As they walked out of the *salle à manger*, Celia spoke to Geoffrey:

'I thought the sparks were about to fly between my aunt and Nadine.'

'They did fly,' said Geoffrey, his cool blue eyes still amused, but the amusement died as he looked at the girl's lovely glowing face.

Oh God, he thought, more moved than he had ever been in his life before, how he wished Celia Frayne had never come to the Villa Psyche—never come into his life. He was in love—quite hopelessly in love. She was everything he had ever dreamed of in a girl or ever wanted. He found her unutterably sweet. And if she but knew it, he was so much on Aunt Tiny's side. To the devil with all this make-up, dressing-up, nail varnish and the rest. Just Celia with the breeze blowing her thick hair, and in that simple cheap cotton dress, making her look about sixteen—that was the Celia he loved; not the artificial gorgeous young woman straight from the *Croisette* in Cannes.

But he had no right to love her, and she must never know.

He moved away from her. He must phone down to the chauffeur's quarters. Turning his head over his shoulder just for an instant, he happened to see Philippe Clermont surreptitiously take one of Celia's hands and carry it to his lips. He saw the passionate glances they exchanged. He shut the study door and taking out a handkerchief, wiped his forehead. He felt almost sick with the force of his jealousy and distress. She was really in love with the fellow. If only it had been anybody else but Clermont whom he distrusted and despised and whom he knew was worthless—a sycophant, who had got Nat on to his side—a fortune-hunter. Nat's niece was penniless, but she might not always be so, and she *was* his niece. Hadn't Philippe got an eye to the main chance? Didn't he hope that she might one day have prospects?

Geoffrey was conscious of the first bitter pain he had ever suffered in mind and heart as he sat down at Nat's big desk and took up the telephone. Mechanically he ordered Jacques to bring the Cadillac at ten o'clock to take them all to the Casino.

All? No, not he . . . he wouldn't go with them. He seldom did. Anyhow he had a new canine patient down at his place, he must get back. And he couldn't bear to spend hours with Celia, watching her respond to Philippe Clermont's advances.

As he put the receiver down, the door of the study was pushed open. Nat's valet rushed in—a nice boy who had not been with him very long. He looked white and scared.

'*Monsieur, Monsieur*, come quickly, please.'

'What is it?'

The valet replied in his own language:

'*Monsieur's* bell sounded once—only once, just now—no more. When I reached him I found him lying on the floor.'

'Lying on the floor?' repeated Geoffrey.

'Yes, *Monsieur*,' the boy almost sobbed, '*Il est presque mort.* He is dying, I am sure.'

'Good God!' exclaimed Geoffrey in a shocked, unbelieving voice.

From the hall came the sound of Celia's happy laughter.

# NINE

NEVER had Celia been more pleased to have dear Aunt Tiny with her. The wisdom, the strength, the sound practical judgment possessed by her was much needed now. Celia was made suddenly painfully aware that she loved this father whom she was about to lose. Whatever he had done in the past, she loved him and she did not want him to die.

The little party that had been so happily preparing to go down to the Casino that night dispersed. The Villa became suddenly shrouded in gloom and silence. The servants went round on tiptoe. The *Comtesse* discreetly sent for a car to take her home. The evening's 'fun' was over—she could see. She would have liked Philippe to accompany her but as Nat's trusted partner and friend, he remained in the Villa—quite genuinely anxious about Nat's condition.

Geoffrey, after one quick look at his employer, had telephoned for his doctor who, in turn, sent to Paris for the specialist whom the millionaire had seen before when he had a thrombosis. The famous Professor Latour-Guillemin had chartered a plane which would bring him down to Monte Carlo immediately.

As soon as Geoffrey knew that the Professor was coming his anxiety deepened. It must be that the local physician suspected the worse.

Now Celia made little effort to conceal what she felt about Philippe. She sat beside him on the terrace, holding his hand, her young healthy face pale and strained.

'I just can't believe that—that Uncle Nat is so bad,' she kept saying.

'You must have courage,' Philippe tried to soothe her, 'Nat has had these bad turns before. He has wonderful resilience.'

'If he's anything like the Nat I used to know he won't give up easily,' seconded Miss Cotland.

She, too, was anxious. Not because she had any love for the man who had ruined her sister's life but because the thought of death must always be a solemn and awful one. It was the absolute end of everything on earth. The grim finality that faces all of us, thought Aunt Tiny—and best faced if one has a clear conscience. She wasn't sure she envied poor old Nat what must lie on his. But she knew that he had been kind and generous to Celia, and that an affection had arisen between the two. It would be a tragedy if it ended so quickly, and if Celia should lose her father almost as soon as she had found him.

They all sat there waiting for the Professor to arrive. The doctor was still upstairs with Nat and a hastily-found hospital nurse. Geoffrey had gone home to take a quick look at a sick dog but was returning almost immediately.

Philippe had taken Celia's hand quite boldly in front of her aunt. She answered the pressure of his long smooth fingers gratefully. She needed his comfort now. She needed his warmth and strength, and the compassion that lay in his brilliant eyes. Dear Philippe—he loved Uncle Nat, too. He had worked with him for a long time.

Celia gave a deep sigh and spoke to Aunt Tiny.

'What chance do you think he's got of survival?'

'I don't know much about it,' said Miss Cotland shaking her head, 'but that nice Geoffrey More told me, after he'd spoken to the doctor, that Nat had had a very bad attack and they only just pulled him round in time. He might get over it, of course—and he might not. That's all anyone can say.'

And there was not much more that the Professor, himself, had to tell after he had arrived, and examined the patient.

Mr. Frayne was in poor shape, he said. But the heart was beating a little more normally now, following an injection, and he might easily live another day or so. But not, in the Professor's opinion, much longer.

'Is he conscious?' asked Celia.

'He came to only for a few moments,' said the Professor, 'and he spoke a name—yours, is it not, *Mademoiselle*? You are, I believe, Celia, his niece.'

She flushed and nodded, too upset to speak. It touched her to think that she had been in her father's thoughts. The Professor went on, gently:

'I should not disturb him just now, but later if he asks for you—go to him. It can do him no harm.'

'Of course I'll go,' said Celia, swallowing hard.

Once more the clasp of Philippe's hand reassured her.

Geoffrey, who was there, was not unaware of those two holding hands. He turned from the sight, his eyes hardening. He had never been more upset in his life than when he had looked on the fallen body of his Chief up there in the bedroom. He was devoted to Nat. The idea that he might die now, at any time, filled him with gloom. A gloom that certainly could not be lifted by seeing Philippe Clermont and Celia so openly exhibiting their feelings for one another.

There was nothing more to be done that night. Geoffrey drove the Professor to the Hôtel de Paris where he was staying. The little bearded doctor who attended Nat regularly was remaining in the Villa in case of an emergency.

It was midnight when Celia went upstairs with Aunt Tiny and said good night to her.

'Isn't this awful? I have a ghastly premonition that—that *he* won't get over it, this time.'

'We must be prepared for the worst,' said Miss Cotland.

Celia, her eyes full of tears, looked at her aunt.

'I'm afraid I made it pretty apparent this evening that Philippe and I are in love.'

'Yes, you did,' said Miss Cotland drily.

'Do you blame me? Isn't he marvellous?'

Miss Cotland bit her lips. She hadn't the heart to tell Celia tonight of all nights when she was facing the first great sorrow of her life, what she, Tiny Cotland, really thought about Philippe Clermont. But something about him made Miss Cotland suspicious despite his strong physical attraction and charm. Suspicious that he was chasing her niece with an ulterior motive. She just could not get that idea out of her mind, and it had grown as the evening went by.

'Oh, Aunt Tiny, I do love him so much!' Celia spoke again and wiped her eyes and blew her nose.

Like a child, Miss Cotland thought. Celia was still so much of a child. That's why she regretted the fact that the girl had rushed into this tempestuous love-affair.

'Don't think about it all too much now. I'm sure things will work out,' she murmured and patted Celia's shoulder. 'But you've got to keep calm now. Run to bed, duckie, and get some sleep.'

Celia nodded and sighed.

'What I'm so unhappy about is that there will be no time to tell my father about Philippe. I did so want him to know.'

'He may yet know. There's still hope,' said Aunt Tiny.

And, sincerely, Miss Cotland prayed for this. She would like to have Nat's opinion on the possible marriage of his daughter with young Clermont. She was sure Nat had his head screwed on the right way, and could advise Celia. After all, he had started this 'uncle and niece' business for the purpose of preventing her from being married for her money. It would be a tragedy, indeed, if he died without knowing which way the wind was blowing, and if M. Clermont were to discover Celia's secret so soon.

It was a night of tension at Villa Psyche. All through the hours, lights burned in Nat's suite. The nurse sat beside him, waiting for him to wake again.

Philippe, at Celia's request, did not return to his apartment but stayed in one of the spare rooms at the Villa. Miss Cotland, tired though she was after her journey, could not sleep, and lay awake until dawn, reading, worrying about her beloved niece's future.

Nat Frayne held on to life.

He gripped it as tenaciously as he had always held on to everything he knew to be of value. He was a tired man and a disappointed one. But he had grown to love Celia. He had no wish to leave her now, nor that sweet life that he had made for himself on the French Riviera. Besides, death in his mind was a kind of defeat. He did not like to be defeated.

The entire household was aware of the fact the next morning, that the great Nathaniel Frayne still lived. His mind had triumphed over his weak wasted body—for the moment, anyhow. That overtaxed heart was still stubbornly beating. He was no longer in pain and able to speak and think with astonishing clarity when the Professor came up to the Villa to see him at eight o'clock.

'How long do you give me?' he asked the specialist grimly.

Latour-Guillemin, with a finger on Nat's pulse, glanced at the nurse—a young pretty girl who was standing behind him. Then he smiled at the millionaire. Tough and a fighter, yes— this pulse was fantastically stronger. But there were other aspects of the case that raised no false hopes in the Professor's mind.

'Well, come on?' muttered Nat, 'I want the truth. None of this hypocritical humbug you fellows go in for . . . Telling a patient there's no need to worry, and that he's got a long life in front of him when he's just about to expire. That nonsense won't wash with me.'

'I'm sure it won't, M. Frayne,' said the Professor in his best English and with a calm smile, 'so I shall be truthful with you.

Your long and useful life is behind you, *mon cher*. I cannot be more explicit.'

Nat nodded, half closing his eyes. He had expected the death sentence. It did not frighten him. He took it as he had taken all the other blows he had received, coolly.

'The knock-out, eh,' he said with a twisted smile. 'Okay. How long?'

'Last night, I would have said a matter of hours. This morning I find your pulse rate more amenable. But there are other unfortunate symptoms which we need not go into—I can only say it will be a temporary respite.'

'A few more hours—or another day?'

'*Peut-être.*'

'Okay,' repeated Nat. 'Tell the nurse to leave us alone. There are things I wish to say to you. I want to see my daughter, too.'

'Your daughter?' repeated the Professor in surprise.

'Yes, Celia, my so-called niece. She is my own child.'

'Indeed,' said the Professor, raising his brows, 'you are to be congratulated. She is a beautiful girl.'

'Does it surprise you?'

'That she is your daughter? Yes and no. Nothing really surprises me any more in this life, *Monsieur*.'

Nat gave one of his old sardonic chuckles.

'Well, it's going to come as a surprise to quite a few people in this house, I assure you. But they've all got to know. My Will will inform them if I don't. I've left her everything.'

'She will be lucky,' said the Professor with a healthy respect for his patient's financial position.

'She is already lucky because she has something I've never had, and which I envy her, my dear Professor.'

'Which is?'

'Faith,' said Nat Frayne. 'A beautiful, touching, sincere faith. She believes in a God and a heaven and hell and judgment throne and all that old fairy story which deceives so many millions.'

The Professor raised his brows.

'Maybe it is no deception, *Monsieur*. Maybe your—your daughter is right.'

'It's just another gamble, eh? You're either on the winning number or you aren't.'

'I think time has proved our belief in God to be more than

94

a gamble, *Monsieur*,' said the Professor drily. 'If you ask me, I think *Mademoiselle* is on a certainty.'

'Ah, then *you*'re a good Christian. I'm not, you see. I'm an agnostic.'

'Each man must live and die as he thinks best.'

'Too true! And now could you send for my daughter—just in case the sands of time run out before I tie up all the loose ends.'

The Professor went out to find the nurse. Only a few moments later Celia was sitting by her father's bedside holding one of his hands in hers. A cold thin hand, yet she noticed with interest and faint surprise (although she should not really have felt astonishment) how like it was to her own. The same shape —the same sort of knuckles and nails—reproduced in herself on more feminine lines. But she was like him in many ways. And she was conscious of a very real relief and joy at being able to talk to him again—surprised at his normality—the strength of his voice—delighted to watch the old quizzical ironic lift of the bushy brows as he looked at her. Nathaniel Frayne was not dead yet—far from it.

'Sorry I gave you such a fright,' were his opening words.

'Please don't *ever* do it again.'

'I daresay I shall. Only next time it will be the end.'

She pressed his fingers.

'Don't, please!'

'My darling child, you've got to face up to the fact that I'm for the high jump any moment now. But it oughtn't to worry you. Not you with all your belief in the "Better World To Come".'

'You're being sarcastic,' she said gravely and reproachfully.

He gave his short chuckle.

'Okay. Skip it. We won't argue about religion. But it's nice to have you around, honey. I've grown rather attached to my daughter, you know.'

'And I to my father,' she whispered using the forbidden name rather shyly, and lifted the cold fingers to her warm young lips.

'Darling,' said Nat, 'when we're alone I like to hear you call me that. In time everybody will know—I've left you everything, Celia. You'll be a very rich girl.'

She felt a sudden choking wish to burst into tears but controlled it.

'I don't want to talk about that. It's wonderful to have money but you're so very much more important.'

He sighed. There was only one other woman in his life who had found money less important than love . . . the little French wife whom he had lost so tragically. Sometimes Celia reminded him of Marie-Thérèse. Marie had had the same fresh naïve charm—nothing mercenary about her. And she too used to have Faith—she had been an ardent Roman Catholic.

How pretty Celia looked this morning in her blue Italian slacks and sleeveless silk jersey. Her hair was burnished with health—her eyes smoke-grey under their heavy black lashes. She was charming, he thought, and felt a pang of anguished regret that he, by his own folly and selfishness, his lack of paternal feeling, had so long neglected her and left her out of his life. Dammit, he thought it had always been his philosophy that one should never regret the things that one did. So far, in his life he had been ruthless. But he was not going to be so ruthless about dying—he could see that. He was being forced to feel sorry about a number of things.

Celia was looking around the big bedroom with its three windows facing the sea, thinking how little she really knew about her father and his personal tastes, other than that he had exquisite judgment. There were evidences of it here; in the tobacco-brown carpet and brown and white chintz curtains of beautiful design; the carved walnut eighteenth-century bed; the beautiful Watteau over the fireplace; the French marquetry chest of drawers; two bronze statuettes holding crystal lamps aloft on either side the dressing table.

It was the first time she had been in her father's bedroom. Venetian blinds kept out the sun. It was cool and beautiful in here—Nat Frayne adored beauty. It would be terrible, she thought, if he had to leave it all. It was *too* terrible even to contemplate his departure—it gave her no pleasure to hear that all his treasures, everything in his millionaire world, would belong to *her*.

'Oh, Daddy,' she said, 'I hate calling you Uncle Nat. You're my father—I *feel* it. I love you very much.'

He saw her lips trembling. He raised her hand and put it against his cheek. His heart thumped a bit too fast and painfully.

'Now, Celia honey. No tears—no heel-taps—just go on smiling,' he said, 'and let your old daddy feel you will be very happy after he's gone. Not yet, dear—not yet. Those fools of physicians have given me some pretty powerful dope—the old ticker is still working. We can still laugh, eh—what?'

Her throat felt restricted.

'Yes, of course!'

Now she felt the need to tell him everything—about Philippe.

'Listen, Daddy. It was your wish that the man I married shouldn't know I was your daughter or heiress. Well, I've found him. I hadn't meant to tell you yet—but I must now. I want to know what you think about him.'

Nat narrowed his gaze upon her.

'So you're in love, honey? I can see it in your eyes.'

'Yes, I am.'

'Well, it can be only with one of two men—the two you've been seeing in this house. Philippe—or Geoffrey.'

'Not Geoffrey,' she said hastily.

'Oh—he's a very good fellow—solid as a rock and with a lot to him. But I rather imagine it's young Philippe? He has all the answers—all the girls go for Philippe,' Nat chuckled.

Celia's colour burned deeper. She looked anxiously at her father.

'Do you disapprove?'

'How far has it gone?'

Her lashes fluttered nervously.

'We just love each other and have admitted it. It was love at first sight. He told me so. He's wonderful. Daddy, you think so too, don't you?'

'I'm very attached to young Philippe. As far as business goes, he's come along well during the last year or two and pulled off some very fine deals. And he's amusing. Yes, I'm attached to the boy particularly as he is a blood relation of my little Marie-Thérèse.'

'Then you do approve,' said Celia eagerly.

There was a moment's silence. Nat Frayne felt very tired. His brain wasn't too alert this morning. That jumping pulse put him off his stroke, he thought. He wished he knew what he ought to say to this sweet child of his. She was very good— he knew that—too damned good, in a way—too liable to get hurt. But he thought he knew Philippe pretty thoroughly. It had never entered his head not to trust the boy. Of course Nat was aware that Philippe had never been without some female around, somewhere, and neither was he blind to the fact that there was an attachment—or used to be—between Philippe and Nadine. But Nat had never censured the boy on account of his love affairs. He was typically French, and inclined to be promiscuous. But like so many, he might well settle down and make a good husband. He had a fine name. He was an experienced man of the world who could look after little Celia. And he knew the business thoroughly. He would manage *Frayne et Cie* for his wife, which was important. Above all he seemed to have genuinely fallen for Celia, and suggested marrying her while still believing her to be just the penniless niece. He could not possibly know the truth. That was distinctly in his favour.

'Daddy,' Celia's voice broke through her father's wandering thoughts, 'tell me you will give us your blessing.'

'If it will make you happy, honey, yes.'

Wild with excitement, Celia bent to kiss her father's cheek.

'Oh, darling, *darling* Daddy, I'm so thrilled. That was all that I needed. Let me bring Philippe to see you. That is if you feel strong enough.'

'Later, dear . . . later. All in good time. But I want to see your aunt first. Fetch her for me, will you.'

As Celia walked to the door, Nat called her back.

'I don't mind you getting engaged to young Philippe but I'd be obliged if you'd say nothing to him—or anything about our true relationship until after—well you know what.'

'Whatever you say. But you're not to leave me. You're not even to contemplate it,' Celia warned him.

'Time will tell,' he said grimly and shut his eyes.

She hesitated, then asked:

'Can't I even tell Philippe?'

'Not for the moment, dear. Let things stay as they are.'

'Very well,' she said obediently.

She went in search of Aunt Tiny. In her youthful fervour—so very much in love—her whole mind was concentrated on the thought of Philippe. She had never seen death—nor had its icy finger so much as touched the fringe of her consciousness, until now. And she could not believe even now that her father was dying. He seemed far too normal.

She felt that she walked on air, knowing that he approved of her attachment to Philippe. Now they could get engaged. They could tell the whole world. It was marvellous.

She found Miss Cotland and sent her to the sick room, then rushed to find Philippe.

He was in Nat's study. He and Geoffrey had been talking, two large account books open on the desk before them. The only times the two men met and talked without animosity were on matters of business—when each respected the part the other played in Nat's affairs.

The moment that Geoffrey saw Celia's glowing face he felt disturbed—wondering why she should look like that when Nat was dying. Surely she realised the gravity of his condition? She gave him an embarrassed smile and said:

'Do you mind if I speak to Philippe alone a moment?'

Geoffrey froze. 'Of course,' he said coldly and turned and walked out of the room.

Philippe looked at Celia with some surprise.

'Darling—wasn't that a bit obvious——?'

'It was, it was,' she broke in, 'and it doesn't matter any more. Oh, Philippe—my love—it doesn't matter!'

She flung herself into his arms. Still astonished, he held her, passing a caressing hand over the rich satin of her hair.

'What *has* happened?'

'I've told him—I've told him about us.'

'You mean—Nat?'

'Yes, I've told him that we love each other, and he approves. He said he was very attached to you and that if it was going to make me happy, he would say "yes" to us getting married.'

Philippe Clermont's heart gave an upward surge of triumph. His hold of Celia tightened. He said, under his breath:

'*Mon Dieu!* Is it true?'

'Quite true. And we must just pray now that he gets better and that his illness is just a false alarm, and that we can soon have a marvellous, glorious celebration of our engagement.'

'*Mon Dieu!*' repeated Philippe. He shut his eyes in case the young girl should see the light of victory in them.

He hadn't expected that victory to come quite so soon. He had anticipated having to wait discreetly for quite a time before he would let Celia 'spill the beans' (wasn't that the English expression?). But of course that sudden heart attack of Nat's—her anxiety and so on—had propelled her into a confession. Supposing the old man had *dis*approved. Well, he hadn't and it had paid handsomely, always being gracious and tactful and charming to the old boy, as well as carrying out all wishes to the letter.

'Celia, my angel!' Philippe exclaimed aloud, burying his face against her hair, 'but this is truly wonderful news.'

'No more need to keep our love from the world. We can tell everybody—Aunt Tiny—Geoffrey More *and* Nadine,' Celia ended with a purely feminine touch of malice which she immediately regretted, for she added: 'I hope it doesn't upset her because I think she is rather too fond of you, Philippe.'

He made no answer. He didn't care a damn what Celia's aunt or Nat's secretary or anybody else had to say when their engagement was announced. But he did have a few doubts about Nadine. She'd be absolutely livid—and because she knew him so well—she might suspect his reasons for this sudden desire to marry Nat's niece. A good thing it was all happening before the old boy died—before anybody knew about Celia's true relationship to her 'Uncle Nat'.

Celia, warm and content in Philippe's arms, thrilled by the thought of being able to break the news to everybody in Villa Psyche, was thinking:

'I wish I could tell him everything, but I can't—I promised my father. But what a terrific surprise it will be to Philippe when he knows who I am. And how glad, glad, *glad*, I am that he wanted to marry me just for myself—when I had nothing.'

# TEN

MISS COTLAND sat beside Nat Frayne looking down at a man whom she hardly recognised, and feeling a certain pity mixed with curiosity.

Here was the man who had broken Mary's heart—her poor sister Mary who had been the pretty, silly one of the family. Tiny had always protected her and cared for her—as she had done in later years for Celia. Goodness, she thought, what a lot of water had rolled under the bridge since Nat walked out of the house and left Mary to weep herself into the grave. And what a change time, and life—and now his fast approaching death—had wrought in Nat's once handsome, intelligent face. He looked grey and shrunken. And yet his eyes met hers with the same mocking diabolical smile that he used to give in the old days when they embarked on one of their frequent disagreements. How they had fought! How they had hated each other—yet respected one another's brains and determination. They had neither of them ever given in.

'Well, Tiny,' Nat spoke first. 'I never used to be very pleased to see you but times have changed. We're too old to hate each other any more.'

'Oh, no we're not,' said Miss Cotland drily, 'I don't think one's ever too old to hate—or to love. It's just that one hasn't quite as much energy.'

'Well, that's what age does to you.'

Miss Cotland smiled broadly.

'Now, Nat, you're a sick man and we're not going to start one of our arguments.'

He shut his eyes and drew a long breath. Tiny's long horse-face with the kindly eyes, her tall, stooping, unfeminine body, brought back so many memories. That old life seemed so far, far away.

He said:

'It's a hell of a long time since we last met.'

'It is.'

'You've made a grand job of my girl.'

'Glad you like her.'

'I'm crazy about her but the fates don't seem to want me to

enjoy having my daughter. A pity. I'd have liked more time with her. She's a sweet thing.'

'And she's good through and through without being boring,' said Miss Cotland bluntly.

He nodded.

'So I've discovered. Usually I yawn my head off in the company of the worthy and respectable.'

'Oh, you—you were never the one to appreciate virtue, my dear Nat,' said Miss Cotland with her tongue in her cheek.

'Maybe I've changed. I certainly appreciate Celia—every little thing about her.'

'Even in the short time she's been out here with you she seems to have developed,' said Miss Cotland.

'Along the right lines, I hope.'

'I hope so, too. But she was a nice child as she was. That Countess-creature seems to have smartened her up a lot and I suppose that's what you like.'

'The "Countess-creature" knows her stuff,' chuckled Nat. 'So you don't like the beautiful Nadine?'

'No, you can keep her. She's a spiteful, vain woman.'

Nat looked at Tiny out of one eye, as was his habit when sizing people up.

'Still my dear outspoken sister-in-law. You never minced words when you took a dislike to anyone. Tell me—what do you think of Philippe Clermont?'

Miss Cotland knit her brows.

'Ah! M. Clermont. Is he what you want for your daughter?'

'Then you know.'

'I know Celia's in love with him.'

'They want to get married.'

Miss Cotland winced and compressed her lips.

'And is that what you want, too?'

He sighed wearily.

'I don't know, Tiny. Marriage is a helluva gamble. Celia's very young and hasn't met many men. I don't want her to make a mistake. But she seems to have fallen hard for Philippe. She begged me to give them my blessing.'

'And you gave it?'

'Yes. I want the child to be happy.'

Miss Cotland shook her head.

'I know nothing about the young man except what I see on the surface. He's got all the charm and looks—but I must say I'd like to learn a bit more about his character.'

'You don't like him, do you?'

'I haven't formed a definite opinion,' Miss Cotland found herself hedging, which was unusual for her. 'On the surface, as I say, he's charming.'

'He has brains, too. Excellent at his job.'

'All the same I'm not sure he isn't too much of a play-boy for Celia. She may seem a simple sort of girl to you but she's deep—thoughtful—and idealistic. Would you say that Philippe Clermont would make the right husband for a girl with ideals?'

'I don't know,' said Nat Frayne. 'Marie-Thérèse always liked him. My brain isn't working. They've fuddled me with their damned medicines. I can only say that I've never found anything against young Philippe, and his father was a good friend of mine. Celia will be marrying into a fine old family. Anyhow—she wants him—she says so—and if he wants her, too—well, that's that. I don't believe in trying to direct the lives of others too stubbornly. I adore Celia. But she—like others, has got to fight her own battles, make her own mistakes and weather the storms like the rest of us.'

'I've no particular wish to sit by and watch my Celia weathering emotional storms if they can be prevented,' grunted Miss Cotland, her face a bit red. 'And I would say it would be wrong to let Celia rush into a marriage after only having known this French boy for a few weeks. I think they should have a long engagement.'

Nat opened his eyes and nodded.

'You haven't changed, Tiny. You were always prejudiced. Something *has* put you against Philippe Clermont.'

'If that is so, it's merely my own intuition.'

'You may be right—you may be wrong. I tell you, love and marriage is a gamble. Celia may be lucky. If Philippe is wrong for her I shall be sorry but I'm a dying man, too tired to work it out for her. You must watch her after I've gone, and do what you think best. Meanwhile let them get engaged—see what happens.'

'I'd have been better pleased if it had been that other young man even if he hasn't got an aristocratic name or a penny piece.'

'Whom are you talking about?'

'Geoffrey More.'

'He's a good lad, but there's been no question of a love-affair between him and Celia.'

'Not on Celia's side, perhaps. But I've watched that boy—the way he looks at her—I just wish if it must be one of the two that it was Geoffrey and not the Frenchman.'

Nat's eyes closed again. Miss Cotland looked at him with sudden anxiety. His breathing seemed to her to be worsening. She was about to call the nurse when Nat once more unclosed his eyes and spoke.

'One thing—a very big one—in Philippe's favour. He doesn't know that Celia is my child. He hasn't proposed to her because he thinks he'll benefit financially. He imagines, as everybody else does here, that she is just my niece and hasn't a penny.'

'Oh, well,' said Miss Cotland, 'as you say—Celia must do what she wants and if she *is* making a mistake, she will have to get on with it. I'll do what I can, naturally.'

Then she added, gently:

'Afraid you and I have never seen eye-to-eye, Nat, but if there is anything I can do for you now, please tell me.'

'Just look after my girl . . .' he whispered, and started to raise himself on one elbow. Then suddenly he gave a low cry. A convulsive shudder shook his frame; his lips turned blue, his eyes stared.

Thoroughly alarmed, Miss Cotland called out to the nurse.

'Fetch the doctor—quickly—oxygen quickly.'

By the time the nurse and physician had reached the bedside it was too late.

It was the end of the road for Nat Frayne.

Miss Cotland looked grimly and with awe upon the white still face of Celia's father. It was a little frightening, she thought, that one moment a man could be speaking to you and the next moment be gone for ever.

Nat—the man of millions—the man of culture, power and prosperity (and of little faith) had slipped with terrifying suddenness through that grim yet fascinating gateway of Death. Perhaps, she thought, at long last he was looking now upon the Face of Absolute Truth. Stripped of all shams, all illusions, all human frailties, he would find the meaning of life and solve the problem which has eluded science and religion throughout the ages.

'Poor old Nat,' thought Tiny Cotland and tears suddenly pricked her eyelids. She turned and walked out of the room to find Celia and break the news to her.

When Celia first heard it she was stunned. She had expected the end yet it had come so swiftly and suddenly it seemed somehow unexpected. It seemed impossible to believe that she had only been talking to her father, watching him smile, half an hour before he died.

The intensity of her own grief was also an astonishment to Celia herself. She had not known this father of hers for long; she had, in fact, thought of him as an enemy rather than a friend during her childhood. In an emotional moment, she burst into tears in Aunt Tiny's arms. Miss Cotland, patting her back, said:

'Keep a stiff upper lip, duckie. Now this has come—you must face up to it and remember you're the head of the household. I'm afraid you'll have to take on quite a bit of responsibility.'

Celia pulled herself together and blew her nose forlornly.

'Oh, lord!' she muttered in an instant of childish helplessness. Then she remembered Philippe. Her face brightened. She added: 'Thank goodness for Philippe.'

'Quite,' said Aunt Tiny drily. 'He'll manage all your business affairs. There's that nice Geoffrey to help, too. I reckon he attends to the financial side and leaves young Philippe to the antique and fine art department.'

'Thank goodness for my Philippe,' repeated Celia.

Aunt Tiny stuck her tongue in her cheek. She was not yet reconciled to the fact that her niece had made a final choice.

'He's gone down to the shop,' went on Celia. 'He'll be terribly shocked when he gets back. Where is Geoffrey? Have you seen him?'

'No. He said something about having to rush down to the kennels because he's got a dying dog there.'

Celia shivered and wiped her eyes.

'Oh, Aunt Tiny—it's such a wonderful life. Why do man or beast have to leave it?'

'It wouldn't do if we all lived for ever, lovey,' said Miss Cotland and gave the girl a little squeeze. 'Cheer up. I know it will please you to hear that your father and I had a friendly chat before he went.'

'Yes, I'm glad, Aunt Tiny. And did you mention about Philippe and me?'

'He brought it up, dear.'

'He was pleased, wasn't he? He loved Philippe because of Marie-Thérèse as well as Philippe himself.'

'He rather favoured a long engagement for you, duckie,' said Miss Cotland guardedly.

Celia looked at her wet crumpled handkerchief in which she had shed some bitter tears. She longed more than ever to belong to Philippe—never to leave him, but she knew that just now, with her father lying dead, and the funeral ahead of them, was no time for consideration of her personal happiness.

But there was the future—the glorious future. Poor Daddy wanted her to be happy and she *would* be; not because of the money but because of Philippe's love.

She said:

'I'd better ring Geoffrey up and tell him what has happened and ask him to come straight back. I've already rung Philippe but he's gone out. Geoffrey will want to get in touch with Daddy's lawyers and—and make all the other necessary arrangements.'

'Don't you concern yourself with that side of it, leave it all to Geoffrey,' said her aunt kindly. She could see from the girl's stricken face and trembling hands that she was badly upset.

It needed only two words from Celia—'*Daddy's dead*'—to bring Geoffrey back to Villa Psyche at top speed. It was only as he was driving there that his mind—shocked by the thought of his good friend and employer's passing—re-registered the title that the girl had used. '*Daddy.*' What on earth had she meant by that? She must have had a mental lapse.

He found her in the study at her father's desk. She was doing nothing. The young figure in the smart Italian slacks and jersey looked strangely desolate. Her face was buried in her hands. Awkwardly he spoke her name:

'Celia!'

She turned. He saw the tears streaming down her cheeks. He was a little surprised that she should feel the death of her uncle quite so intensely, but of course he knew that Celia had a very warm heart under that cool childish exterior.

She said in a muffled voice:

'Oh, Geoffrey, isn't it terrible?'

'It is indeed. I'm exceedingly sorry, please accept all my sympathy.'

'He was unique—marvellous.'

'Yes. I shall miss him not only as an employer but as a very great friend.'

'He relied on you for so many things, he told me so—he trusted you absolutely.'

Geoffrey flushed.

Impulsively she put out a hand, holding a handkerchief to her lips with the other. The big, bronzed, blue-eyed man looked hesitatingly at that slim young hand and then up at Celia's tear-drenched face. All the love and tenderness that he felt for her welled up and threatened his control. In this moment of mutual understanding and sorrow for the dead man, he felt that there was a real bond between them. She felt it too. She put away her handkerchief and clung now to his hand with both of hers.

'Oh, Geoffrey!' she choked again.

'I'm so sorry, dear . . .'

He felt distraught with the desire to snatch her to his heart and comfort her that way. It was pretty grim, he thought, to have fallen in love with her knowing that she was in love with that other chap. They hadn't announced the engagement, but Geoffrey was sure she and Clermont had an understanding.

Then suddenly in this moment of desire to give her his love —give her everything in the world that he had—his normal discretion faded. To hell with Philippe Clermont—that damned Frenchman and all his tricks—all's fair in love and war, thought Geoffrey with blinding passion. He was not going to remain a heroic figure, biting his lips in self-sacrificing silence. He had grown to love this girl with every breath in his body and he was going to tell her so.

'If there is anything I can ever do for you—please remember it,' he said hoarsely. 'I can't tell you how deeply I feel for you. I'm in love with you. I would have asked you to marry me if I hadn't known you care about somebody else. Now I've told you. Are you angry with me?'

'Of course not,' she stammered, 'I'm deeply grateful.'

'And I know you don't care a damn about me,' he added bitterly. 'But I just want you to know that if things become difficult for you and if anything goes wrong—you can rely on me.'

Her eyes widened. Her thoughts turned away from her grief. She was drawn to him. This was a Geoffrey she did not know—an emotional, deeply disturbed Geoffrey with unmistakable devotion written all over his rugged face. Madly in love though she was with Philippe Clermont, she was feminine enough to appreciate another love when it was offered her— to be warmed and comforted by it.

'Dear Geoffrey,' she said, 'dear, dear Geoffrey, I don't know what to say.'

He lifted her hand up to his lips and kissed it.

'Forget it. As I have just told you—I know you don't care a damn about me—but I do about you, and I wanted you to know.'

'It isn't true that I don't care a damn about you. I like you very much indeed. I've enjoyed all the times we've worked together down there with your sweet dogs. I admire you, too. So does Aunty Tiny. So did Daddy.'

Silence. Now for the second time Geoffrey was shocked by that word, *Daddy!* He let her hand fall slowly.

'You mean your *uncle*?'

'No, Geoffrey. He was my father. Everybody's got to know now, so you might as well be the first.'

Geoffrey was astounded. He gave a gasp:

'*Your father*?'

She made haste to explain—telling him briefly of the relationship and of Nat's original reason for wishing to keep the identity away from the world.

'He was so afraid somebody would want to marry me for my money,' she ended sadly.

Geoffrey's mind leapt uncomfortably to Philippe.

'And does Clermont know nothing?'

'No—nobody knew it.'

Afterwards, Geoffrey reproached himself for harbouring malicious and suspicious thoughts of his rival but now in this split second he found himself wondering whether Philippe Clermont had not known, *somehow*. Geoffrey had been in close association with Philippe for a long time. He knew so well the Frenchman's light nature concerning women—his numerous *amours*—and the sensuous type that attracted him. Nadine de Sachelles was that type—not the simple, delightful English girl. Why had Clermont made such a dead set at her, unless he had known something about the money?

Afterwards, of course, Geoffrey had to give Philippe the benefit of the doubt. To tell himself that if he, Geoffrey, could fall so much in love with Celia at first sight, why not another man? Anyhow this staggering news put an even greater barrier between himself and—Nat's heiress. For he was no more than Nat's personal assistant with small means behind him.

'It's all rather fantastic isn't it, Geoffrey?' he heard Celia's rather forlorn voice.

'It certainly is. All I can say is—I'm glad I told you how I felt before I knew you were Nat's daughter.'

Her heart warmed towards him. She hated the thought of anybody being hurt. She could read the naked pain in Geoffrey's very blue eyes. Aunt Tiny had, of course, agreed that Geoffrey had grown too fond of her—but Celia had not realised to what extent. She put out a hand to Geoffrey again with a gesture that he could not refuse. He took the warm young hand and pressed it.

'Thank you,' she said, and looked up at him with so much beauty and sweetness in those smoke-grey eyes that it wrung his heart and deepened his sense of loss and pain. 'Thank you for what you've said to me. But believe me I would never have imagined you the type to go after a girl for her money. Never.'

'Thank *you*,' he said, and dropped her hand and turned from her. He felt that the emotional outburst which he had allowed himself had been disastrous and done neither of them any good.

Then Philippe Clermont rushed into the room. Wordlessly, Celia flung herself into his arms. Geoffrey, white to the lips, walked out and shut the door.

# ELEVEN

A MONTH had passed since Nathaniel Frayne was laid to rest in the English Cemetery in Monte Carlo.

During that month Celia found herself having, perforce, to say goodbye to her extreme youth and carefree approach to life. Her whole life changed, and with it vanished any ideals that she might have cherished that life as Nat's daughter and heiress could be simple. Not even Aunt Tiny's presence and help, nor Philippe's thrilling love, could make it that.

Now, of course, everybody at the Villa Psyche, to say nothing of the English community who lived around them, knew about Celia's true identity. The local papers chronicled it. Celia woke up one morning to see her name in headlines.

Intense fervent young French reporters flocked to interview her. English representatives of the British national Press flew out to do their share of questioning and photography. This was news. A romance to interest the world. The internationally famous art-dealer of *Frayne et Cie* had re-discovered the daughter of his first marriage—brought her out to Monte Carlo as his niece in order to prevent her being run after for her millions—and died, leaving her his entire fortune. It was a nine-day wonder. Celia found herself very much the focus of attention and interest. Letters poured in from Nat's friends from all over the Continent and America. In addition, after a decent interval of time following her father's funeral, she had announced her engagement to Philippe Clermont. That, of course, added to the general interest. One paper published a photograph of Celia, arm in arm with her fiancé, standing by the grotto in the grounds of Villa Psyche, looking at the beautful water-nymph that had recently been transported from Italy. It was here that they had first admitted their love for one another, Celia told the Press.

Under this picture were the words:

MILLIONAIRE NAT FRAYNE'S DAUGHTER AND HER FIANCÉ, NEPHEW OF THE LATE DUC DE FRAGONARD, ONE OF THE ASSISTANT DIRECTORS OF FRAYNE ET CIE.

There followed a little paragraph about Philippe's family, not forgetting to add the fact that Philippe had believed Miss

Frayne to be a penniless niece when he asked her to marry him. So, Miss Frayne proudly assured the Press, her father's wishes had been carried out.

All this publicity was somewhat alarming to Celia although it had its amusing and exciting moments. And with Philippe at her side she could always 'cope', (as she told Aunt Tiny). He was marvellous. He could tackle anybody. And they were both happy—oh, so happy! She was sure darling Daddy would be glad if he knew.

But Miss Cotland was not happy. For some extraordinary reason that intuition of hers continued to bother her and she just could not like Philippe as much as she wanted to. Nor was she particularly pleased about that magnificent emerald ring which Philippe placed on the finger of her niece explaining that it had belonged to the one-time *Duchesse*, his aunt, who had given it to him for his future bride. He had become quite voluble on the subject of that emerald. He had meant, he said, never to marry—then Celia walked straight into his life and his heart. He had intended to present the ring to his poor little cousin Marie-Thérèse when her child was born. Now it was in its rightful place, on the hand of the future *Madame* Clermont.

All this sounded fine and Celia, besieged and overloaded though she was by family business and her new responsibilities as mistress of Villa Psyche, was blissful. The one thing that Aunt Tiny needed was the assurance that Philippe was genuine. Celia, of course, believed in him implicitly. Rather in defiance of Aunt Tiny she repeatedly told her how astounded Philippe had been when, on the morning of her father's death, she told him about their true relationship.

'You know he even offered to walk out—not to hold me to my promise to marry him,' she said proudly. 'Darling Philippe, he couldn't bear me to think that he might have been one of those fortune-hunters Daddy dreaded.'

Aunt Tiny listened, nodded and kept her own counsel. But she continued to caution her niece not to name the wedding day until next year.

To this, of course, Philippe made strenuous objections.

'He's terribly in love with me,' Celia explained to her aunt, 'and he doesn't want me to wait too long. He'd like us to get married straight away without a fuss or a big wedding.'

Aunt Tiny so far forgot her vow never to interfere in other people's lives as to beg Celia not to do this.

'Everything's happening too suddenly, duckie, give yourself time. Get your bearings. It was your father's wish as well as mine.'

'Philippe and I are so much in love,' Celia argued, then added with a little laugh, 'but I'll try and make him understand.'

'I never did like rushed weddings,' muttered Aunt Tiny.

There was somebody else who didn't like the idea either and that was the *Comtesse* de Sachelles. She had received one or two major shocks after Nat died—the first when she heard that the 'penniless little Miss' was his daughter, the second, (later on) when Celia's engagement to Philippe was announced and celebrated by a family dinner party. Nadine was invited to this but she did not go. She had grievances of her own to nurse. She looked with a very jaundiced eye upon the whole proceedings. She had lost her handsome and attractive boy-friend and lost him to Celia which was a bitter blow. She had also lost a wealthy Sugar-Daddy in Nat Frayne. She looked like losing everything. She treated Philippe to a bitter scene.

'Don't tell me you didn't know which way your bread was buttered. I know you too well, *mon cher*,' she said.

She had gone down to his flat late one evening. He had been avoiding her up till now but when he opened the front door she walked in and told him she was standing no nonsense. She even threatened him.

'I shall tell your sweet pure little bride just how far things went with us.'

Philippe was much too pleased with life to be intimidated. He was sure of his prize—and everything that went with it. Besides marrying Celia, Nat had left him a small legacy as well as an interest in the firm. He had absolutely nothing to worry about now. He looked at Nadine in an ironic way. This was not the subtle elusive woman who had played so 'hard to get' for so long, when he hadn't a sou. He reminded her of it.

'You only want me now because I'm solvent, and because I'm likely to be a lot more than that once I get control of my wife's fortune.'

'You're a devil,' Nadine said and tears of rage sparkled in her large dark eyes. 'A heartless, greedy devil.'

'Now come, my darling,' he mocked her. '*You* have been the cruel greedy one up till now. I have had to put up with all your moods—and exigencies. It was you who used to call the tune and make me dance to it. You used to visit me when you wanted a little love and you liked my kisses, didn't you? But you were not at all keen on marriage, *chérie*. No—not on being tied to a hard-pressed young man who was always in debt. Nat kept me pretty short—as you know. In any case, why this attitude from a woman who has had an eye on Geoffrey More? He's going to be at a loose end shortly. You can amuse yourself with him. Oh, I know he wasn't willing before, but he should be more so now. He's nuts about Celia and she won't look at him, and if I have my way he'll soon be right out of the Frayne household. I reckon he might drop like a plum into your beautiful arms. I suggest you go and hold them wide open to him.'

Nadine, walking up and down the small elegant *salon*, furiously smoking a cigarette, turned and glared at Philippe. She was infuriated by his air of self-confidence and superiority. Now that she was about to lose him for good and all, she remembered how well they had suited each other as lovers. She had come often to this flat, and he to hers. Physically they used to be unable to keep out of each other's arms. It had been a mad affair, controlled only by their mutual acceptance of the fact that they could not afford to marry. But in Nadine's life there had never been a lover like Philippe, and never would be again. She trembled violently with the force of her own feeling.

'I shall tell that girl you are my lover,' she stammered.

'She already knows that you and I have had some kind of affair but she is not interested. My past is my own. I suggest you don't try and tell her the sordid details about us. It will only end in humiliation for you, *ma chère*.'

'You stupid fool!' she sobbed the words at him. 'You and that girl could never really hit it off. You'll be bored to tears with her before the end of the honeymoon.'

He shrugged his shoulders. His almond-shaped eyes sparkled with malicious amusement.

'That may well be true. But I shall never get bored watching her sign the cheques. Oh, the lovely lolly! And after all, why shouldn't I inherit some of it? I'm Nat's cousin by marriage.'

'You knew,' said Nadine in a deadly voice. 'You *knew* that she was his daughter.'

'Prove it, my darling.'

'I will! I will! I'll find some way of making her realise just why you are marrying her!' Nadine cried in a high shrill voice.

He looked down at her. She was an extraordinarily beautiful

113

woman. She still had a strong magnetism for him. It was flattering to think that those large glittering eyes expressed such hot desire for him—that all her rage and crazy jealousy were on account of him. He thought of the many times when she used to refuse to meet him, to be involved with him. This was an amusing change. One of Philippe Clermont's greatest failings was his vanity. And there was a strongly sensuous side to him which made him more vulnerable than an older, colder man might have been. It was satisfying to see Nadine de Sachelles in this state and it would be a pity, he thought, not to take advantage of it.

'You have the most magnificent eyes, *ma chère*,' he said in a low changed voice, put out a hand, pulled the dress down from one of her brown shoulders and kissed the satin-smooth flesh.

Immediately she melted. The next moment they were clinging together in one of those violently passionate embraces that they had shared on other occasions. He kissed her until she was breathless.

'Magnificent,' he repeated the word, 'and I don't mind admitting I am sometimes bored by the good little girl up at Villa Psyche. But I assure you, *chère*, that I intend to marry Celia. Nevertheless, I see no reason why you and I should not continue to meet, providing you drop this stupid jealousy, and the quite foolish idea that I knew Nat's secret. I shall have plenty of money, and plenty of spare time in the future. Can our friendship not continue, *belle amie*?'

Nadine made no answer but pressed her lips to his again with desperate passion. It was almost as though she was silently defeating Celia *and* Geoffrey, who didn't want her, by those kisses. Philippe wanted her still. He was worth having these days; and he wasn't married to Celia yet.

Then her mind ceased to work and only the beautiful body that Philippe found 'so magnificent' was wholly alive to the thrill and urgency of the moment.

At half past five in the golden mist of the summer dawn, Philippe Clermont let Nadine out of his apartment and escorted her down in the lift. Her car was parked outside the block of flats. She drove away in it quickly feeling a good deal more satisfied and confident of the future than when she had arrived.

A man, with two large dogs on a lead, had just turned the corner. He saw the woman get into the small blue Renault which he recognised as the *Comtesse's* car. Geoffrey More had been up all night with his sick dog. It had, unfortunately, died an hour ago. He always felt sad when one of his pets expired. He and the vet had fought so hard for its life. He felt deeply depressed. He missed Nat and he was particularly concerned about the situation at the Villa. He had made up his mind to hand in his notice. It had become intolerable to him to stand by and watch Celia become more and more deeply embroiled with Philippe Clermont. Unable to sleep, Geoffrey had decided to bring two of his convalescents out for a walk while there was no one around, and the day was yet cool. His home was not far from the block in which Philippe lived. Then he had come across the Renault, and a moment later he saw the familiar figure of Nadine, wearing a white sleeveless dress, with an emerald chiffon scarf tied over her hair, emerge from the building. Keeping well out of sight in a doorway Geoffrey watched the last passionate embrace between Nadine and the man who was seeing her off.

Sick at heart, he turned and walked back to the kennels. So *that* was it! That was how things still were between Clermont and the *Comtesse*. And this was the man who was actually engaged to Celia and trying to urge her into a marriage before the summer ended.

Geoffrey thought of Celia's fresh pure face, her natural charm and innocence, her deep religious belief in both God and man. Oh, how damnable! he thought, what a catastrophe! And what the *hell* could he do about it?

He could hardly go to Celia and tell her bluntly that her fiancé was carrying on an intrigue with Nadine at the same time that he was protesting love and fidelity for her, Celia.

Geoffrey was in such a state when he went up to Villa Psyche to work that morning that he could hardly concentrate on his job.

Miss Cotland found him in the study when she came downstairs. She wanted some more notepaper. Celia had used the last, just now. Celia was not a good correspondent, and her aunt was having to stand over her and make her answer the many people who had written to her after seeing the announcement of her engagement in the French and English papers. She had just left Celia at her *escritoire* up in her own room, plodding through some of this correspondence.

Miss Cotland looked curiously at Geoffrey. The young personal assistant was sitting at his late employer's desk looking slightly distraught. Tables and desk were littered with documents, papers and account books. Miss Cotland felt sorry for Geoffrey. He had a great deal to do and she had thought once or twice that young Clermont ought to be more help to him. But Philippe, when discussing the business side with Celia, always declared that he was immersed in buying and selling for *Frayne et Cie* and had no time to give Geoffrey any assistance. Anyhow, he said there were two under-secretaries to work for Geoffrey—an Englishwoman of middle age, and a French girl who came up every day to help with the correspondence. There were also solicitors, both French and English, to grapple with death duties and tax problems. It was all very 'big business' of course. Celia Frayne was head of the show in name only—she was really like a small ship being carried along on a mountainous sea, scarcely knowing in what direction she was going.

'You look a bit off colour, Geoffrey,' said Miss Cotland who had become good friends with the boy.

He took his pipe from his mouth, stood up and turned to her. She was quite shocked to see that his eyes were red-rimmed and his face looked quite exhausted.

'Off-colour is an understatement of how I feel this morning, Miss Cotland,' he said grimly.

'Anything happened?'

'Yes.'

'Can you tell me?'

Geoffrey knocked his pipe on the fender—then carefully scooped the bowl out with the end of a match. His lips smiled bitterly.

'No—I suppose you'd call it a personal matter which I must keep to myself.'

'I'm so sorry.'

He looked up at the long, bovine, kindly face of the big woman and felt warmly towards Celia's aunt. She was a great personality, he thought. A fine woman. If she weren't at Villa Psyche he would have felt a great deal more anxious than he already did about Celia. After a moment he said:

'I don't think I shall be here much longer, Miss Cotland.'

'Oh—why not?' she asked uneasily.

She could see that something had very seriously upset the young man who had been Nat's personal assistant and head secretary for so many years. But she did hope he wasn't going to leave Villa Psyche. He was so much to be trusted. She felt that Celia needed his devoted, honest service. At the same time she was well aware that he was in love with her niece—which must make it hard for him to remain under the same roof—in such close association with Celia, having to watch her prepare for a wedding with Philippe.

Miss Cotland sighed. It seemed a pity life must hold so many snags, she thought. Snags, wherever one looked! Here they were, in this gorgeous villa, with Celia in a terrific position. Celia who a short time ago had been a penniless little typist. Yet there was something wrong. Very wrong, and Miss Cotland sensed it. She realised that Geoffrey sensed it, too.

She had always been a blunt outspoken woman. Yet she hesitated from coming out into the open over this particular matter. She was too afraid of doing and saying the wrong thing. She kept telling herself that it was Celia's life. Celia's choice. She, her aunt, *must* accept this. At the same time the more she saw of young Geoffrey, the more she wished Celia had fallen in love with *him*.

It was a beautiful day. The summer had by no means ended. The temperature was still in the high seventies. The sky was a deep clear blue this morning and the half open slats of the Venetian blinds let the golden sunshine filter gently through. Miss Cotland looked round the walls at Nat's fine collection of books, and a portrait of him over the fireplace. A Graham Sutherland—one of his many treasures. A masterly reproduction of that sardonic, interesting face. Oh! what a pity poor Nat had died so young, and was no longer here to guide Celia. To keep them all together, Miss Cotland thought, a trifle grimly. Without the head of the household, where so much money was involved, there was bound to be trouble. They needed his firm steadying hand at the helm.

Suddenly Miss Cotland said:

'Wasn't it Mr. Frayne's wish that you should stay on and run things for Celia? Didn't he mention this in his Will?'

'The Will was made before he knew that Celia was going to marry Philippe Clermont,' said Geoffrey brusquely. 'He, as Celia's husband, will obviously want to do all the managing.'

Miss Cotland hummed and hawed.

'They're not married yet.'

She saw Geoffrey change colour. He turned and shuffled through some of the documents on the desk but she knew quite well that he didn't see them. Of course, she thought sadly, all this boy's trouble was wrapped up in Celia. He was hard hit.

Fancy her little Celia getting all these men to adore her, this way! And it wasn't as though she was a slinky glamour-girl-cum-temptress. She was just a lovely sweet youngster with a charming nature, an unprejudiced outlook on life and a capacity for enjoying everything which probably the men found rather exciting.

It was interesting to Tiny Cotland to look on and see what Celia was making out of life—how she had grown in stature mentally since she took the plunge and flew down here to her father. Tiny knew that Celia wasn't nearly as easy and simple as she appeared. There was too much of her father in her for that. She trusted people but they only had to put one foot wrong and betray that trust and they would be 'out'. Of that, Miss Cotland was certain. Celia had a will of her own *and* ideals, and with each succeeding day, Miss Cotland seemed to watch her increasing in judgment and wisdom (over everything and everybody except Philippe).

She had tackled her new important position with extra-ordinary good sense and equanimity. And she did not delegate all the responsibility. She had her own ideas on how Villa Psyche should be run—who should be asked there, and who not. Knowing that Celia disliked the *Comtesse*, Miss Cotland had half expected her to bar Nadine from further invitations to private parties. But she hadn't done so. She had in fact said to her aunt:

'I think it would be rather mean of me to exercise my new authority by ignoring Nadine. After all, whether willingly or unwillingly, she did take a lot of trouble turning me into the chic Miss Frayne that Daddy wanted me to be. And she was a friend of his. And,' Celia had added with a rather touching bravado, 'I think she used to be good friends with darling Philippe.'

*Good friends!* Miss Cotland had thought over the words at the time, sniffing. She'd like to bet her bottom dollar that the 'Countess-creature' had had more than a platonic friend-ship with *Monsieur*-Don-Juan-Clermont, as she privately called him.

But in the kindness of her heart, Celia continued to extend the hospitality of Villa Psyche to the *Comtesse* who was now, of course, being most friendly and charming to her. *She* knew which side her bread was buttered, thought the caustic Miss Cotland.

Celia had also become mistress of the house in fact, by clamping down on the undesirable activities of some of the staff. Nat had allowed himself to be robbed right and left. A good quarter of the food went home with the married chef every night, added to which he was carrying on a clandestine affair with the pretty girl who waited at table. Celia had got rid of them both. She was not prepared to accept exquisite cooking at the price of thieving. But Annette and the butler were faithful and devoted servants and the other maids and gardeners remained and had transferred their allegiance from *Monsieur* to *Mademoiselle*.

Thinking now about Nat's Will, Miss Cotland recalled the fact that he had left a bequest of £5,000 and one of his many cars to Geoffrey. He had forgotten none of his friends. He had made this Will so it appeared only a fortnight after Celia had joined him.

Miss Cotland spoke now to Geoffrey:

'How are your little patients this morning?'

'I have only one sick terrier—the others are just strays, waiting for homes.'

'That reminds me,' said Miss Cotland, 'up till now my niece hasn't had time to think about everything but she did mention to me last night that she was thinking of asking you to let her have Gigi—you know, the one she adopted.'

Geoffrey bit his lip. It gave him a pang to remember Celia working with him down at the kennels—taking such a sweet earnest interest in them. He answered:

'Surely M. Clermont won't care for mongrels about the place——'

'I think she wants Gigi for herself and not for M. Clermont,' observed Miss Cotland tartly.

Geoffrey suddenly turned and looked her squarely in the face.

'When are they going to get married, Miss Cotland?'

She turned uncomfortably from the pain in those honest and attractive eyes.

'I really don't know, Geoffrey. First she says quite soon—then she says later on—she can't seem to make up her mind.'

'Surely she has no doubts?'

'About her feeling for him? No, I don't think so. But I think she's concerned because she knows her father wanted a long engagement and Celia would be quite willing to wait until the New Year. But Philippe is trying to rush her.'

Geoffrey's mind flashed to the picture of Philippe letting Nadine out of his flat at five-thirty this morning. He gritted his teeth.

'Oh, damn,' he said under his breath, '*damn!*'

At this point, the study door opened and Philippe Clermont strolled in.

Miss Cotland eyed him over her horn-rimmed glasses. The nigger-in-the-wood-pile, she thought. Well, no wonder he had such a hold over Celia. He certainly was a good-looker. Talk about Greek statues . . . over six foot of feline grace . . . with that golden-brown skin and those liquid eyes . . . and the careless, yet careful attention to his appearance. Black linen slacks, white silk shirt, and black scarf. Bare feet in dark red sandals, a half-smoked cigar between his fingers. Miss Cotland had noticed that he had lately been smoking Nat's special brand of cigars. Just as she had watched him pouring out the drinks in the evening as though he had already taken over his position as head of the household. Yet, as usual, when she looked at him with positive dislike, he broke through her defences with his easy charm and made her realise that no woman, even one in the fifties, could be impervious to the strong masculine attraction exuded by Philippe Clermont.

He came straight up to her, took her hand and bent over it. '*Bonjour, ma chère tante.*'

He had lately taken to calling her that.

'Morning, Philippe,' she said briefly.

'Where's that enchanting niece of yours?'

'Writing letters. Now don't interrupt her—she's got to get them done.'

'Dearest *Tante*, I have every intention of interrupting her and taking her to swim on this divine morning,' he laughed. 'You come with us, and I'll teach *you* how to water-ski.'

His eyes, sparkling with laughter, were hard to resist. She found herself laughing with him. What a devil he was. What chance had Celia? Yet why worry about him if he made the girl happy? She had nothing concrete against him.

'Get away with you,' she said, 'and please leave Celia alone for another hour. She *must* write some letters.'

'To please you, *chère Tante*—anything,' he said gaily.

Then he looked across the room at Geoffrey who was once more seated at the desk with his back to them. Philippe's expression altered. It became rather ugly—not that Tiny Cotland could see it.

'I have some business to get through with Geoffrey, anyhow,' said Philippe.

Miss Cotland left the two men to themselves.

Up till now any talks that the two men exchanged in Nat's study had been confined purely to business. Geoffrey had expected it to be the same this morning. But he found M. Clermont a little less pleasant than usual once Celia's aunt had left the room. His tone changed. He seated himself on the edge of the desk, crossed his arms and looked with a certain insolent superiority at his English colleague.

'Well, *mon cher* Geoffrey . . . you still seem to be finding a great deal to do with all this . . .' he waved a hand around the untidy room, 'although I wonder if it has been really necessary for you to go through so many files and deed boxes.'

'It has been *quite* necessary,' said Geoffrey.

'You seem to have assumed the position, shall we say of Chief Controller these days,' drawled Philippe.

Geoffrey reddened. Now that he was made aware of Philippe's actual antagonism, his own proud stubborn blood rose to meet it. He stood up and looked Philippe straight in the eyes.

'I was Nat's personal assistant while he was alive. I know about most of his affairs and he entrusted me with clearing up his personal correspondence and other papers after his death. With a man like Nathaniel Frayne, this cannot be done in an hour or a day or a month.'

'You have two junior secretaries.'

'They have both been fully occupied in the library, where you will find them this morning hard at it. You may remember, Nat willed a large number of books and papers of historic and artistic value to various universities and museums. Everything has had to be found, catalogued and packed. Added to which Probate has not yet been granted and until it is, there is an enormous lot for me to do—quite apart from your own job of helping to clear up the business side in Cannes.'

Temporarily defeated by this explanation against which he could hardly argue, Philippe thrust out his lower lip and narrowed his gaze upon Geoffrey. He had never liked him. He had always been jealous of Nat's affection and trust in Geoffrey and also been annoyed in the past by Nadine's penchant for the Englishman. He wanted him out of the house—out of

Celia's life, too. Not that Philippe was uncertain of Celia's love—he could congratulate himself that she was crazy about him, but he disliked the fact that Celia still held Geoffrey in friendly regard—and that even now, at times, she went down to the kennels and helped with those damned dogs. Philippe was no dog-lover.

Philippe said:

'You were so much in Nat's confidence I'm curious to know if he ever told you about Celia being his child?'

'No, he did not.' Then like a flash Geoffrey shot a similar question at Philippe: 'Did he ever tell *you*?'

'Certainly not,' came Philippe's quick retort. But in a split second of indiscretion he let his gaze wander to that little drawer on the left side of the desk which had contained the fateful copy of the letter he had originally read, the one concerning Celia. Geoffrey noted that glance. Then Philippe said:

'I've been wondering, also, what happened to the little key Nat used to carry around with him—the key of his private drawer.'

'It was on his bed table with his watch and wallet containing a photograph of the late Mrs. Frayne,' said Geoffrey curtly. 'I handed them all over to Mr. Wentworth, his English solicitor. They were returned to me to deal with as I thought best.'

'Shouldn't they have been given to Celia?'

'Eventually they will be. But Mr. Wentworth, when he was here the day afer Nat died, considered that the key, at least, should remain with me for the moment until I had sorted out the contents of the private drawer.'

'And have you done so?'

'In fact, no. I completely lack idle curiosity, if that is what you are driving at, Philippe,' said Geoffrey coldly. 'I am quite sure that that drawer contains only Nat's most private correspondence and I am at the present wholly concerned with his other papers which need immediate attention—particularly those relating to financial affairs which are of interest to the French and English tax valuers and collectors——'

'I must congratulate you on your admirable foresight,' said Philippe with a faint sneer, 'but I rather think you have taken on a little more authority than your position in this household warrants.'

Geoffrey went scarlet.

'May I ask what you mean by that?'

Philippe slid off the desk. Avoiding Geoffrey's blue piercing gaze, he opened a fresh box of cigars which lay on the big desk beside the blotter. He took one and pierced it. The whole gesture reeked to Geoffrey of insolence and it infuriated him. It distressed him, too, to remember that numerous times he had watched the Chief take a cigar out of the box like that, light and smoke it while he dictated his letters. God! How he wished Nat was alive today! Loving Celia without hope was one thing . . . but to see her marry this French fellow who, in Geoffrey's opinion, was a complete and utter cad—was another.

'Merely that you take too much on yourself,' said Philippe. Geoffrey snapped:

'I resent that, Philippe. I think it is you who are taking on an excess of authority. You are not my employer. I do not intend my actions to be questioned by you. I have my work to do and I know exactly what Nat wanted of me. I shall carry out his wishes.'

Philippe also reddened but he still did not look at Geoffrey, but the long slim fingers holding the cigar trembled. Philippe was having some difficulty in controlling his hot temper.

'All very worthy, my dear Geoffrey, but I suggest that you remember your position—and mine.'

'What exactly is my position?' asked Geoffrey, in a freezing voice.

'That of a paid employee, which you still are, despite the fact that we've all been very friendly in the past and so on. But Nat, you know, would have been my father-in-law if he had lived and I always *have* been a distant relation, as my cousin was once married to Nat. And very soon I shall be Celia Frayne's husband which, surely you realise, puts me right at the head of the table——'

Geoffrey felt slightly sick. He, too, was having to exercise control. Peace-loving though he was, he had never felt more inclined to knock a man down. And he could do it if it came to a straight fight. Philippe looked wonderful, but he was flabby; the type who was given to excesses. Geoffrey led a more regular life and he had boxed for his public school and later for Oxford. It would have given him immense satisfaction to land a straight right on the Frenchman's sneering, rather womanish mouth, and knock a couple of those glistening white teeth out of position. Geoffrey's hands doubled. His own teeth clenched. He said:

'Now I know just where we stand.'

'Good. And as we understand each other, I suggest you hand in your resignation at once. You can leave Nat's affairs quite safely to me.'

'That,' said Geoffrey, 'will be for Celia to decide.'

'I'm not having her brought into it,' said Philippe in a loud blustering voice.

'Much though I regret it, I'm afraid she will have to be brought into it. Until she is your wife I regard her as my employer and if I hand in my resignation it will be by her wish and hers alone.'

Now Philippe lost a modicum of his self-possession.

'Don't think I'm ignorant of the fact that you're rather keen on Celia!' he said furiously. 'But you won't get very far with her so it's no good hanging round, acting the British bulldog.'

That was too much for Geoffrey. He made a quick movement towards the Frenchman, his right fist doubled. He saw Philippe's pale face sweating with sudden fear and astonishment, near to his own. He heard the high-pitched voice:

'Get away from me . . . I'll have you arrested for assault . . . I'll . . .'

Philippe stopped, choking. The still unlit cigar dropped from his fingers. He shook violently with mingled fright and astonishment. He had not expected violence from Geoffrey—neither did he wish to taste it. He was only too well aware of the Englishman's muscular strength and his own inability to defend himself if it came to a showdown.

It was at this moment that they heard Celia's voice outside the study door.

'Hi—you two big businessmen—can I come in?'

It was an anticlimax and a respite. Perforce, both men cooled down. Geoffrey turned away from Philippe who picked up his cigar and with trembling fingers began to light it.

Celia walked in.

# TWELVE

CELIA entered her father's study with a light step and a light heart. She was completely unaware of the little drama that had been taking place. She had every cause to feel happy this morning—not only because it was so beautiful and she would soon have a blissful session at her favourite sport—swimming and aqua-skiing—but because she was so much in love. Being in love made a girl so very happy—so much happier, she kept thinking, than knowing she had only to sit down and sign her name on a little pink cheque and she could have hundreds of thousands of francs in her purse at any given moment.

But while writing her letters she had found time to think about one or two things that she could now do for people less fortunate than herself. This last month had been too busy—too fully occupied so far—for her to think about those people. But this morning she had made a list, and was going to show it to Philippe and discuss it with him and perhaps ask Geoffrey to see to the financial side. There was that woman, Mrs. Mumford, who used to do daily work for herself and Aunt Tiny at Battersea. She had six children and her husband was an invalid. She was an honest creature and a faithful worker. Sometimes she had looked so tired and worn that Celia used to hate to watch her scrubbing the kitchen floor. Aunt Tiny used to give her food to take home—and dresses to cut down for herself. But now Celia was going to see that poor Mrs. Mumford's life changed as miraculously as though she had won a football pool (her husband was always trying to make the odd pound that way). It was awfully difficult for Celia to realise that she was virtually a millionairess but she could, she knew, pay a substantial sum in to the bank for the Mumfords, and buy them a cottage by the sea which was Mrs. Mumford's dream.

That was only one of the good deeds she meant to do. There was also her girl-friend at the office—Joanna Page. Jo needed help badly. She was one of the brave ones. The eldest of a family of five small children with a harassed musician for a father and a never-well mother, Jo parted with most of her salary to help swell the home exchequer. Celia would send Jo a fat cheque and later have her out to Villa Psyche for the first real holiday of her life; the others had been spent looking after her small brothers and sisters in some cheap seaside boarding house.

'How lucky I am!' Celia kept thinking.

She adored Philippe. Sometimes when Aunt Tiny accused her of spoiling him and giving in to his every wish she felt that perhaps it was true. She *was* weak with Philippe. He was hard to resist. All that was warm and passionate in her nature reponded to the passion in his. When at times she thought about things quietly she was almost afraid of this love. It was not the quiet steady devotion she had always dreamed about. It was a fierce flame devouring her. When she was with him, she was not herself. It was by no means a peaceful sort of relationship. He was clever and subtle in his love-making. He never outraged her feelings and seldom tried to break down her resistance. But he made her acutely conscious of her own young ardent body and of the undoubted fact that sex played an important part in one's life; that love was not always romantic in its purest, most idealistic sense. It was a little disturbing to Celia to feel the clamour of her own desires. Philippe's caressing hands, his long experienced kisses, sometimes left her breathless and exhausted; with the curious sensation that she was drowning. Yes, it was almost like that. As though she dived into deep water and found it difficult to come up. She would pull away from him and say:

'No—no more—don't kiss me any more, *please!*'

Immediately he would do as she wished and tease her.

'Still in the fifth form! My little schoolgirl, wondering what life's all about,' he would say, his handsome eyes full of amusement.

But she knew that it wasn't quite like that. She was no schoolgirl. She was like any other girl of her day and age—fully aware of facts—of the sensual claim that two ardent young people, very much in love, can have upon each other. It was just that she didn't want to lose her head completely *now*. She wanted to wait until she was Philippe's wife. Although Philippe never actually said so, she feared that he considered that idea a little prudish; even boring. Thus it was that when they were in each other's arms at the height of their passion, she felt furthest away from him. This gave her something to think about. She found it disquieting. She could not possibly have discussed anything so personal with dear Aunt Tiny, so she kept it all to herself. And she kept telling herself that everything would be different when she and Philippe were married. There would be no need then to worry about *anything*.

The other night, he had taken her down to the Casino to watch him playing *chemin-de-fer*, which she found only faintly amusing—although he seemed to enjoy it. Everyone at the Sporting Club knew him. He was obviously a regular gambler. They seemed to Celia to be playing for very high stakes. She was still so unused to being rich, it positively flabbergasted her to see her fiancé lose a big bank, shrug his shoulders and draw a fresh packet of ten thousand-franc notes out of his wallet. Finally he lost all he had brought and borrowed from her. He lost that then stopped playing.

'I'll pay you back first thing in the morning, *ma mie*,' he had said. But he hadn't done so. She supposed he had forgotten. She hadn't the slightest intention of reminding him but found herself wishing that he *would* pay her back. It *was* a debt of honour. In her opinion, even one's husband should pay his wife back his gambling losses.

But once she and Philippe were back at Villa Psyche, they switched on the radiogramophone and danced together for an hour. She had been wearing his favourite of all her new model dresses—tailored white crêpe that made her slim young body look as though it were moulded into the material. It showed up her rich tan. During one of the dances he kissed her, put a hand against her throat and kept whispering her name urgently:

'Celia, *Celia*!'

She had put both arms around his neck and felt her ardour leaping to meet his. Then his fingers caught at her necklace—a turquoise collar—and broke it. She had wanted to stop and pick up the beads, but he said:

'Let it go. *Mon Dieu!* I love you—I want you so much. You drive me crazy. You don't know how beautiful you are—a hundred times more beautiful than when I first met you. Celia, *Celia*, tell me you want me too.'

'You know I do.'

'Then——?'

But that was one of the times when she suddenly went cold on him and no longer wanted to be kissed or caressed. She moved away, trying to laugh.

'Darling—we're often a little mad at times like this. It's four o'clock in the morning. You must go home, and I must go to bed.'

He had grown sulky.

'I don't believe you really love me.' He had smoothed back his hair and lit a cigar. She could see him shaking. She was trembling herself. She found herself thinking that passion was a terrible as well as a beautiful thing. *But I can't let myself go as he wants me to. I can't.*

'I do love you, honestly,' she told him. And knelt down and began to pick up the scattered turquoise beads. There were tears in her eyes. At times like this she felt almost panic-stricken because everything seemed to have happened to her in such a big way and in such a short time. She had found a father—and lost him. She had become almost a millionairess in her own right. She had discovered what love was and found a future husband in one of the most attractive and handsome young men on the Riviera. Yet none of it could really change the real Celia she had always been, the girl who used to live quietly, simply, in that little Battersea flat, with Aunt Tiny.

Suddenly she found the tears pouring down her cheeks. She had raised her face and looked up at Philippe imploringly.

'I do love you,' she said. 'But please, Philippe darling, try to understand me. It may be different with other girls—I may seem stupid. I've certainly discovered various complexes and difficulties in my own nature that I never knew existed. But forgive me. Everything will be different when we're married.'

He had knelt down the floor beside her, taken both her hands, kissed them gently and wooed her back to a sense of security.

'*I'm* the one that needs a lecture—not you—I just let my heart run away with my head because you're so divinely attractive, darling. I love my "fifth-form girl". I worship her. I would not want her to change into the sort of female who is so used to petting and love-making that she yawns while it's going on . . .' Then Philippe had laughed and made her laugh until she felt completely happy again.

Before he left the Villa he had said:

'Never let me upset you again and swear you'll go on loving me. I couldn't bear to lose you now.'

After he had gone, she felt as passionately in love with him as ever. The next day she received a magnificent bunch of pure white roses from Philippe. They were special blooms and had been flown from Brussels. With them was a note:

*'I love you. Please forgive last night and tell me that you'll marry me before the end of September. I want to take you away— right round the world—just you and I, alone on our honeymoon.'*

Of course she had adored the note and the white roses. But when she discussed the possibility of a September wedding with her aunt, Miss Cotland was still against it.

'Do be guided by me, duckie, and wait until the end of the year. Not only in order to make sure you're doing the right thing but because I feel it would be wise to wait until all the legal and business side is settled. You want to start off on your honeymoon knowing all that is behind you.'

When Celia repeated this to Philippe he went tense with anger and lost patience with her for the first time.

'This is your old aunt—she's always the one who doesn't want us to get married quickly. She's a jealous old so-and-so. She just doesn't want to lose you. She knows that after the wedding she'll have to go back to England and stop stage-managing you.'

That had made Celia feel both alarmed and upset.

'Oh, what a horrid thing to say, Philippe. And quite unjust. It *isn't* only what Aunt Tiny thinks. It's what I feel, too. Maybe you've got me all wrong but I'm not the sort of girl who wants to be swept off her feet and rushed into things. Perhaps I'm wrong for you altogether, Philippe. Perhaps you'll always find me priggish or boring or something, and we oughtn't to get married at all——'

She had deeply resented the way he had spoken about her beloved aunt. She knew, of course, that she would have felt heartbroken if Philippe had agreed with this and broken their engagement. But she had to be frank. It was an intrinsic part of her nature. She just wasn't the sort of girl that any man, even Philippe, could twist round his little finger. She must retain her sense of independence—have a will of her own. What she said seemed to shatter Philippe completely. He stood absolutely silent for a moment, staring at her, then said:

'I deserve that. I know I do. It all boils down to the same thing—that I love you too much and I get carried away. We've got to learn to know each other better. You are right. I'm fully aware that you are a more self-possessed practical person than I am. Thoroughly English in fact. I'm Latin and a bit excitable and I find it *hell* waiting for our marriage. But if you stop loving me, Celia—if you leave me—I shan't want to live—that's how much I love you.'

'You mustn't say things like that,' she had exclaimed.

'I mean it,' he had replied. 'I realise that you hate me to be possessive. I suppose that's what makes you so damnably attractive. Most women *want* to be possessed. You preserve your integrity in the most remarkable fashion. I find it fascinating and rather frightening. But I'll never again ask you to hurry on our wedding. I swear it. Just to prove how much I love you I'll wait patiently until you feel absolutely ready to name the day. Only go on loving me, go on believing that I love *you*.'

If this was exaggerated and over-emotional, it nevertheless made the strongest possible appeal to Celia's feminine vanity. She could not fail to believe that Philippe loved her. Neither could she tolerate the idea of sending him away. She wanted him as much as he wanted her. It was, as he had said, just that they were different in their approach to love. He even added words to the effect that he was really very fond of her *chère tante*. But it was always the same. This longing for her drove him mad. *And* he had a suspicion that *la tante* did not really like him.

Before they parted company, Celia was as deeply in love with Philippe as ever.

She had almost made up her mind to compromise and suggest that the wedding should take place at the end of the year—say, on December 1st which she knew was Philippe's birthday. It would be a wonderful, marvellous celebration and wedding, all in one. She made up her mind to tell Aunt Tiny and Philippe of this decision some time tomorrow. She was quite sure that all their restlessness and over-emotionalism would vanish once they were married, and alone. They were with so many other people now; the Villa was always full; and although she loved Aunt Tiny with all her heart Celia did sometimes resent the fact that Miss Cotland was so against her marriage to Philippe.

Celia, however, was not the type to be depressed or worried about anything for long and when she got up this morning she had felt her old happy optimistic self. After all there was nothing to be depressed about. Everything was marvellous—including Philippe!

But once she walked into her father's study her good spirits vanished. Philippe looked positively ghastly, she thought in dismay. She turned to Geoffrey and saw that he, too, looked odd and unlike his usually impassive self. The atmosphere between the two men seemed to be charged with antagonism. The cheerful 'good morning' which Celia had begun to say, died on her lips. She said:

'What on earth's happened? You two look like a couple of thunderclouds.'

Philippe wiped the perspiration from his forehead and neck and gave a short laugh.

'You came almost in time to witness what might be called an "ugly scene", my darling,' he said, breathing hard.

Celia stared from him to Geoffrey. The latter looked her in the eyes for a moment then turned and took characteristic refuge in a pipe.

Celia, who had been carrying a towel and swim-suit under her arm, tossed the bundle on to a chair. The morning was hot. She had put on a yellow and white sun-suit. She wore no make-up except lipstick. Her tanned face was already oiled in preparation for the fierce sun.

'What on *earth* has happened?' she asked again.

Philippe gave another unpleasant laugh.

'Our dear Geoffrey has just proved that he is not quite such a peaceful gentleman as we thought him. He has been quite violent this morning. In fact, if you hadn't come in, my sweet, I'm sure I would have been flat on my back by now. Knocked out by the one-time heavyweight champion of Oxford University, Mr. G. More.'

Celia's cheeks went pink.

'What *are* you talking about, Philippe?'

'You'd better ask *him*,' said Philippe pointing at Geoffrey, and largely because he didn't want to betray himself to Celia by being too unpleasant, he walked out of the room.

Left alone with her father's secretary, Celia gave an embarrassed laugh.

'My goodness gracious—what *is* all this in aid of, Geoffrey? Were you really going to knock my future husband down?'

He could sense the coldness and disapproval behind her laughter. He swung round to her, taking the pipe out of his mouth.

'I'm sorry, Celia, I'm afraid I was.'

'Good gracious me,' repeated Celia, 'I'd very much like to know why.'

'It's quite impossible for me to explain,' said Geoffrey.

'But you must. I must know—surely you see that.'

'I tell you I can't explain except that we had—words—he got my goat. I lost my temper. That's all.'

She felt dumbfounded and looked it.

'But, Geoffrey, you're not the sort of man who goes round losing his temper and hitting people. What on earth provoked it?'

'I can't explain,' he repeated. 'A great many things led up to it. Of course I know you're going to marry Philippe and that he hates my guts. The sooner I quit Villa Psyche the better. He told me I wasn't wanted here before we had the row. I said what I felt then—that as your father asked me to stay and look after everything, I meant to remain. But now, feeling as I do, I've changed my mind.'

'Changed your mind?' repeated Celia and her heart sank unaccountably low. 'But why?'

He felt agonised. It wasn't going to be easy to tell this girl whom he loved so much that this was 'goodbye'.

'Geoffrey, why do you want to go?' she demanded.

'Because as I told you,' he said, 'your future husband doesn't like me and he made it plain to me that the sooner I quit the better.'

Now Celia blushed hotly. She seated herself on the edge of the desk and nervously locked her fingers together.

'Geoffrey, this rather shakes me. I didn't dream that you and Philippe were so unfriendly—although I knew you weren't exactly buddies. You're such different types,' she ended awkwardly. 'But I can't *believe* Philippe asked you to leave.'

'I'm afraid he did.'

'This is absolutely ridiculous!' exclaimed Celia. 'You were my—my father's confidential secretary and assistant, and now you are mine. Philippe can't just tell you to—*quit* like that——' she waved her hand towards the window.

'Don't let it worry you, Celia, I can take care of myself.'

'You mean you intend to go?' her voice sounded so incredulous and worried that it warmed his heart. It was good to know that she did not share her fiancé's ill-feeling towards him.

'I think it's too unpleasant for everybody in the circumstances, Celia. It might be best for me to leave.'

'You can't possibly—with all my father's things still in a muddle—why, you told me only the other day you hadn't got through half his papers.'

'I admit there is still a good bit to do, and will be, until Probate is granted.'

'Then, Geoffrey, you can't go.'

A slight glimmer of sardonic amusement came into Geoffrey's eyes.

'My dear, is that an order to stay?'

She slid off her desk. Her lips were compressed. Those wonderful grey eyes of hers were very expressive, he thought, and she was uncannily like the Chief when she drew her mouth into a thin hard line. But of course he had come to the conclusion long ago that soft sweet little Celia had quite another side to her. She was a person to be reckoned with.

There followed a short sharp dispute as to whether he should leave or not and it ended in Celia losing her temper which was something he had never seen before. She marched to the door and flung it open.

'Well, I'm going to put a speedy end to *this*. You're just being plain stubborn. I don't want you to leave and I'm going to tell Philippe so.'

Once again Geoffrey felt elated by her obvious wish to keep him here, but he hurried after her.

'Please, Celia——'

'No, I'm not going to have this,' she said, her eyes flashing. 'My father relied on you and I do, too. You can't just march out because of some ridiculous misunderstanding with Philippe.' And now she raised her voice and called out: 'Philippe, *Philippe*, come here. I want you.'

Geoffrey pulled at the lobe of his right ear. His face was puckered. He had never felt more awkward. What a darling she was! And so sweet of her to have this faith in him—but the last thing he could do, even to please her, was accept any patronage, or condescension from that damned Frenchman!

Perhaps it was fortunate that Philippe was not to be found. Jean, the butler passing through the hall, told *Mademoiselle* that M. Clermont had just gone out in the car and left a message that he would return to take *Mademoiselle* for her swim in about half an hour. Celia went back into the study, her face still bright pink and mutinous.

'I suppose Philippe's in a huff, too. It really is all too stupid.'

Geoffrey felt inarticulate. He just shook his head at her. If only she knew what Philippe Clermont was really like, he thought. Oh *God*, if he could stop her from marrying that fellow, he'd gladly fade right out of her life and never see her again.

She said:

'I'll talk to Philippe when I see him but this really is *my* show, Geoffrey. Philippe can do all he wants about the personnel in Cannes but *I* run this house and I refuse to accept your resignation.'

His gaze fell before hers.

'It's very good of you to want me to stay,' he said in a low voice. 'I appreciate your trust in me, but I still have not explained to you why I nearly hit Philippe, have I?'

'You lost your temper, you said so. Well—I lost mine just now. We all do at times.'

He felt a sudden return to good-humour and grinned.

'You're really very, very sweet,' he said.

She tilted her head, and said:

'I'm not at all, I assure you. I feel furious.'

'Okay, you want me to stay and clear up the secretarial side of things. I'll do so and we'll leave personal feeling out of it.'

'But you know, Geoffrey, that personally I have the greatest admiration for you.'

'Well, let's not talk about that,' he said hurriedly.

She was forced to remember that Geoffrey was supposed to be in love with her. Aunt Tiny was always saying so. She also was forced to remember that Philippe had accused him of threatened violence.

'Oh, dear, I wish you'd put an end to all this mystery and nonsense and tell me why you and Philippe came so near to a fight.'

'I'm afraid that is out of the question. It was a personal matter between Philippe and myself.'

'Well, I'll make him tell me if you won't.'

Geoffrey had never felt more in love with her or more heartbroken to think that she was going to hand herself over completely to Philippe. She was such a charming adorable mixture—she could be so naïve and unsophisticated—and such a child. Yet she had proved herself since her father died of being a tough little businesswoman, with sound judgment and a will of her own. He could only suppose that Philippe had such a strong physical attraction for her, she failed to see the real man under the fascinating mask. He thought of some of the things that Philippe had said during their heated discussion this morning; and of Nat's key to that drawer in the desk. *Philippe had wanted to get at that drawer.* Geoffrey was positive. But why? Suddenly he said:

'Look, my dear, don't worry any more. Forget the fact that your fiancé does not like me—or vice-versa. As you said, I'm *your* employee not his. I think half the trouble is that I told him so.'

Celia frowned. Really Philippe must have been very tactless and silly, and Geoffrey was over-sensitive. She said:

'Okay. Let's forget it. But please stay on, Geoffrey. Honestly, I don't think we could manage without you.'

He smothered the longing to take her in his arms and kiss her. He inclined his head.

'Thanks. Thanks, very, very much, Celia. I hope I'll never betray your trust in me, and as soon as I've got everything straight, of course, I'll resign.'

That brought her fresh confusion. She was going to marry Philippe which meant that he would, of course, become head of her household. But she was so fond of Geoffrey—she had grown so used to him around the place. He was always so helpful and considerate—she did not really want to lose him. Oh, she *must* try and make Philippe see him in another light. She was sure the whole thing was sheer jealousy. Flattering though this was, she deplored it. She was also rather cross with Philippe for sacking Geoffrey out of hand without so much as asking her what *she* thought about it.

Suddenly Geoffrey pulled a bunch of keys from his pocket, undid one of them, and handed it to her.

'I'd like you to have this. It belongs to that drawer,' he nodded at Nat's desk. 'The top one on the left. He always kept this key on his person. I feel that you are the one go to through the drawer. The key was on his table with others beside his bed. I handed them straight to Mr. Wentworth and he returned them all to me a couple of days ago. Some of the trouble between Philippe and myself was over this key. He wanted me to give it to him.'

'No—really?' Celia's eyes widened. 'But it has nothing to do with Philippe. Daddy's private things, I mean.'

Geoffrey remained silent. Celia spoke again:

'And you haven't been through the drawer yourself.'

'No.'

'Well,' said Celia, walking to the desk and sitting down in her father's chair, 'as Philippe seems to have walked out in a bit of a huff and I'm in no hurry I might as well go through the drawer right now.'

Geoffrey stood smoking and watching as she unlocked Nat's

private drawer. She pulled out an envelope that was on top of some other papers and held it out for Geoffrey to see.

'It's marked "*Strictly Private*" but it's not sealed down. Maybe you had better read it.'

'I don't like reading other other people's private letters but I suppose I must,' she said.

A few seconds later she handed it to him with a somewhat sad smile.

'It's only a copy in my father's own handwriting of the one he sent to London after he had traced me. I remember every word. It is telling me all about my parentage and how he wanted me to come out here as his niece.'

'I see,' said Geoffrey slowly.

His mind worked—leapt to all kinds of new possibilities. An open envelope and in it a copy of the letter that informed Celia as to who she really was. That was interesting. And wasn't it possible that Philippe Clermont had seen it—read it? Could there have been such an occasion? Were his suspicions founded on facts as well as intuition? He glanced at Nat's revealing letter then gave it back to Celia who returned it to the drawer. Geoffrey smoked his pipe in silence, watching her. She found some other letters—one which she put in her bag, turning tear-filled eyes to him.

'It seems to be the last letter my poor mother ever wrote to father. He must have had *some* sentiment about her. I'd like to keep this. There are two bundles—obviously love-letters from his French wife, Marie-Thérèse. Please burn all these things some time, Geoffrey. And there's this miniature—look—I suppose this is Marie-Thérèse?'

'Yes, it is,' said Geoffrey.

'Poor Marie-Thérèse,' said Celia sighing. 'I'll keep her miniature. It's very beautiful and I think my father would prefer me to have it rather than let it go to a stranger.'

'I'm sure he would,' said Geoffrey.

'There's absolutely nothing else in this drawer that can't be thrown away as far as I can see. A facsimile of his Will which we've already got, and a bundle of English five-pound notes which you might lock in the safe.'

'Okay,' nodded Geoffrey, but his mind was still on that copy of Nat's original letter to Celia. He felt thoroughly uneasy, trying to work out in his mind *if* and *when* Philippe could have seen it. If he had at any time had access to that drawer?

Then Philippe came back. He seemed to have recovered

136

from his ugly mood completely. He was as gay and charming as ever. He went straight up to Celia who gave him a rather reproachful look, kissed her hand, and said:

'Sorry, angel—let's go and have that swim now . . .' then he even addressed Geoffrey with civility. 'Look, Geoffrey, I've been thinking things over. I really did not mean half I said. I was in a hell of a mood. Forget it, will you?'

Celia, who had been prepared to have a show-down with her fiancé, was relieved. But her large shining eyes were still reproachful as she said:

'Well, I don't know what it was all about, but let's *all* forget it. Geoffrey's a tremendous help to us and you know it, Philippe.'

'Oh, of course,' he said, 'I fully agree. Now, come, my sweet, we've wasted too much of this radiant morning already. The car's waiting.'

'I'm going to take Aunt Tiny with us whether she wants to come or not. I'll go and fish her out,' said Celia, feeling vastly better now that she thought the storm had blown over.

Geoffrey said nothing. He alone felt uneasy.

If it hadn't been for Celia's wishes nothing would have induced him to stay at Villa Psyche one day longer. He watched Philippe with a lynx-like scrutiny. He could have sworn that the Frenchman's gaze kept turning to *that drawer*. A sudden thought struck Geoffrey. The key was still in the lock. Philippe had no idea whether the drawer had been opened and examined by Celia, or by him, Geoffrey. He walked towards the door; as he did so Philippe called after him:

'I was rather too hasty—you understand? *Of course* you mustn't leave us, Geoffrey.'

'Thanks,' said Geoffrey in a tone of ice. 'I shall certainly remain until my job's over. Then we'll think again.'

Ten minutes later, Celia, her aunt, and Philippe had driven off in the Cadillac. Geoffrey had waved goodbye to them. An atmosphere of friendliness and ease was restored to Villa Psyche. Now that he was alone Geoffrey walked back into the study and opened Nat's drawer.

*The unsealed letter marked 'Strictly Private' had gone.*

Geoffrey's pulses jerked uncomfortably. His cheeks reddened. He whistled under his breath. So that was it. Philippe *had* seen that letter before and he had pinched it just now, meaning of course to destroy it, hoping that Celia neither knew, or would ever know, that it had ever been there.

# THIRTEEN

PHILIPPE CLERMONT had to come to grips with himself. Once he had cooled down, he had decided that he had acted like a lunatic with Geoffrey. And he had been mad to underrate Celia's character. She was no sweet simpleton to be pushed around and influenced even by the man she was going to marry. She liked that ruddy fellow, More, and her aunt liked him, too. The pair of them were on Geoffrey's side. Anyhow, he, Philippe, had no possible cause for jealousy so far as Celia's affections went. She was much too much in love with *him*. It was just that she wasn't going to be bulldozed into firing Geoffrey at a moment's notice (as Philippe had wanted). And Geoffrey on his part would not be easy to deal with. What on earth had possessed him to walk into that study and sack him, Philippe asked himself.

He bobbed up and down on a raft on the bright blue water beside Celia that radiant morning; going over all the events, in his mind. He didn't fancy a fight with the one-time boxing champion. Up there in Nat's study, Geoffrey's fist had looked very menacing indeed. Better to steer clear of him. Go he must, once Celia was *Madame* Clermont, Philippe made up his mind to that but he must be more patient and tactful for the present or he might put Celia's back up and that was the last thing he wanted to do. She was damned difficult—this little English girl whom he had at first thought so pliable. It was easier dealing with a purely physical type—like Nadine—whom a man could twist around his little finger just by appealing to her very sensuousness. But there was a good deal more to Celia Frayne than *that*—as he was finding out to his cost. Nat had never been easy. *She* was a chip off the old block. No, thought Philippe, I must play my game a little more cunningly.

The best thing he could do now was to make no further reference to this morning's ugly dispute. Celia seemed to be avoiding it so he followed suit. But he was damned glad he had got hold of that incriminating letter, just in *case* she might think he had seen and read it before he proposed to her. He must remember to put a match to it as soon as he got back to his flat.

Now he set out to be his usual, delightful, companionable self. They had been swimming together for an hour, leaving Aunt Tiny under a beach umbrella with her tapestry work.

Philippe always had a healthy respect for Celia as a swimmer. She was a superb diver, too. An American boy had been overheard to describe her as 'real cute' in that white swim-suit that fitted her like a glove and showed the extreme smallness of her waist, and the satin-brown tan of her slim rounded arms and tapering legs. In his fashion Philippe was in love with his young fiancée. Of course he found it easy to be in love with any pretty girl. But he had to admit that what he called Celia's prudish streak often frustrated him. He was glad he hadn't turned his back completely on Nadine. There were moments when *she* could be a menace, but she still appealed to his worst side.

Celia, her brown oiled face turned upward to the sun, opened sleepy eyes and glanced at Philippe. She thought how handsome he looked—how difficult it was to be cross with him. She had only brought up Geoffrey's name once.

'I still don't know how you two got quite so hot and bothered but please never let it happen again. And try to be nicer to Geoffrey, please, darling.'

'If I'm not, it's because I'm so jealous of you,' he had answered.

'I don't understand that,' she had said, giving him one of those frank penetrating glances that made him feel uncomfortable. 'When two people love each other as we do, surely we should trust each other implicitly. Why *should* you be jealous of Geoffrey or of any other man?'

'It's the way Geoffrey hangs around you,' said Philippe. 'I find his attitude insufferable at times. But because you like him—I'll do my best to put up with it.'

Celia had burst out laughing.

'You do make me laugh, Philippe darling. Sometimes I really do not understand you at all.'

'Well, it's not only on my side. Our dear secretary does not like *me*, and you know perfectly well why.'

That had brought the colour to Celia's cheeks but she had continued to laugh and tease him.

'Then you should be sorry for poor Geoffrey and nicer to him just because you've got me and he hasn't.'

He had swum close to her then, tasted the salt on her lips with a quick possessive kiss and swum away, shouting, '*Tu*

*me fais peur!* You frighten me, Celia, with your cool logic.
I'm going to let myself sink. I am about to commit suicide.'

He had gone under and she had dived under with him laughing, feeling her body tingle with the joy of life and love and
forgetting all the disquieting events of the morning. They
had surfaced again clinging to each other's fingers, as gay and
happy as children. With all his genius for making a woman
feel loved and adored, Philippe won her back to a state of
complete contentment.

She would not allow him to go back to business after lunch.
She felt a sudden need to prolong this happy, carefree com-
radeship and to get away from the Villa and everybody in it.
She was eager to tell him the conclusion she had come to about
their wedding. She would make him drive her out into the
country—up into the mountains to a little place she knew
where they could sit under the trees by a heavenly trout
stream and drink China tea with a lemon in it and eat *fraises
de bois* with thick sour cream. They had been there once before and she had adored it. There, this afternoon, they would
settle the date for their marriage.

Philippe could drive the Cadillac. They wouldn't be
bothered with a chauffeur. They would be quite alone—that
was what she wanted to be—alone with her lover—her
spoiled, jealous, adorable Philippe.

He wanted to stop at Cannes on the way and give an order
to his secretary at *Frayne et Cie*. But he must go back to his
flat first, he said. He must change out of his beach clothes
after the heat of the morning. So it was decided that she would
return to the Villa with Aunt Tiny and he would pick her up
there.

She felt on top of the world after those hours of relaxation
and fun. She looked forward to the picnic. When she looked
in the study and saw Geoffrey still sorting papers, she felt
sorry for him. It couldn't be much fun having to sit in and
work on a day like this. In the renewed fervour of her love for
Philippe and her happiness in life, she wanted to say or do
something to make Geoffrey feel happy, too. He was so very
nice. She *hated* to feel that he was seriously in love with her.
He just *mustn't* be. She liked him. He mustn't be hurt through
her. She *must* try and find some nice girl to attract him.

Celia ran into the study and said in a breathless voice:

'Oh, hello! It's been *terrific* in the water this morning.
Geoffrey, do stop work. You're **a** demon for it. Take the

afternoon off. Find someone to go and have a swim with you and picnic.'

He stood up, smiling down at her. He found her naïve friendliness and concern both delightful and tormenting. He adored Nat Frayne's daughter from the tip of that short, proud, freckled nose to the slim brown feet with their rose-tinted nails.

He said:

'It's sweet of you but I have far too much to do.'

'Please—to please me, take some time off.'

'I'll have to see later on how things go.'

She ran her fingers through her tangled hair. He thought how enchanting she looked. The sun-kissed face, throat and shoulders seemed to have acquired an even deeper tan since he saw her last.

'It's been a heavenly morning,' she sighed stretching her arms above her head. 'I hate to think of anyone cooped up in a study with the sun and the blue, blue skies shut out by Venetian blinds.'

'You're very kind,' he said, and turned from all the beauty and sweetness that were so maddeningly out of his reach. He kept thinking; *Oh God, what am I going to do about that letter? Oughtn't I to warn her?*

'I'm so glad everybody's got back their sense of humour,' Celia went on, happily. 'Let's try and keep things that way. My father would have hated there to have been any unpleasantness, and I know Philippe doesn't mean half he says. He'd hate you to go, honestly, Geoffrey.'

'Perhaps I *want* to go,' broke from Geoffrey before he could restrain himself.

'No—stay till we get married at any rate,' Celia pleaded.

He shut his eyes wearily. He could see that she was unconscious of the pain she inflicted on him by making remarks like that. And it was a pain tangled up with a thousand fears for her and her future. He felt worried to death and wondered whether or not to take Miss Cotland into his confidence.

He looked at his wrist watch and hurriedly changed the conversation.

'Frightfully sorry—I must bolt—I'm not lunching up here today, I've got to go home.'

'By the way,' she said, 'I'd love to have Gigi. Will you bring her back with you?'

'Are you sure?' he hesitated. 'She isn't very beautiful to

look at, you know, although she has the most endearing ways . . . But whether Philippe . . .'

'If *I* want Gigi I'm going to have her,' broke in Celia tossing her head.

'I'd like you to have her,' Geoffrey muttered, and with a hasty 'See you later——' walked out of the room unable to bear a single moment more alone with Celia.

Celia called Aunt Tiny to come and talk to her while she changed for her picnic, putting on slacks and sleeveless top. She brushed her hair and pinned it up high on her head, took the sun-tan oil off her face and began to make-up a little. Miss Cotland watched her. She found it quite incredible listening to Celia's gay chatter, feeling the warmth of her radiant happiness and remembering the shy, reserved and sometimes diffident little Celia of the old days. At one time she used, Miss Cotland well knew, to feel so out of things, less glamorous than the other girls, even a nonentity. She seemed now to have emerged like a gorgeous butterfly from its chrysalis, and of course that made Miss Cotland happy. But at times it also alarmed her. She could not help wondering whether it would last. Especially when she heard what Celia had to tell her about the row between Philippe and Geoffrey.

'It's all right now,' said Celia airily, 'but it might have been unpleasant. Poor Geoffrey was quite crushed by the thought that Philippe had tried to sack him.'

'I should think so——' Miss Cotland snorted indignantly. 'Philippe had no right to do it you know, lovey.'

'He's so jealous of me,' Celia sighed.

'Well, for all the interest you take in poor Geoffrey, he needn't be,' said Miss Cotland.

'I'm terribly fond of Geoffrey,' Celia sighed again, 'but I'm just not in love with him, and Philippe is, after all, my future husband.'

'Well, I only hope you know what you're doing, Celia.'

'Of course I do. There have been times when I haven't quite understood Philippe's rather un-English excitable ways, but I think I do now. He's the most blissful person to go out with, you know. Such enormous fun. I'm longing for this afternoon.'

'You can't,' said Miss Cotland, 'build your whole life round having *fun* with a man. There are other more serious aspects of marriage, my girl.'

Celia burst out laughing.

'*Darling* Aunt Tiny—you're a scream! I dote on you!'

And I, thought Aunt Tiny, dote on you, my little Celia, but I wish you'd take this idea of marriage more seriously. It seems to be impossible for you to see Philippe Clermont except through rose-tinted spectacles. He just *isn't* what you think him. *Of course* he wants to get rid of Geoffrey who is such a man—such a reliable friend. He wants to get complete control of you—and this household. He'd give *me* the sack if he could!

With these gloomy thoughts Miss Cotland went down to lunch. She and her niece lunched on the terrace—a perfect meal served by the white-coated Jean. The two of them discussed plans for December 1st. Miss Cotland having had the news broken to her that this was to be the deadline date for her niece's marriage, accepted it and put on a good face. She would stay with Celia until then she declared. After the wedding she would go back to Battersea.

'I shan't like that,' said Celia.

'Neither shall I, but I don't think *Monsieur* Clermont would like it if he found me still here when you got back from your honeymoon,' said Miss Cotland drily.

Celia bit her lip. Her mood was gay and she felt confident about the future but she did wish that Philippe wouldn't be quite so difficult—about Aunt Tiny *and* Geoffrey. Geoffrey had said that he was leaving as soon as he had cleared up her father's documents. That prospect didn't please her, either. She would hate him to pass out of her life—he seemed an integral part of her father, of his old life.

Philippe, meanwhile, let himself into his flat in a mood less pleasant than Celia's.

He had put on a good show while they were swimming and aqua-skiing but his vanity had been horribly deflated by the scene with Geoffrey More. He could neither forget it nor forgive the Englishman. Neither could he blot out the memory of his own fear; the way he had sweated and flinched when Geoffrey threatened him. He had had to capitulate but it was humiliating to know that Geoffrey had won the contest with Celia on his side. There were moments when Philippe felt like breaking Celia's pretty little neck because he couldn't completely dominate or subjugate her to his will. But once he had complete control both of her and of *Frayne et Cie* she'd have to toe the line, he told himself.

His ill-humour further increased when he found Nadine de

Sachelles sitting on the sofa in his *salon*, sipping a cocktail, waiting for him.

He hadn't seen her for a few days. He didn't really want to see her unless he was in the mood for love—love of the kind *she* offered. He certainly did not want that just now.

She looked her handsome and fascinating self—as usual faultlessly dressed, in an orange linen suit; no jewellery except three or four heavy gold bangles. Her sloe-black eyes gleamed at him smilingly.

'You are surprised?'

'Very,' he said shortly.

'Well, try to look a little more pleased.'

'I am delighted,' he replied stiffly, 'but you know me—*mon trésor*—I like warning.'

And he thought: *I must remember to get my latch key back ro m her. She can't keep it—it's too dangerous.*

'I have helped myself to a drink—I knew you wouldn't mind.'

'Of course not, *chérie*, have you come to lunch?' he asked on a note of sarcasm.

'Well, I thought you might like to see me for an hour or two, then I can make you an omelette. You like my omelettes. It's the only cooking that I do well,' Nadine smiled, put down her drink and held out both arms. 'Come here, Philippe. Stop looking like a handsome, sulky little boy. Something's upset you. I know the signs.'

He set his teeth. Nothing irritated him more than to find Nadine in an amorous and playful mood when he was feeling the antithesis. But he was so used to her reactions. To be rude and unresponsive would put her in a bad mood and make it difficult for him to get rid of her. The best way was to make love to her first, then tell her he was busy. He threw himself on the sofa, kissed both her hands, then her neck.

'*M'm!* That perfume of yours is most exciting. It's "*Femme*", isn't it?'

'How well you know.'

'You're a most exciting woman, Nadine.'

She put her tongue in her cheek. Her long lashes flickered up and down.

'A pity I'm so impecunious. I can't compete with your little heiress, even if *I am* more exciting.'

'Oh, don't let's start that,' he begged.

She curved an arm around his neck and drew him down to

her. He was warm and glowing from the sea and immensely desirable to her. Since his engagement to Celia Frayne her old passion for him had redoubled in fervour. She no longer cared whether Geoffrey More looked at her or not. She had given him up. Philippe was more her kind. She wanted Philippe. She wanted him so desperately and continually that she had begun to hate Celia Frayne as she had never hated any human being in her life before. She wished to God she had never worked so hard to make that girl presentable. It was bitter irony to know that it was *her* taste and brains that had turned that little nonentity with her frightful clothes into the attractive glamour girl of today. It positively maddened her to know that the day of Philippe's wedding to Celia was drawing nearer and that soon she, Nadine, would have to stay out of his life except for any odd visit she cared to make. There could never be any more sudden exciting moments like this. Stolen, impromptu, heavenly meetings.

She reached up and kissed him.

He caught fire from her and for the moment the shadow of Celia slipped away. They surrendered to their mutual passion, in the cool elegant room that was shielded from the sun's rays by the striped awning on the balcony.

A while later, Philippe lit a cigarette and took a drink into his bathroom, in order to take a shower. He had accepted Nadine's offer to stay and make an omelette; after which he would 'shelve her' and go to his appointment with Celia.

As he left the room, Nadine noticed a piece of white folded paper lying on the carpet half under the couch. It looked like a letter. It must, she thought, have dropped from Philippe's pocket. She picked it up and glanced at it idly. But after one glance she changed colour and began to read the contents earnestly. She walked towards the kitchen as she did so. She read the letter twice, then examined the date. She whistled excitedly under her breath.

'*Tiens!*' she said aloud.

This had been written by Nat Frayne before Celia came out to Monte Carlo. It was marked 'copy' in Nat's own handwriting, and in his businesslike way he had also written: '*Original sent to my daughter, Celia, care of her aunt*' (and it gave the Battersea address).

The information did not interest Nadine. She knew it all anyhow. But what was of absorbing interest was the fact that this letter *had been in Philippe's possession*. So he had known all the way along that Celia was Nat's daughter and heiress. Nadine had thought as much. He had lied—denied it. But this was proof. What, in heaven's name, he was doing with the letter this morning, she could not imagine.

She heard him calling. She slipped the letter into her bag.

He was standing in front of his dressing chest, brushing his damp ebony-black hair. How handsome he was, she thought. How smug and self-satisfied, too. She despised him yet was mad about him. She wanted to live with him. *She wanted to kill him.* She hardly knew which. But the sight of his complacency was annihilating to a woman of her vanity. She might have sympathised with him for wanting to get hold of the Frayne fortune through a mean trick, and even condoned it, if he hadn't made one or two serious mistakes. Looking at her reflection in the mirror, now, he said:

'By the way, *mon ange*, I wonder if you would let me have my spare key.'

At once she was on the alert. Her expression changed.

'Have you lost your own?'

'Yes——' he began.

But it was too late, for she had seen the latch key attached to his car-keys on a ring, on top of the dressing chest. She gave a twisted smile.

'It seems to be there, my darling,' she said sweetly. 'So maybe you'd give me the real reason why you want back the one I have had for so long.'

He shrugged his shoulders. He really didn't fancy any more rows today, and he had begun to regret, in the extreme, letting his affair with the *Comtesse* de Sachelles continue for so long. He had been flattered at first by the attentions of so beautiful and glamorous a woman but lack of money had made it impossible for him ever to suggest marriage to her, and she hadn't been all that anxious for marriage herself when their liaison first began. So it had drifted on in a lazy, easy sort of way with which they had both seemed content. But now Nadine was becoming far too possessive. Her visits were too frequent. At this juncture he couldn't risk anyone finding it out and reporting it to Celia.

'I do wish you'd get it into your head that I'm not a free agent as I used to be,' he said irritably.

'No, you're engaged to all that nice lolly,' she sneered.

He gave her a quick look.

'Was that a reproach?'

'You know I don't like it, Philippe.'

'You also know that as far as you and I are concerned, I have never had enough money for us both.'

'Nat left you a bit, plus your directorship in the business. You aren't penniless, *mon cher*.'

He turned on her.

'Listen, Nadine, we've been over this far too many times. The facts must be quite clear to you.'

Her long fingers with their red varnished nails tapped her bag as though feeling the letter inside it.

'It *is* quite clear, believe me!' she said.

It was at that precise moment (for no particular reason) that Philippe remembered the letter which he had put in his pocket after he left Villa Psyche to take Celia on the beach and which he had not yet had a chance to destroy. Up till now he had forgotten it. He muttered:

'Don't let's carry on with this stupid, senseless conversation and spoil what we've had together.'

Nadine looked at him bitterly.

'It's already spoiled.'

'If you'll pardon me,' he said coldly . . . 'just one moment . . . I've lost something . . .'

She stood smoking, watching him as he went through the pockets of the slacks and jacket that he had worn on the beach. She knew exactly what he was looking for. She felt coldly malicious. He hurried out of the room. She imagined him searching the *salon*, diving frantically under all the cushions—under the sofa—even in the bathroom. When he came back she could see how worried he was. He cleared his throat and said:

'You haven't seen a letter lying around, have you, Nadine?'

'A letter,' she repeated glibly. 'What letter?'

'A business letter. I must have dropped it.'

Her eyes narrowed. She felt cruel, feline, thoroughly revengeful. Let him look for the letter. She wasn't going to help him. It served him right if he felt nervous and anxious. She went up to him and touched his cheek.

'You're not going to take my key away from me, lover-boy, are you?'

That was when Philippe made a fatal mistake—totally unaware of the force of the weapon she was holding. In an instant of acute irritation, he pushed her caressing hand away.

'Oh, leave me alone. Yes, I *do* want my key back. I can't

carry on with this. You've got to see it for yourself. Our affair must come to an end, Nadine—greatly though I regret it.'

She went white. He had hit at her pride as well as her passion. And the passion died in consequence. Only pride remained and with it an unquenchable thirst to get her own back—in a big way. Not only back on him but on Celia Frayne. Celia these days received her with delightful good manners when Nadine went up to Villa Psyche, but it never failed to infuriate her watching Celia taking her place as mistress of the house; calling the tune and making them all dance to it. Celia—now the pampered pet with Philippe's expensive engagement ring on her finger. *But if I die for it*, Nadine thought, *I am going to get that ring off before I am finished.*

She kept silent, her breathing uneven, her body trembling with rage. It was Philippe who spoke again, driving the nail yet deeper into the coffin of his own hopes.

'In fact, I think it will be much better that we don't meet any more after today, Nadine. It's all been wonderful while it lasted, but I've just got to settle down now and do the right thing by Celia. I refuse to deceive her any longer; surely you respect my feelings!'

Then Nadine turned on him, her eyes large, furious, flashing.

'You damned hypocrite!' she said, flung the key at him, walked out of the room and out of the flat.

## FOURTEEN

ONE morning, about three weeks later, Celia sat with Aunt Tiny at her *escritoire* in her bedroom, sending out wedding invitations. Aunt Tiny, spectacles on the end of her nose, had volunteered to address envelopes. They were preparing at last for December 1st.

The Venetian blinds were not down as usual. The big beautiful bedroom was gloomy. Outside there were stormy skies, and a wind whirling the leaves across the garden. It was as though the vivid colours of the Mediterranean had been suddenly blurred by a grey veil, and all the gaiety, all the joy had gone. The golden summer was ending. The mistral had been blowing for the last twenty-four hours and the temperature had dropped considerably. The air seemed full of dust which made everybody's head ache.

This morning when Celia had been down by the harbour after a shopping expedition she had watched almost in surprise the unaccustomed sight of the leaden choppy water, and the sleek white yachts and motor launches rising up and down agitatedly on the swelling tide. Behind the town the hills rose like dark shadows that disappeared into cloud. In the gardens and terraces of the cafés chairs and tables had been put away. Everybody said that tonight it would rain.

For Celia there was still plenty of warmth and comfort in her bedroom and she had switched on the shaded candelabra on her desk but she felt that the mistral was blowing into her heart as well as across Monaco.

Miss Cotland kept looking at her, noting the varying changes of expression on that young charming face and worrying because the fine brows were constantly knit and she chewed her lips while she wrote. Not, surely, just with the exertion of the job, which she should have been thoroughly enjoying, but because she was inwardly ill at ease. Aunt Tiny knew that and could make a pretty good guess as to why.

Recently, things had not been going quite as smoothly for Nat Frayne's heiress as in the past. There was an 'atmosphere' in the house; and a certain tension in the girl which Miss Cotland observed every time she saw Celia after she had been for any length of time with her future husband.

Celia had not said anything. She continued to talk about her trousseau and plan for the wedding, two months ahead, and to behave as though that was all she wanted in life. But she had lost some of that old breathless enthusiasm and undiluted delight in life. Tiny Cotland had a pretty shrewd idea that Celia was no longer dead certain she was doing the right thing by marrying Philippe Clermont.

Miss Cotland had absolutely nothing to go by but her own observation, and she would not have dreamed of bringing matters to a head by any tactless comments or questions. Miss Cotland was far too wise and patient a woman for that. But she herself felt heavy-hearted while she addressed the envelopes to all the hundreds of friends Nat Frayne had once gathered about himself, and who knew Philippe and the *salons* of the famous Art Collector who had branches in London, Paris and New York.

Suddenly Celia put down her biro and turned to her aunt. As she did so, it struck Miss Cotland that the girl had lost weight. She had once mentioned this but Celia had given a rather nervous laugh and said she was glad because she was getting plump from all the rich Continental cooking. But Miss Cotland didn't like those new hollows in Celia's cheeks. That new thin face made her look so much older. Her aunt also missed the old childish curls and waves. She wasn't sure she liked Celia's new chic smooth hair style—high on the head and with a white Greek bandeau. But the dark blue jersey suit she wore edged with white braid was, of course, very smart. For the first time this summer, Celia had put on stockings—and shoes instead of sandals. It all made Miss Cotland sad; winter was approaching, and with it the end of her old dear familiar association with Celia. Lately, Philippe had been putting himself out to be extra charming to Miss Cotland, but she still couldn't abide the thought of Celia becoming *Madame Clermont*.

Celia said:

'Aunt Tiny, I've never really kept anything from you, have I?'

'Never, my dear,' smiled Miss Cotland, also laying down her pen and reaching for a cigarette.

Celia got up and began to walk up and down the room. She paused in front of an enormous jar full of bright pink carnations on a gilt and marble stand. Every morning the gardener sent in masses of these favourite flowers of the Mediterranean, to help beautify *Mademoiselle*'s room. Celia buried her face in the spicy sweet blossoms for a second, then said:

'Do you remember ages ago when I thought I'd got a crush on that young naval lieutenant I met at that Christmas dance I went to with Jo Page?'

'I do.'

'I didn't eat for two days and felt quite sick with misery because he didn't phone me, after saying he would.'

'Yes,' sighed Miss Cotland, 'you were only eighteen then and it was your first "crush".'

'And then there was that boy I met when we were on holiday and who used to swim with me and thought my diving so marvellous—Jack Something-or-other. How awful! I've forgotten his surname. He was the first one ever to kiss me and I thought something would come of it but it didn't. And there was Peter Wallis at the tennis club who fell for me completely but *I* didn't like *him*. All those little affairs which seemed so important at the time and one suffers a lot then realises, once the Big Thing comes, that they were all mere pin-pricks and meant nothing at all.'

'I expect they did, you know,' said Miss Cotland, cocking an eyebrow. 'Everything that happens is of importance and has a bearing on one's life. One doesn't forget one's first kiss any more than one forgets one's last. Even *I* had one boy-friend . . .' she broke off with a laugh.

'Aunt Tiny, what happened? Why didn't you marry him? You've never told me.'

'It's simple, my darling. He preferred somebody else.'

'Oh dear! How perverse life can be!'

'If you want to know, he looked exactly like Geoffrey More,' said Miss Cotland drily.

'Is that why you've had such a sneaking affection for our Geoffrey since you came here?'

Miss Cotland grinned.

'Possibly. But I like him for himself, not only because he looks like my one-and-only. I think he's a man in a thousand, our secretary. To be quite frank, I consider Philippe has been beastly to him and it has been very decent of him to stay on. I think he's done it largely out of respect and affection for your father's memory and to keep an eye on things for you.'

Celia began to walk up and down again. The grey day and the mistral made her feel nervous and depressed. She said:

'Yes. Geoffrey has been awfully kind. I do admire him. I like him awfully, but——'

'But Philippe is your man,' put in Miss Cotland bluntly.

Now suddenly Celia stood still, twisting the big valuable engagement ring around her finger, her face puckered.

'Oh, Aunt Tiny, I wish I knew and understood certain things.'

'What don't you know or understand?'

'What really goes on in Philippe's mind and heart. Even what goes on in his private life. There! Now I've come out with it—I've told you—you might as well know—I *don't* feel as confident and settled about Philippe as I used to.'

Aunt Tiny's heart gave a great leap of hope which she immediately suppressed because she didn't think it would be wise to exhibit it.

'And how's that?'

'Well—all kinds of things have unsettled me. When we talk together, he kind of mesmerises me. I can't think straight —he seems to take control of my mind and my emotions. I know I am in love with him. I find him the most fascinating man in the world. But I don't like what goes on *underneath*.'

Miss Cotland drew a breath at her cigarette and looked steadily at her niece.

'You mean you think he's capable of pulling the wool over your eyes and you don't want that. You aren't that kind of a girl. You're too honest and open. Isn't it so?'

'More than that. He behaves in a sort of *odd* way occasionally.'

'Here it comes,' thought Aunt Tiny triumphantly. 'She's beginning to see him as he really is. By jingo, as Nat used to say, wouldn't it be a cinch if she found him out in time!'

'Tell me more, dear,' she said aloud.

Celia sat down at her dressing table and began to play with a scent spray; not looking at her aunt.

'You remember that day we went out for a picnic up towards Grasse—after the row with Geoffrey. Philippe and I had dinner at that little place "*Lou Mas*" in *Cannes-la-Bocca*, run by that Frenchman, *Monsieur Le Cesne*, who was a friend of father's—an expert on old china?'

Miss Cotland nodded.

'Well—Philippe was in the strangest state that day. Something had upset him. He made love to me almost wildly——'
Celia's cheeks reddened and her breath came quickly at the

152

mere memory of the crazy fashion in which Philippe had embraced her when they were alone up there in the mountains by the trout stream. How he had tried to appeal to all the sensuousness in her nature, and besought her to marry him at once; not wait for December. He had told her that it was the force of his passion for her that drove him to distraction. Well, Celia told her aunt, half of her responded, the other half retreated. (That half which Philippe never understood.) But the more he had pleaded with her, the more, somehow, that reluctant side gained ascendancy over the other.

'I told him once and for all that I just did not want to be rushed, and he was most unattractive about it, and hardly spoke to me on the way home. For days he seemed cooler towards me as though trying to make me change my mind *that* way. I think it put the devil in me——' she gave an uneasy laugh—'I just wouldn't give in and finally he did, but it left a mark. I couldn't somehow feel so secure with him any more.'

'Quite,' said Miss Cotland drily.

'Then his attitude towards Geoffrey has been so absurd. He wasn't very pleasant about Gigi, but I insisted on having her.'

Gigi, the waif and stray to whom Celia had become 'godmother', was now out for a walk with the kindly Annette. Celia, herself, had become devoted to the little dog who adored her, and slept in a basket beside her bed. She couldn't imagine Philippe ever making friends with the little animal. And she had been thoroughly annoyed when he said:

'I wouldn't have minded so much if you had wanted to waste your time on a nice smart-looking poodle, but I hate mongrels.'

'Well I don't,' she had snapped, 'they're often the most clever and most affectionate of animals.'

They had quarrelled over Gigi.

Nowadays Celia was well aware that Philippe, who could be so charming and sparkling and amusing most of the time, could rapidly change into a sulky boy when he was thwarted. He just couldn't seem to accustom himself to the fact that she had a will—and tastes of her own.

'What else?' asked Miss Cotland.

There were plenty of things. One outstanding one—in all Philippe's plans for the future he spoke of flying her from one of the capitals to another—combining business with pleasure, furthering her interest in antiques and the fine arts. That side of him she admired, Celia said, and she would be a funny girl if she didn't want to see Paris, Vienna, Rome—all those fascinating places he had so often visited. Also she was sufficiently her father's daughter to want to learn more about his business. Philippe was at his best when he was concerning himself with it. But he had a weakness—and one which Celia was the last girl to appreciate. She put it rather bluntly to Miss Cotland this morning, her colour heightened, her eyes averted.

'Let's face it—Philippe is a bit over-sexed. I know the French are supposed to be more like that than the English but it upsets me when I know his mind is harping on it all the time. And I watch how he looks at other girls—how he treats them. Then there's the day that I walked unexpectedly into his office in Cannes and found him with a smear of lip rouge on his cheek that just wasn't my colour . . .' she laughed unhappily. 'But it was the same colour Martine, that rather attractive secretary of his, uses.'

She didn't want to be a prig or a prude. She just didn't like promiscuity, and if a man behaved that way before marriage, what might he be like *afterwards*? Perhaps it was silly of her, she said, but she knew she would be miserable if Philippe turned out to be the unfaithful type of husband. To her, love was something sacred and binding. She had remembered arguing with her friend Joanna Page, back home, on this very subject. Jo was the nicest type, but she personally had a notion that 'men were different' and should be allowed the odd infidelity.

'I'm afraid I didn't agree then and I don't now. I'm just not like that. It all worries me,' Celia concluded.

'And have you told Philippe any of these things?'

Celia pursed her lips.

'Yes and when I do he just laughs and teases—calls me "his fifth-form girl" or that kind of thing. And of course he has got a tremendous influence over me, Aunt Tiny, I feel that if I couldn't see him any more I'd be terribly unhappy *but*——' She shrugged her shoulders helplessly.

'H'm,' Miss Cotland gave a fond and anxious look at Celia. 'It does rather sound to me as though you feel you're in a kind of trap and you don't know how to get out and you're afraid that even if you managed it, you wouldn't know which way to go.'

'That rather describes me,' said Celia with a miserable laugh.

'Well, you'll have to make up your own mind and form a definite decision before we send these . . .' Aunt Tiny tapped one of the envelopes. 'It isn't too late to end the whole thing and shut up shop. I know it'll take courage but you'll have to face it if you do decide you won't be really happy with Philippe.'

Now Celia put her face in her hands and Miss Cotland saw to her dismay that the girl was crying. With the tears came a further confession. This morning, the *Comtesse* de Sachelles had telephoned and asked her if she could have a long private talk with her.

'About Philippe, she said . . .' Celia blew her nose rather dismally. 'As though she had something to tell me about him which I wouldn't like. Of course I've always rather suspected that Philippe and Nadine——' she broke off, twisting her handkerchief around her fingers . . . '*Oh, I hate the whole thing,*' she ended, 'I'm so mixed up, Aunty! The thought of breaking with Philippe and not marrying him now that we've got so near to the wedding appals me. I don't know whether I'll ever have the strength to send Philippe away. But I'm *not* happy about him. I'm *not*, Aunt Tiny.'

Now she was sobbing openly and Miss Cotland put her arm around her, comforting her as she used to do when Celia went to her with her childish woes. She could see that the girl was upset and uncertain of her feelings and far removed from the happy confident Celia who had entered into this engagement in the first place.

'I know *you* would be glad,' said Celia, 'you've never liked him and neither has Geoffrey.'

'What we feel is of no account. It's what you, in your own heart, want, my dearest child.'

'Sometimes I wish I *were* a kid again—the old Celia who hadn't a sou to her name. I wish I wasn't going to get married, and could just go down to *Madame* Pavette's house and help Geoffrey with the dogs. Life's become much too complicated for my simple tastes.'

Tiny Cotland's heart leaped for the second time that morning, with the fervent hope that her prayers were going to be answered and that she was not going to have to stand by and watch Celia throwing away her life on a man who was totally unworthy of it and would only end by breaking her heart. It was so wonderful, she thought, that Celia had made her own observations, formed her own opinions and reached this pitch entirely on her own—without being influenced by *her*.

And there was something else she liked very much indeed—and that was the naïve way in which Celia, who was candid and realistic, had spoken of Geoffrey. She had thought of his home, his work, as a refuge for herself.

'*I'm jolly well going to tell him*,' Tiny Cotland decided with a certain defiance and tactlessness entirely foreign to her.

'Now as to this business of Nadine—do you intend to see her and hear what she has to say?' Miss Cotland inquired.

'No,' said Celia, 'I don't think I want to discuss my personal feelings with Nadine or hear about hers.'

But it was too late. Annette came into the room.

'*Pardon, Mademoiselle, but Madame la Comtesse de Sachelles* is in the little *salon* hoping to see *Mademoiselle*. Jean is serving coffee to her.'

'Oh, Aunt Tiny, *see* her for me——' began Celia.

'Darling,' said her aunt, 'I'd do anything for you and you know it, but I'm not going to let you lose your backbone. Whatever the Countess-creature has to say I think you should hear it and deal with it personally. You've gained a lot of self-confidence since you've been out here. Don't lose it. I know you're feeling mixed up and a bit frightened but this is the turning point in your life. Face up to it, lovey. If you're going to give Philippe back his ring—so much the better as far as I am concerned. But yours must be the choice. And somehow—I don't quite know why—I have a feeling your little interview with Nadine may tip you over the edge.'

'Very well—I'll see her,' said Celia with a grimace.

She sat down at her dressing table, removed the tear stains from her face, put on some fresh make-up then went downstairs to face the Frenchwoman. She looked as cool and soignée, as attractive now as Nadine had originally helped to make her.

# FIFTEEN

GEOFFREY was going through one of the last of the deed-boxes marked '*Nathaniel Frayne*'; destroying letters and documents which were of no further value, and of no use to the dead man's daughter.

The mistral was still blowing. Geoffrey had a blinding headache. He loathed these windy days on the Riviera, having had a touch of sinus which always made him feel stuffy in the nose, and short-tempered. He also knew that Nadine had called to see Celia and that the two women were now in the little *salon* talking together. He wondered a trifle gloomily what Nadine was up to. She was capable of doing and saying anything. He had an idea that she hadn't been as friendly with Philippe as she used to be, because when he had last seen her she had hinted darkly that she was 'through with Philippe', that their 'friendship' had come to an end. There had been a nasty look in her magnificent eyes that had made him uncomfortable. One never knew what was going on with those two and Geoffrey's one fear always was that between them Celia might get hurt.

*She*, he had noticed, hadn't recently been her bright sparkling self. Nobody at Villa Psyche seemed very pleased with life except Philippe who went about with his usual air of arrogance and conceit which Geoffrey found so detestable.

As for this wedding day which loomed on the horizon—Geoffrey could hardly bear to think of it. He was certainly not going to be here on December 1st. He had made up his mind to that. He could not watch Celia and Philippe Clermont being made man and wife—even if he had to send himself a telegram saying that some relative was seriously ill and that he must leave Monte Carlo immediately. Then it would be the end. He would never come back to Villa Psyche.

Not long ago he and dear Miss Cotland had had a long talk about things. Somehow, deeply reticent though he was, Geoffrey had found himself confiding in her, telling her what Celia meant to him.

She had guessed. She told him so. She was very, very sorry —and when he had made it plain that he would have to resign from Celia's employ because of his feelings, she had shaken her head sadly and told him that it was more than a pity. They both seemed to agree that Celia was making a mistake and that she was bound to discover it in time—when none of them would be here to help or comfort her. Her aunt had said that Celia was the type that having found she had made such a mistake, she would abide by it because of her personal integrity. That thought had destroyed Geoffrey's peace of mind for days and nights. The whole thing had become a nightmare to him. He had fallen in love with Celia so deeply and abidingly that he felt that if he could not get her (and that was right out of the question) he would never marry. There would never be another girl in his life—or his heart.

Headache or not, he was suddenly pulled out of his deep despondency when Miss Cotland came into the study this morning and returned his recent confidences with one of her own.

She told him exactly what Celia had been saying upstairs just now. And when Geoffrey heard it, his own heart leaped with the sort of acute satisfaction and hope that Celia's aunt had just experienced. His strong square face burned under the tan. His eyes looked very blue. He put a pipe between his teeth and began to walk up and down the study restlessly. He cleared his throat nervously.

'I'm darned if I know what to say, Miss Cotland.'

'It certainly is a bit of a problem. It surprised me, I can tell you, Geoffrey, when she suddenly stopped writing invitations and this all poured out. Do you know, her doubts seem to have started on that day you had the fight with Philippe?'

'I'm not surprised,' he muttered.

'And what's that Countess-creature doing here this morning?' Miss Cotland added uneasily.

'Oh, she's capable of anything,' said Geoffrey.

The two—the elderly spinster and the boy—who had become such friends over this emotional championship of Celia had no further time to exchange ideas. Suddenly the study door opened and Celia rushed into the room. She looked, Miss Cotland thought, thoroughly upset. She was trembling. She held a letter in her hand. Her big grey eyes glanced from her aunt to Geoffrey.

'Oh—so you came down here, Aunt Tiny! I was going to ask Geoffrey something privately but you might as well hear it. I always tell you everything, anyhow.'

'*Now* what's happened?' asked Miss Cotland.

'First of all,' said Celia, very red in the face, 'Nadine has informed me that for absolutely ages she has been living with Philippe and has been doing so up to a few weeks ago, when she quarrelled with him. That's a nice thing, I *must* say. If I'm supposed to be broadminded and agree with Jo that "men have a right to be different" I'm afraid I shall just have to be thought a prig. Because I'm not going to accept it.'

Geoffrey, who was staring at the slim, shaking figure and who read the deep hurt, the bitter pain in those beautiful soft eyes, muttered an oath under his breath.

'Damn Philippe—and damn Nadine for giving the girl such a shock in such a crude way. *Or wasn't it the best thing after all?*'

Miss Cotland exclaimed:

'Oh, my *dear*, how absolutely hateful for you. I'm so very sorry.'

'Nadine, of course, has hated me at heart ever since I got engaged to Philippe,' said Celia. 'I can't say I admire her for this sudden treachery. But she's got what she wanted. I no longer have the slightest intention of marrying Philippe, now or ever.'

Neither Geoffrey nor Miss Cotland spoke, but their glances met, loaded with relief.

Then Celia tapped the letter she was holding.

'It was what Nadine told me about this that finished me. Geoffrey . . .' she turned to him . . . 'you have seen this letter?'

He looked at it. He had known of course that Philippe had it, but wondered how it had come into Nadine's dangerous hands. Celia enlightened him.

'Philippe dropped it out of his pocket at his flat and Nadine was there and saw it and she thought *I* ought to see it, and be made to realise that the contents had been largely instrumental in making Philippe go all out to get me before anyone realised who I was. In other words *he's* known all the time that I was going to be a rich girl one day.'

'Celia,' said Geoffrey quietly, 'that letter was still in your father's desk in his personal drawer on the morning that Philippe quarrelled with me. The fight began by his demanding the key. He must have taken it when I was out of the room, because I refused to give it. Then I found the letter gone after you two had driven off. You remember?'

'I can remember very plainly.'

'I can't swear that he had seen it before but I suspect that he did, because of his anxiety to get hold of it again. Having stolen it, he obviously meant to destroy it so that you would never know of its existence.'

Miss Cotland was listening intently. She had nothing to say, because she was not in this, but she found every word of absorbing interest. Poor little Celia, what a shock! She looked quite ill, Miss Cotland reflected pityingly.

'The fact that he wanted that letter so badly points to the fact that he *had* already seen it,' said Celia. 'And Nadine has told me many other things that confirm that suspicion. She even pitied me——' Celia gave a harsh unhappy laugh. 'She said she *knew*, because Philippe had told her so, that I wasn't his type and that it was my money and the position he'd hold as my husband that he wanted. Then he meant to go on with his affair with her.'

Miss Cotland uttered an exclamation of disgust.

'All the same,' put in Geoffrey, 'one can't prove anything beyond the indisputable fact that Philippe took that letter, and was careless enough to let Nadine find it.'

'I think you'll have to see Philippe and ask him about all this,' said Miss Cotland, who was always more concerned with the rightness of behaviour than conduct of an irresponsible nature.

But Celia sat down at her father's desk and put her head in her hands. She said in a muffled voice:

'No. I don't want to see him. I don't ever want to see him again.'

It took all her courage to face the meeting with Philippe. She dreaded the scene which she knew to be inevitable with a man of his disposition. But she agreed with her aunt that it would be cowardly not to see him. So, that same evening, when Philippe returned from a business trip to Paris, he found a shock awaiting him. When he walked into the Villa, which he was now in the habit of doing without being announced, he was met by Miss Cotland in the hall. She said somewhat tartly:

'Good evening. You'll find Celia in the study.'

'What is she doing there——?' began Philippe.

But Celia's aunt had vanished. With a shrug of the shoulders, Philippe sauntered into the study. He looked forward to a glass of his favourite sherry and one of the late Nathaniel Frayne's cigars. He was also feeling smug and self-satisfied because he had come upon a *Degas* belonging to an impoverished French nobleman and bought it, this morning, at a good price. It was just in time for London where *Frayne et Cie* were holding an exhibition of French masters this winter.

He was also pleased because he had lunched with a certain gentleman to whom Philippe had for a long time been heavily in debt—in a big way. The said Frenchman had been pressing for payment but now that he knew the marriage with Miss Frayne was fixed for December 1st, he was willing to wait. Philippe would have no more trouble. It had been an agreeable meeting—on both sides.

Celia was standing by one of the bookcases—looking through a rare volume of English hunting prints. One, in colour, showed the vivid pink of the huntsmen's coats. An exquisite setting of oak trees, lush meadows and green hedges and the hounds rallying to the master's horn on a golden autumn morning. It had made her wonder how she could ever have anticipated settling permanently in France. England was *England* and her native home. She would go back there. She would buy a country house and live there with Aunt Tiny, and try to forget these last few months in Villa Psyche. All the beauty and elegance of her father's fabulous home had been poisoned by the unhappiness of her engagement. She felt as crushed and miserable as any young girl would feel who sees her first dream of love disintegrate—turn to the ashes of bitterness.

She faced Philippe, her heart pounding nervously. Quite unconscious of what he was about to hear, Philippe looked with satisfaction at her, noting the elegance of the golden velvet dress which, because the evening was chilly following the mistral, had a touch of mink at throat and wrists. She really had improved. He had to hand it to Nadine for that. She had turned the little girl into quite a *femme fatale*. He advanced towards Celia with outstretched hands.

'*Ma petite fleur*——'

He spoke in the old throaty, haunting voice which used once to mesmerise her—turn her very bones to water. Tonight suddenly she found it too theatrical, even a trifle absurd. He was fantastically good-looking in his dark-grey suit, a red carnation in his buttonhole; tasteful grey silk tie. As he drew nearer her, she caught the fragrance of brilliantine from his thick dark hair. (He had obviously had a 'cut and shampoo' in Paris.) The attractive almond-shaped eyes smiled amorously into hers. *And it made her feel sick.*

'No—don't kiss me, please,' she said.

His hands dropped to his sides.

'But, my *dear*!——'

'I'd like you to sit down. I want just to talk to you for a moment,' she interrupted. She had to summon all her strength of character, that strength that she knew she would need because his physical attraction for her had been enormous and she was terrified that he might play on it—that it wouldn't be too easy to break away, no matter how deeply she resented all that he had done.

'Sit down, Philippe,' she repeated.

Immediately he took offence. That, she thought, was typical. She had always rather worried about what she called his 'touchy' side, but had hoped it would improve once they were married. He used to excuse himself on the grounds that it was because he wanted her so much that it produced this nervy, hypersensitive state. He said:

'Well, this is a nice welcome home, I *must* say.'

Quietly, Celia took a small leather box which lay on her late father's desk and handed it to Philippe. He stared at it unbelievingly.

'What in the name of fortune——?'

'Yes, it's my ring—our engagement ring,' she said in a quick nervous voice, and her long lashes flickered. She found it hard to look at him. 'Our engagement is over, Philippe.'

He was dumbfounded for a moment. Then, his face scarlet, he exclaimed:

'Are you out of your mind? What's happened in my absence? My dear, *darling* Celia, when I said goodbye to you on the telephone this morning you said you were just about to write the invitations for our wedding.'

She, too, coloured.

'I know. I owe you an apology, I suppose, for having let things get this far. For the last few weeks I've been terribly worried and uncertain about—about us, and I suppose I ought to have told you so right away. But initially it's your fault, if it hasn't been a success. I did love you, Philippe—I loved you very much and I hoped we were going to be terribly happy together!' she added in a low troubled voice.

He stood like a man rooted to the spot. The healthy colour ebbed from his cheeks. Then he drew a deep breath and said:

'This is staggering. I don't begin to understand you.'

She pressed the case into his hand.

'Take this, please.'

'I don't want the damned thing. I want *you*.'

Now for the first time in her life Celia resorted to sarcasm. She said:

'Do you? Or is it that you want all that you'd have got *with* me?'

He gasped.

'What a damnable thing to say!'

Now she took the fatal letter—that letter to herself which her father had copied and handed it to him.

'You lost this, Philippe. Do you want it back? Would you like to read it again?'

This was certainly something he had not expected. Celia, watching him, thought that he looked positively ghastly, and guilty enough, as he unfolded that sheet of paper and stared at it.

'Where did you get this?'

Then she dealt him the second blow.

'From your mistress, the *Comtesse* de Sachelles.'

Thoroughly unnerved he remained inarticulate. He was usually ready with glib words and explanations, but this time he was not prepared. It was too sudden, too hideous. When he did speak, he could only stutter:

'You—you're crazy, Celia. Nadine is not my——'

But Celia interrupted, holding up a hand.

'Oh, please spare me a lot more lies and excuses. Whatever happens, do let's both be honest with each other now. You've told me a good many lies, Philippe, but I beg you to tell the truth now.'

He had begun to shake perceptibly. He went on stammering:

'It's an old story . . . that business with Nadine . . . before you came into my life. It's been over for a long time.'

'You're determined to go on lying to me,' broke in Celia in a cold voice. 'Okay, carry on.'

'If she's told you any different, she's a liar!'

'I don't think so. As you've always known, I've never been very attached to Nadine, but I think she's in love with you and she told me the truth because she was jealous and disappointed. Also I know she was in *your* flat that morning—that's where you lost the letter. She found it.'

'I'll make her sorry for this!' began Philippe on an hysterical note, and stopped, handkerchief to his lips.

Now, as Celia looked at him, all the veils were torn aside. The rose-coloured glasses were smashed. She saw him as he was—and it wasn't a pretty sight. She knew without further doubt how right Aunt Tiny had been—and what a terrible mistake she would have made if she had married Philippe.

'Please don't start cursing Nadine or anybody but yourself,' she said. 'Your behaviour has been the absolute *end*. I don't know how you could have done any of the things you—you've done to me.'

'What have I done? What else?' he shouted, throwing the letter and the ring on to the desk with a clatter. He was beside himself with fury, with almost murderous rage towards Nadine de Sachelles. He was aware now that he must, indeed, have dropped that letter in the flat on that day Nadine had cooked lunch for him. She had found it, and made good use of it, too.

'You've no proof——' he almost snarled the words at Celia, 'and I think it's outrageous of you to treat me like this.'

'You're a fine one to use the word "outrageous" to anyone else!' she said indignantly.

'Anyhow, what is there in this letter to upset you?'

'You took it out of my father's desk.'

'That's a lie. Geoffrey More gave it to me.'

'*That* is a lie,' Celia parried.

'So *he's* been at you too! He wanted to marry you himself, so he's done his best to put you against me.'

Celia flushed and then gave him a look of utter scorn.

'How typical of you to make such a remark.'

'Do you deny that he's in love with you.'

'I refuse absolutely to discuss Geoffrey with you at this stage of our affairs.'

'The next thing you'll be telling me is that *you* want to marry *him*!' said Philippe, beside himself with anger. He felt crushed by a positive load of anxious thoughts. If he didn't pull off this marriage with Nat's daughter it was going to mean ruin for him. He couldn't possibly pay his debts just on the money he received as a director of the firm—certainly not with that damned fellow, More, and his accountants watching the profits.

Celia said:

'I think you're the most despicable person I've ever met. I only wonder why I ever thought I loved you. I must have been out of my mind.'

Then Philippe collapsed. As Celia feared, he resorted now to appealing to her as a former lover. He literally grovelled, on his knees, begging for her tolerance and understanding. He was in the grip of complete hysteria. He bathed her hand in tears and kisses. She could hardly hear what he babbled except that he was trying to pretend that he had not seen this letter until quite recently, and that he had *not* asked her to marry him, as Nadine said, for her money. Neither had he known who she really was when he proposed to her. He loved her. He adored her. He couldn't bear it if she sent him away.

Celia stood still feeling ill, and quite unnerved. She had never thought it possible that a man (who called himself a man), could behave like this. It was too frightful. And the awful thing was that the more Philippe pleaded the colder she became and the more determined to abide by her decision never to see him again. Finally Philippe stood up, wiped his eyes with a silk handkerchief then looked down at her with a tortured expression.

'Oh, God, *God*, don't send me away! I do truly love you, Celia. Whatever I've done in the past, I love you now and I want you to forgive me.'

'Okay. I'll forgive you. It just doesn't matter any more. But I'm not going to marry you. Please Philippe, let me go now. I can't stand much more of this.'

'You really mean it, Celia.'

'Yes, I'm afraid so.'

'You believe all these awful things against me?'

'Yes, I'm afraid so,' she repeated, red with embarrassment and her own private misery.

Philippe Clermont knew when he was beaten. He surrendered. He put his face in his hands.

'I wish I'd never been born,' he whispered.

Celia chewed at her lips, and almost wished that *she* had never been born, then, because she was at heart a very kind person, said:

'I'm terribly sorry, Philippe. But I thank you for the . . . the lovely times we did have together. Just let's try not to poison the memory of them all by this horribleness.'

The childish appeal scarcely moved him. He was too embittered. He had lost more than she imagined. He muttered:

'I'm sure your father would have been sorry. He liked me.'

Celia winced. She would have liked to have said at that moment: '*He didn't really know you* . . .' but she resisted the temptation. Then after a moment, she said: 'It will be best if we don't meet any more.'

He lifted a haggard face to her.

'But what about the business—*Frayne et Cie*—we're so

closely associated. We can't just split over our personal grievances.'

Celia was ready for this. She and Aunt Tiny had talked things over and decided what she must do.

'I shall be leaving France—and selling Villa Psyche,' she said. 'I don't feel I want to live here any more. I've known a lot of joy here and a lot of pain, too. I think it's best that I sell up and go back to England. You and I won't have to meet. My . . . my lawyers and the various other directors who were Daddy's friends, can negotiate the business side with you, Philippe.'

Even in that moment when he knew that he had lost her, Philippe Clermont's mind swivelled to his debts and various other commitments. With a quick sulky look at her, he said:

'No doubt you won't want me in the firm any more. Maybe *Frayne et Cie* would like to buy me out.'

And he would ask a jolly good price for his shares, too, he thought. He'd make Celia pay for dishing him like this.

'That might be best but it will all have to be talked over,' agreed Celia.

Now he could see that there was not the remotest chance of wooing or winning her back, Philippe's worst side reasserted itself. He looked at her with a sneer.

'So you intend to sell up and go back to London. No doubt your excellent secretary, Mr. More, will go with you.'

Celia went dead-white. It was not so much the implication behind Philippe's sneer as the fact that he could put it into such words that upset her. After all, he had been her first love —this handsome attractive young Frenchman who at his best had had all the graces, all that any man could give of gay companionship and loving. It was a terrible come-down; such a grim toppling of her ideals, such utter destruction of her faith. She had hoped to part from him in friendship. In this hour she despised him. As for Geoffrey—nicest, most gentle, most decent of men—she wasn't going to answer Philippe's gibes about him. But if anything, Philippe planted an idea in her head. The idea that she might, indeed, ask Geoffrey to go with her and Aunt Tiny back to England until such times as he felt that his job—the job he had always carried out so faithfully, despite Philippe's persistent unpleasantness—came to an end.

Philippe, already regretting what he had said, was preparing to cringe again, but the look in Celia's grey scornful eyes defeated him. She walked past him and out of the study, closing the door behind her.

He stood absolutely still for a moment, doubling and un-doubling his fists, trembling with nerves and anger. He could hardly believe that Celia had given him back his ring. He could hardly believe that he would never now hold that place which he had played for, as Celia Frayne's husband and business manager. *Nom de Dieu*, what a gigantic fool he'd made of him-self!

Then he thought of Nadine de Sachelles. His face went red with fury, his eyes gleamed. He picked up the telephone and got through to her apartment. But it was not Nadine who an-swered the telephone; it was her maid.

'*Madame la Comtesse* is out, *Monsieur* Clermont,' said the girl who knew him well.

'Where is she to be found, Marianne?' asked Philippe in his silkiest voice.

'I do not know, *Monsieur*.'

'What do you mean, you do not know?'

'*Madame* has left Monte Carlo.'

'Left Monte Carlo for where, *idiote*?' demanded Philippe, his temper rising again.

'I do not know. But really, *Monsieur* Clermont, I do not know,' now came the tearful reply. '*Madame la Comtesse* left no forwarding address. She said I was to tell anybody who rang that she was going to let this apartment, with me in it, for the next six months or even longer.'

Philippe had never felt more thwarted. Not to be able to get his own back on Nadine, riled him beyond words. He tried to wheedle, then to bribe Nadine's address out of Marianne. But it seemed that the girl really did not know where her mistress had gone. But, she said, she had heard *Madame la Comtesse* mention to a friend that it might be a very long way away, perhaps even to America. She had always intended to visit some distant cousins of hers in the States.

With an oath, Philippe put down the receiver. He looked around the study, tugging at his collar. The sweat was pouring down his neck. He felt hot, although the evening was cool. It was goodbye to all this—to Villa Psyche—to everything that had really meant quite a lot to Philippe—as well as a final farewell to Celia. Now that he had lost her she had begun to seem the most desirable woman in the world. How he could have played his cards so abominably, he could not think.

He glanced at the painting of Nat over the fireplace. Graham Sutherland had caught that cynical half-amused grin that had so often played about Nat Frayne's lips. It looked alive. And Philippe, staring at it, was filled with fresh regrets. Nat had died believing in him, fond of him. Poor little Marie-Thérèse, his cousin, had adored him. Through her he had come into the firm. But they were dead, and everything had gone wrong and the living despised him. He had no one to blame but himself. In this moment, he remembered Celia's young enchanting face and slender grace, and groaned. She had loved him so much; so trustingly at first. There had been nobody else but him. *Bon Dieu, how he had blundered!*

Philippe wiped his face and neck again, then automatically reached for the box of cigars on the desk, took a couple, stuck them in his pocket, lit a third, then walked out of the study and out of Villa Psyche for the last time.

For Celia the rest of that evening was the unhappiest phase of her life. She had kept up an appearance of cool dignity during the scene with Philippe but once she was alone with Miss Cotland, she broke down.

'I've sent him away—it's all over—oh, Aunt Tiny, it's all over!' she kept sobbing.

Miss Cotland cradled the girl in her arms, smoothing the beautiful red-brown head, hurt because her darling was hurt, yet unable to avoid feeling an utter relief over the broken engagement.

With her usual discretion and wisdom, she said little. But she assured Celia that she had done the right thing.

'He was an attractive devil but a bit of a villain. Your father entirely misjudged his character, my dear. But that was like poor Nat—he used to take violent fancies—then find himself being let down. Oh, I'm so glad, lovey, that you found this all out in time.'

There was nothing left for Celia to say. She was sick to the bottom of her soul, but because it wasn't very pleasant for any girl to discover just before sending out the invitations to her wedding that the man she had adored and trusted was no good.

Finally Celia dried her tears and faced her aunt, nose shiny, eyes bunged up with weeping. She made an announcement.

'Everything's over here as well. I shall get Geoffrey to put Villa Psyche up for sale. I want to give most of the staff immediate notice and just leave Annette and Jean, whom I can trust, as caretakers, and a gardener, and I want you to take me straight home to England, Aunt Tiny.'

'Darling, don't do anything in a hurry. You've had a nasty shock. You want to get over it before you act hastily in any way.'

But Celia looked round her beautiful bedroom and shuddered. All the valuable trimmings—the gorgeous pictures and flowers—that wardrobe packed with expensive clothes and furs—none of it seemed any longer worth-while. She had become a 'glamour-girl' at first to please her father, then Philippe, and now both of them were gone. Nadine de Sachelles had gone, too. Celia would not, she thought, be stupid and pretend she wanted to go back to being the gauche, badly-turned-out young thing who had first come out to Monte Carlo. She had learned lessons she would never forget. But somehow she felt she wanted to put Villa Psyche and the whole environment right behind her now.

'Don't try and persaude me to stay on here. I *want* to go home,' she said.

'But, my dear—you'll never settle down in our flat again——' began Aunt Tiny.

'I don't intend to. My father left me a fortune and I shall spend it, but in the way I want—not as Philippe would have wanted—which was recklessly—leading a life without meaning. Nor even by running father's business. I want to get rid of that too.'

Aunt Tiny's long kindly face puckered a little. Her eyes blinked behind the horn-rims. My goodness, she thought, this child has grown up and no mistake.

'Oh, well, my dear,' she said mildly, 'you must do as you think best. You're the boss.'

Celia began to cry again quite heartbrokenly. She didn't really want to be the boss, she wept, she hated taking authority. She hated the whole turn events had taken. She had loved Philippe. In the old happy days at first when she had believed in him and his love for her everything had seemed so wonderful.

'Your life will seem wonderful again, my darling,' Miss Cotland tried to comfort her.

Then Miss Cotland brought up Geoffrey's name. She felt sure, she said, that dear Geoffrey would see them through the next few muddled weeks. Celia couldn't do better than leave everything in his hands.

At this point, Celia stopped crying and drew in her breath, remembering how outrageous Philippe had been about Geoffrey. She could hear his voice, sneering:

'*So you intend to sell up and go back to London. No doubt your excellent secretary, Mr. More, will go with you.*'

Celia threw her head back defiantly, dabbing at the corners of her tear-filled eyes.

'At least one can believe in a man like Geoffrey and feel he won't let one down. I shall put him in charge of everything. He can deal with it all for me over here and then he can join us in England and see to the sale of the London branch, and while he's doing that he can live with us.'

Miss Cotland knew that it was very wrong and much too previous but she felt her old heart give a positive leap of delight.

'Well, that's not a bad idea,' she said with as much nonchalance as possible, then added with a twinkle: 'But I can't see us all getting into the flat in Battersea, lovey.'

'No, of course we couldn't. I've got other plans. What I hope is that you'll agree to sell the lease of the flat, Aunt Tiny, and make your home with me. I shall buy a lovely house. I've got the money so why not? I want to live in the country—not too far from London but where I can have a beautiful garden.'

'Well, that sounds very nice, lovey, but I wouldn't want you to think you've got to be burdened with me all the rest of your days.'

'*Burdened!*' repeated Celia indignantly. 'That's the last thing. If you hadn't come out to stay with me, and I hadn't had your help and advice I might have rushed into a mad marriage with Philippe *weeks* ago.'

The door opened. Gigi trotted in. Celia went down on one knee. The little dog bounded on to her lap and tried to lick her cheeks. She was always frenzied with delight at seeing Celia again, after the shortest parting. Fondly Celia regarded the pet. Gigi was comic, with one black ear and one brown, and short, curly, multi-coloured coat. One could only guess at her ancestry. It was very mixed indeed. But she had the most beautiful golden eyes and she had turned into an obedient and engaging companion.

'You'd like a big English garden and fields, wouldn't you, Gigi,' murmured Celia.

The practical Aunt Tiny pulled at one ear and added:

'Plus six months in quarantine.'

'Oh dear, she'll hate that!'

'Never mind, lovey, she's used to being down in Geoffrey's kennels—and they say all the dogs are well treated in the quarantine place. They get used to it—like children at boarding school.'

Gigi jumped into her basket to play with a rubber bone that had been bought for her that morning and which she chewed with apparent relish.

Celia walked over to her dressing table and idly fingered a gold and enamel-backed hairbrush which had her initials on it. Then she dropped it as though it were a hot coal. Philippe had given her that beautiful set—brought it back from Paris one day.

'*For my one and only love,*' he had said in his caressing voice.

She ground her teeth. *One and only*, indeed. One among many!

Oh, what a devil! (as Aunt Tiny had said). How she hated his memory now. How she wished she had never let him touch or kiss her. And how utterly, *utterly* thankful she was that she had never surrendered all that he had so repeatedly asked for. Celia threw the brush down on the table with a clatter.

'I'm going to pack up every present Philippe has ever given me and send them back to him.'

'Jolly good,' muttered Aunt Tiny. 'I'll pack them up for you myself and include a pound of sharp nails.'

Celia gave the faintest laugh—the first for a very long time.

'Oh, Aunt Tiny, you are marvellous—I don't know what I'd do without you.' Then she added: 'Where *is* Geoffrey?'

'He went home after that talk you had with him and I haven't seen him since. I'm a bit surprised. As a matter of fact I expected him back this evening. I asked him to dine with us.'

In Celia there stirred the sudden need to see Geoffrey. He was so absolutely reliable and strong and *clean*, and somehow all that she had lately learned about Philippe Clermont had made her feel anti all men. All men save Geoffrey! she decided.

'I think I'll ring him,' she continued, 'in case he's being tactful and thinks he oughtn't to come up tonight. I just refuse to sit down and go on crying. Why behave like a stupid heartbroken little fool, even if I *am* one? Maybe there's a film on that we can all go and see. Tomorrow you and I'll have to write and tell everybody about my broken engagement.'

'Not at all,' said Miss Cotland, 'we will just put advertisements in all the French and English newspapers.'

'There'll be an awful lot of other business to see to, won't there?' sighed Celia.

'You can leave most of it to Geoffrey.'

'I will,' said Celia and marched to the telephone.

It was *Madame* Pavette who answered that call. When she knew who it was who wanted *Monsieur* More, she broke into a slightly incoherent torrent of words. Celia, who had learned quite a lot of French during her engagement to Philippe, could make out fairly well what she was saying.

Disaster had threatened Geoffrey's Home for Dogs. It appeared that when he had got home at midday he had found all but one of his 'boarders' gravely ill. So ill that he had had to send for his friend, the young French veterinary surgeon, who diagnosed acute poisoning. After some investigations he and Geoffrey decided that some fiend must have crept in while *Madame* was out shopping, and thrown poisoned meat into the kennels—or it might even have been a neighbour who resented the dogs barking. Perhaps they would never know, but it was certainly the work of a maniac, *Madame* Pavette told Celia, tearfully. The poor dogs were *terribly* ill. *She* would never forgive herself because she had not gone out to look at them earlier. Only they had all been so quiet she thought they were happy. *Monsieur* was in a dreadful state, down there working with them, now—refusing to leave them. He wouldn't come in to lunch, or tea. He was quite distraught. And she could not help him. She did not mind animals but she could not *nurse* them. It would make her ill, too, she wailed.

'I shall come along at once!' said Celia, deeply distressed. 'Say nothing to *Monsieur*. I will just arrive.'

The surprised Miss Cotland now witnessed her niece tearing off her smart dress, rushing into black jeans and a thick jersey, explaining while she did so what she meant to do.

'Poor, *poor* Geoffrey—he won't be able to cope alone and it must be *awful* for him to see the dogs all suffering. I must help.'

'But, darling——'

'No, Aunt Tiny, don't try and stop me,' broke in Celia. 'I simply must help Geoffrey. He's been so good to me—to *us*. Think, if Gigi had still been there, and died. Don't wait dinner for me, Aunty. Ring for the car now, darling. And find me some old towels—I'll take down as many as Annette can give you. And bottles of disinfectant, and some brandy. We'll have to make a sort of hospital down there, I can see.'

'Bless you,' said Aunt Tiny and went off to do as she was bidden. Maybe this would divert her from her personal griefs and be far better for her than a cinema. There was nothing Celia liked more than acting the Good Samaritan.

It wasn't going to be a pleasant job but Celia would do it without blenching.

'And she'd have done it even if she had still been engaged to Philippe Clermont and if he'd kicked up about it,' thought Aunt Tiny. 'But oh, my goodness, I couldn't be more glad she isn't going to marry him now.'

## SIXTEEN

A GOOD four hours later, Celia and Geoffrey sat in the little *salon* up at Villa Psyche. They were drinking hot coffee and eating sandwiches Miss Cotland had just foraged for and made for them herself. The staff had gone. And now Aunt Tiny had gone up to bed, too, leaving the two young ones alone.

Celia looked exhausted—and felt it. Geoffrey was less physically tired but still very upset. All was well with the exception of one unhappy death of a small puppy which had been so undernourished when it first came that it had no chance of surviving the effects of the poison absorbed. But the other animals were alive and likely to remain so. When they had left the kennels just now they were sleeping under sedatives. Peace had been restored.

Geoffrey, with Celia's permission, now lit a pipe. He had been thankful for that late meal and for the fine cognac he swirled around the huge brandy goblet that Miss Cotland had given him. Over the rim of the glass he looked at Celia with the warmest gratitude in his eyes.

'I can never thank you enough for coming down,' he said, 'you did a grand job.'

'You and the vet did most—I was merely the kennel maid,' she laughed.

'The kennel maid very often has the toughest job,' said Geoffrey.

'I enjoyed being able to help,' she said, 'if one can use that word "*enjoy*". I never saw anything so pathetic as those poor creatures—all so ill, and writhing in pain. How some people can be so fiendish, I don't know.'

'One wonders,' said Geoffrey.

He had never been so angry in his life as when he had gone down to the kennels earlier today and seen what had happened. Of course he had informed the police, but even if they found the culprit, nothing could undo the misery that had been wrought.

Geoffrey looked with fresh admiration at the young girl who sat opposite him drinking her third cup of coffee. How utterly thankful he had been to see her when she turned up at the kennels, he thought. He had been feeling so heartsick, so anxious about the poor animals—it had been heaven to see Celia, ready to help him—to go straight into action—overall on, arms full of towelling, baskets full of bottles of disinfectant, and tins of special invalid food in case he needed them. She had thought of everything.

At first he had begged her to go home. It was pretty grim down there at the kennels, he told her—no sight for a woman. She had been quite cross with him.

'What sort of a person am I if I can't stand a few nasty sights and sounds, loving animals as I do?'

So he had let her stay and welcomed her assistance.

'Come on, then, Florence Nightingale,' he had said with a grim effort at humour, and led the way through the dark yard. They had been hampered at first by lack of light. And that was where Nathaniel Frayne's daughter had come to the rescue with both ideas and money. She had sent the chauffeur down to an electrical shop in the town. He knocked up the owners and bought practically all the biggest and best electric torches in the shop, bicycle lamps as well. Eventually Geoffrey and Celia had plenty of light to work by. The young vet had been a godsend, bringing all his medical knowledge and skill to their help. By the time they had finished with stomach pumps, enemas and injections, the wretched dogs had survived and improved. Fortunately, the poison they had been given was not as instantaneously lethal as was intended.

Now Geoffrey said:

'I'll never forget tonight and I do thank you from the bottom of my heart, Celia.'

'I'll never forget it either,' she said softly.

'It was hell until you turned up. Your arrival seemed to raise my morale and give me tremendous hope. I had felt quite despairing while I was at work alone with the dogs. The vet couldn't come at once and old Pavette was useless.'

'I think it's wonderful that we've only had one death,' said Celia.

Somehow he felt enormously stimulated by that word 'we'. It was so good to feel bracketed with her. He loved her so very much. Just like that . . . dusty, dishevelled, untidy hair falling about smudged cheeks, lines of fatigue under her eyes. She was kind and courageous and all the things he had ever thought a woman should be.

He said:

'I've been so busy with the frightful happenings down at

the kennels, I haven't had time to ask you about your own affairs.'

She changed colour and averted her gaze. It made her feel sick to remember Philippe. She had forgotten him while she worked with Geoffrey.

In a few short words she told Geoffrey now what had happened.

'I'm sorry,' he said in a low voice, removing the pipe from his mouth. 'I'm afraid it must all be very distressing for you.'

Celia gave an unhappy laugh.

'It would have been made much worse if I had found it all out after December 1st, wouldn't it?'

'That's true,' he nodded. And he thought:

'*God, what a break! What a mercy*—but the poor little thing must be wretched. She won't realise what a lucky escape she has had—just at first.'

Now suddenly to his dismay he saw two big tears trickling down Celia's tired face. She herself was conscious that those tears had only escaped because she was so utterly worn out tonight both in mind and body. It had been a dreadful day. Hastily she drew the back of her hand across her eyes.

'Sorry,' she muttered, 'don't take any notice.'

The man who loved her so devotedly sat still a moment, staring at the bowl of his pipe. It wrenched his heart to see those tears. Of course, he knew she had been infatuated with that damned Frenchman. It must be grim for her. Pretty humiliating, too. That was what irritated Geoffrey most. The fact that Clermont had repaid her sincere and absolute affection with complete lack of scruple or integrity.

Suddenly he got up. He put down the pipe, walked over to the forlorn young figure in the black jeans and grubby jersey and put an arm around her shoulders.

'It must be a helluva shock to you, Celia. And I repeat— I'm damned sorry—but I honestly feel that if the Chief—your father—knows about this (and I'm sure he does) he'll be thankful it is in time. He wouldn't want you to be miserable for the rest of your life.'

Somehow, after that, she never quite knew how, she found herself in Geoffrey's arms, and she was crying with her face pressed against his shoulder. He was smoothing the tumbled hair back from her forehead, saying all sorts of kind, comforting things. There was no passion in the embrace—they might have been brother and sister, or just old familiar friends. But she felt certain it was right that she should be like this with him. She could trust him absolutely. It was blissful to be able to cry, and be comforted—feel secure in a man's arms—really secure. He was the sort of person who would never do the things Philippe had done.

'Don't cry, you'll get over this, you know. It's all going to be all right,' Geoffrey kept saying.

'I'm sure it will. But it's been so *beastly*.'

'Of course it has. It's terrible to have one's faith and trust broken after you've given it.'

'Philippe *must* have seen that letter early on, and found out who I was before we became engaged—mustn't he, Geoffrey?'

'To be quite honest, I don't know for sure, but I'm ready to swear it is likely.'

'It's not very nice to know you were just wanted for your money,' said Celia in a low voice.

'Darling,' said Geoffrey (the endearment slipped out), 'I'm quite sure he grew to love you for yourself. You're so very sweet.'

She lifted a flushed, tear-wet face.

'He didn't love me at all. It couldn't be called *love*.'

'Try to forget about it,' said Geoffrey awkwardly.

'I expect I will—in time. And Geoffrey——' now she drew away from him feeling a trifle embarrassed, 'you will stay and look after my affairs, won't you. You will join us in England after I have found a house?'

'Well, it will want thinking over,' said Geoffrey cautiously.

'Oh, you must, you must,' she exclaimed. 'Aunt Tiny and I have agreed that we can't manage without you. I'm going to find a lovely country house. And I'm going to do something else. I'm going to build some really wonderful homes for lost and stray dogs and get you to organise it all and put in the right people to manage them.'

Now he smiled, delighted because Celia seemed to have some real motive for existence, weighed down though she was by her personal sorrows. He gave a little laugh.

'And what happens to my kennels in Monte Carlo?'

'Well, you know *Madame* Pavette says you can't keep on there much longer, because people complain. It isn't a suitable place. I'll buy some ground just outside the town and build another place with a French person to run it, and we'll call it the *Geoffrey More Home*.'

'Not at all. It will be the *Celia Frayne*.'

'Never mind what it's called—we'll organise lots of similar Homes all over the Continent,' she said eagerly. 'That's what I shall spend some of my money on. Oh, I do want to spend it on something worth-while.'

'You really are a darling, Celia,' he said impulsively.

Her eyes suddenly glowed. Her spirits lifted.

'And you will come to England and stay with Aunt Tiny and me, while you settle your affairs at the London *salon*? I really mean that I want to sell the whole organisation and if Philippe Clermont wants to stay on as a director in Cannes, I don't care. I shan't have anything more to do with him and neither need you.'

'That'll suit me,' said Geoffrey.

'Then you *will* come over to England—you promise?'

'I promise,' he said and held out both his hands.

She placed hers in them. She felt the warmth and strength of his fingers around hers—gripping them closely. She looked up into those very blue eyes and she felt as though she had nothing to worry about any more. Absolutely nothing. And the pale cynical ghost of Philippe Clermont slipped just a bit further into a recess in her mind; into the dark forest of forgetfulness.

# SEVENTEEN

FIFTEEN months later, in the large square hall of a big stone-built house near Rye, two women, a young and an old, were busy with Christmas decorations. Holly in the traditional manner, behind the pictures. Great baskets of yellow chrysanthemums tied with enormous cellophane ribbon on the plant stands in the corners. Mistletoe hanging from the centre light—the eight crystal candlesticks of a beautiful old Venetian chandelier.

Outside, it had begun to snow. Just a few gentle flakes drifting down from the wind-torn sky. A northern wind which would bring more snow in its wake. But inside Grebe Place it was warm. Central heating and the enormous log fire burning in a fireplace that could boast of a carved stone mantelpiece that dated back to the Tudors, kept out the cold. Two tall windows, draped by mulberry-coloured velvet curtains overlooked a scene that would have delighted any artist's heart. Grebe Place stood on the crest of a hill, and one could see from the windows across the sweeping lawns and clipped hedges and orchard, down, down to the coast where this morning the wind had whipped a stormy sea into grey waves tipped with white.

Celia and Aunt Tiny were preparing for Christmas.

Tomorrow was December 24th. There was a big Christmas tree already decorated, in the drawing room, and Christmas fare piled in the larder. Upstairs, an Austrian maid who had been with Celia for the last six months was preparing three guest rooms. One for Joanna Page, one for the young engineer to whom she was now happily engaged. And the other—the guest room that Celia liked most, because it had a round turret with fascinating mullioned windows, and the best view of sea and windswept coast—was for the guest dearest to her heart. Geoffrey More.

She had not seen Geoffrey for three months.

Miss Cotland, perched on a ladder somewhat perilously, adjusting holly behind the portrait of Nathaniel Frayne which hung in the place of honour over the Tudor fireplace, looked from that famous painting down at the slim figure of Nat's daughter. Celia wore dark blue slacks and a white loose-knit jersey with a polo collar. She looked well and gay. Still with that touch of 'chic' which she had gained in Monte Carlo. But somehow to Aunt Tiny she was so much more the *old* Celia, a young girl with unclouded brows and faith and serenity renewed in her big grey eyes.

It had been a wonderful fifteen months so far as Aunt Tiny was concerned. She was thankful to feel that it had been equally good for Ceila. Of course the girl had suffered at first—struggled through many unhappy, trying days after her broken engagement. But now she was convinced that what had happened had been all for the best.

Celia kept glancing at the grandfather-clock which stood at one side of the big hall.

'Geoff should be here from the airport any moment,' she said.

Miss Cotland came down from her ladder and lit a cigarette, looking rather smug and satisfied.

'Yes, so he ought,' she said.

And she spoke casually but she didn't really feel casual about it. She was, she told herself, almost as excited as her niece at the prospect of seeing Geoffrey again; of knowing that he would be spending Christmas, and perhaps longer, at Grebe.

Heavens, how that young man had worked on behalf of Celia and the Frayne estate over these past fifteen months! Miss Cotland reflected. No one had worked harder. He and he alone, she always told Celia, was responsible for the smooth running of the whole concern; for the careful wisdom with which he had helped both Nat's lawyers and business managers to wind up Nat's big estate and dispose of the business.

Now it was all over. *Frayne et Cie* retained its famous name but had passed into other hands. Miss Frayne had come out of it very well.

Celia had never stopped being astonished by her own riches and the power that so much money could bring. But she had not let it go to her head, which delighted Aunt Tiny. In fact, the latter often thought that the girl didn't spend enough on herself. She was forever sending fat cheques to those whom she knew to be in need. And already (with Geoffrey in mind, of course) she had set the ball rolling for this chain of Homes for Destitute Dogs which she intended to build and finance wherever she could—starting with France, Spain and Italy. There were dog-lovers on the Continent who were only too happy to co-operate and only too glad for her financial assistance.

At this moment, Gigi, curly coat sopping wet, paws muddy, dashed out of the door that led through to the kitchen and sprang at Celia, leaving very definite marks on the clean blue slacks.

Celia laughed and pushed her pet away.

'Oh, Gigi, you little monster! Go out to Anny and be dried.'

Anny was the Austrian maid who, with her friend Truda, the cook, ran this big Tudor house most efficiently, with the help of two 'dailies'. The gardens, which were extensive, were looked after by two gardeners of different nationalities; one an Englishman and one a Polish refugee.

Anny came to rescue Gigi and Celia's mind slipped back to the day when she had first landed in England and had to leave her dog in quarantine. How agonised poor Gigi had been at first; and how many tears Celia had shed. Geoffrey had been with her on the day she left Gigi. Then he had travelled to England with her and Aunt Tiny because he had felt that they needed him. And how true it was, because they relied on him for everything.

The first few weeks back in the Battersea flat with Aunt Tiny had not been very happy for Celia. It had been too sudden a break from the glamour and luxury of Villa Psyche and the wonderful Mediterranean weather. And she would not have been human if she had not sometimes regretted all that she had left behind of love and loving. Even though Philippe's recent actions had spoiled the beauty such memories might have held for her.

But Geoffrey had been wonderful. And later, after he had disposed of his cherished Dogs' Home in Monte Carlo and left *Madame* Pavette for good and all, he had flown over to London whenever she needed him. It had been he who helped her find Grebe Place, then shipped over some of the finest antiques from her father's home—the loveliest pictures and ornaments—the most beautiful books.

She had wanted to keep some of the treasures that Nat had spent a lifetime in collecting. And she had told Geoffrey that she must find a home worthy to house them.

Grebe Place turned out to be just that house. It was one of the most beautiful examples of Tudor manor houses on the Sussex coast, and the fact that it stood in rather a cold windy spot did not deter Celia. She felt that she was likely to enjoy such a complete metamorphosis from the *Côte d'Azur*. Aunt Tiny had sworn that the harsh climate would kill her but she was still very much alive, and really preferred the place when it was finished to Nat's exotic villa. She never did like the Continent.

Grebe Place had come on the market just before last Christmas. Celia and her aunt moved into it in the spring of this year. Now they were thoroughly settled and, Celia thought, not for the first time, this morning she was very happy. Happier than she had ever expected to be again after that affair with Philippe Clermont. She had incidentally heard only the other day from one of her father's employees in Cannes that after Clermont resigned his directorship in *Frayne et Cie* and sold out, he had gone to South America and nobody had heard of him since. He had, her informant had added, left a sea of debt behind him on the Riviera.

Celia did not care. She did not feel she minded one little bit now *what* happened to Philippe. Her brief tempestuous love affair and the engagement which had brought her so perilously near to disaster, seemed so far away—as though they had never happened.

Life had gone on . . . as Aunt Tiny had said it would . . . Celia had learned to be light-hearted again and to gather up a few new ideals and dreams as time went on. And she enjoyed immensely the ability that her fortune gave her to help those who needed money—really needed it. Like Mrs. Mumford with the big family. Celia had settled *them* in a bungalow near the sea and had the pleasure of seeing those six children playing on the beach at Rye, knowing that it was through her that they all looked so well and brown, and that the terrible strain had been lifted from their poor mother.

Celia had been able to help Jo's mother too, and it was at one of her parties at Grebe Place that Jo first met the young man she was going to marry.

It looked like being a good Christmas—one of the best of her life. This lovely old Manor house, full of her father's glorious things, lent itself well to the very meaning of Christmas.

And now Geoffrey was coming.

It was no longer only with a mild interest that Celia anticipated Geoffrey's visits. He had been down here many times this year, either on business or for a social week-end. Their friendship had ripened and their liking for each other increased with each meeting, of that she was sure. Nowadays she saw him in a new light. Not just as her father's one-time personal assistant, but as her own close friend. She had become very much aware of the fact that she had been all too blind when she first went to live at Villa Psyche. *Stupid*, she called it, ever to have let herself be hypnotised by Philippe's easy charm and handsome face. Aunt Tiny, as usual, had been right. *Geoffrey*, as a man, was so much more worthwhile.

She knew that he was in love with her. She had known that for a long time. What she had not been quite sure of was how she felt about him now. Her feelings were rather mixed at the moment. But she could be certain of one thing—he had grown to mean so much that when she had first invited him here for Christmas (by letter, to Paris, where he was still busy) and he had written back to say he couldn't be sure of getting away, she had been ridiculously upset.

'*He must come!*' she had said to Aunt Tiny.

She had arranged such a marvellous party for Christmas Day and Boxing Night—a private dance in Grebe Place. Everybody was coming—all the good friends she and Aunt Tiny had made in the neighbourhood. And among them, one or two young men—attractive in their way—who made a point of coming to see Celia quite often. After all she could offer a good hard court for tennis, a magnificent swimming pool, perfect food and wine; all in fact that a young woman of means had to offer. Quite obviously she was a 'catch' these days. One of the richest girls in England. As Jo had said to her: 'You could marry anyone!'

But Celia didn't want to 'marry anyone'. She didn't want to become involved in any meaningless love-affairs, either. She had no intention of repeating that mistake of fifteen months ago.

But she knew suddenly when she received Geoffrey's semi-refusal to join them for Christmas that she did want him . . . tremendously. So, in her direct uninhibited way, she sat down and wrote a long letter telling him that he'd just *got to come* or she'd 'never speak to him again'.

She had received a telegram the next day.

'*Couldn't stand not hearing you speak to me again. Will come. All my thanks.*

*Geoffrey.*'

It didn't take her a few moments after reading that wire to realise that it was more important to her than any of the impassionate and flowery love-letters she had ever received from Philippe Clermont during their engagement.

She was even more pleased when there arrived by air an enormous box of those beautiful carnations which she had always loved in Monte Carlo, with *'Merrie Christmas from Geoff'* on the card. Anny had unpacked the flowers and put them in the drawing room. Celia had taken the vase up to her own bedroom—that very special room which had a magnificent view of the sea.

The carnations were there on her dressing table now, bringing with their spicy fragrance a faint nostalgic memory of that other lovely bedroom in Villa Psyche which used to be filled with flowers. Yet it made her all the more sure that she was much happier here in her Sussex home.

She heard a yapping from Gigi, followed by the deeper bark of the two Alsatians which were kept out in the kennels and which she had taken in because they had both been under sentence of death—hopeless strays. They were now extremely happy and friendly to her—her watch-dogs for Grebe Place. Aunt Tiny was always warning Celia that if she didn't curb her love for animals she would soon be starting a Dogs' Home of her own—she was as bad as Geoffrey.

Celia flung down an armful of holly which she had just taken up and ran to the front door. A massive studded oak door with the gloss of the centuries on it, like the linen-fold panelling throughout all the halls and corridors. She knew that this must be Geoffrey. He stood there, bare-headed, with a powdering of snow on his ruffled hair, looking a trifle pale and nipped by the cold. The north wind was bitter. But his eyes were as Celia always remembered them—as blue as the sea on a summer's day—warm and smiling. He stretched out both hands to her.

'Celia—hullo!'

'Hullo, Geoff!' she said shyly, and placed her hands in his.

His heart beat remarkably fast at the sight of that beloved figure in the slacks and white jersey. She looked marvellous, he thought, cheeks so pink, grey eyes so bright. She had put on a little weight, which was good too, because she had been far too thin when she left France. He liked that short hair again. That upswept glamour-girl hair-do hadn't really suited her.

Every time he had seen her during the last year and three months he had found Celia more beautiful—more desirable. But he never allowed himself to lose his head over her for one single instant. He loved her with all his heart but that was as far as it could ever go, he told himself resolutely. She must always remain his late Chief's daughter—far removed from him, except as a friend—and employer.

Nevertheless their friendship had ripened and he would have been blind if he had not begun to feel that she relied on him absolutely these days, and liked him, too. As never before he had been certain of that fact, when he received her letter making it impossible for him to refuse her invitation to spend Christmas at Grebe.

Now, linking arms with her, he walked into the warm firelit hall and greeted Miss Cotland.

'Good to see you!'

'Very good to see you, Geoffrey. How's the South of France?'

'Oh, I'm not there any more, you know. Didn't Celia tell you? I left for Paris about a month ago. As soon as the Cannes *salon* changed ownership. I've had a lot to do lately with the Paris representative.'

'But isn't it all wound up yet?' asked Miss Cotland.

'Yes, absolutely. But I really didn't think we were going to get through before this year ended. That's why I wasn't sure I could get over to England for Christmas.'

Celia laughed. She stood in front of the fire with her hands in her pockets looking rather like a cheeky boy, he thought. She would never really grow up, never, thank God; or become self-important. (As important as the wealthy Miss Frayne had a right to be.)

'I bullied you into coming, didn't I, Geoff?' she asked.

'I didn't need much bullying,' he smiled back and pulled out the pipe which she must always associate with him. Geoffrey and his pipe were inseparable.

'I'll go and find Anny and get some drinks going,' said Miss Cotland.

'I hope you won't be bored,' said Celia, giving Geoffrey a very feminine look through her long lashes. 'My friend Joanna Page is arriving to stay with her fiancé John Cooke, and we're going to have a big party for lunch on Christmas Day and a dance on Boxing Night.'

'It sounds positively hilarious to me,' said Geoffrey, 'I'll have to polish up my dancing. I haven't set foot to floor since I danced with you—and that's a long, long time ago—in Monte Carlo.'

'Well, the Twist's out,' said Celia cheerfully, 'and there's a new dance in, I believe, so we'll both have to learn it.'

Geoffrey stuck the pipe between his teeth and grinned at her.

'You asked me if I'd be bored. That's a thing I'm never likely to be with you.'

'Thanks,' she said with a bow.

'You're just the same.'

'In what way?'

Now he flushed a bit self-consciously.

'Every way. Whenever I come here I always think you make such a marvellous home out of any place you're in. *This* seems like coming home to me.'

'That's the nicest thing you've ever said to me, Geoffrey.'

'Your father made me feel the same in his home,' said Geoffrey, looking up at the portrait of his old Chief.

'I'm glad,' she said, 'glad that I do the same.'

'You're really happy here, aren't you, Celia? You really like life in Rye?'

'I adore it,' she said.

'And you're still full of plans—for dogs, I mean?'

'Still full of them. My solicitors are busy making inquiries into the question of finance, tax and so-on should we build these places on the Continent.'

'I'm longing to hear all about it.'

'Yes, because you'll be in charge of proceedings, won't you?'

And then suddenly, to her astonishment, Geoffrey looked away from her and said in a low voice:

'I'm not altogether sure of that.'

'Oh, why not?' she exclaimed.

He stood silent. There was so much disappointment in her voice—and undisguisedly in her eyes—that it hurt him. He was bound to realise how she felt but he put it down to the fact that it was only because she wanted him to run her Homes. The truth never entered his head. He was conscious only of the one indisputable truth—that *he* loved *her* so much that he could not bear to go on seeing her. He would be bound to give himself away if he did, and that he must not do. *Never* would he risk letting her think he was a second Philippe—out for her money. It would be too awful.

She looked flushed and upset.

'But why have you changed your mind and decided not to organise those Homes with me?' she began.

But she had to stop, because Aunt Tiny returned with Anny and the sherry bottle, and a clean dry Gigi who leapt joyously into Geoffrey's arms.

'Bless the girl—she remembers me!' said Geoffrey, as he cradled the dog in his arms.

'Of *course* she does. Didn't you originally rescue her from death?' said Celia slowly. *Very* slowly. All her excitement and joy had vanished. She could not imagine why Geoffrey should have changed his mind so suddenly. She had an awful presentiment that he meant to walk out of her life. She was amazed by the pain that idea brought her. It drove all the colour from her cheeks.

Perhaps Miss Cotland sensed that something was wrong. She saw the expression on Celia's face, finished her sherry and made herself scarce again saying that she had to go and find some more evergreens.

Once more Celia and Geoffrey were alone. Both of them standing by the bright gleaming fire. Outside it was growing darker. Snow was beginning to fall heavily now. It was a lovely scene. Geoffrey mentioned this, but his enthusiasm brought no reaction from Celia. She asked:

'Why have you changed your mind about the dogs?'

'I don't know,' he said shifting uncomfortably from foot to foot. 'I just thought I'd do something else.'

'You mean you've lost interest in dogs?'

'You know that's not so. I never could.'

'But *you* know that if you don't organise it all with me I'll have to give up the whole plan.'

He refused to look at her. He felt very uncomfortable indeed and only too well aware of the thrill of her nearness, and the familiar odour of the perfume she used.

'Something's happened. You must tell me,' she persisted.

'Oh, well—we'll talk about it some other time——' he began.

But she was not to be diverted.

'Geoff, I'd be absolutely heartbroken if I had to give up our project.'

'Somebody else could run it for you.'

She was bitterly disappointed and made no bones about it, as she continued to argue with him. Finally she resorted to feminine weapons. She became illogical and emotional.

'You're fed up working for me, I suppose. You've found something better. I think it's horrid of you!'

He opened his mouth as though to deny this, then closed it again. He looked down at her angry young face and felt suddenly tortured. He loved her so much, and it would be so disastrous to tell her so.

'Oh, do let's stop this, Celia——' he muttered.

Her eyes widened. She put the back of her hand against her lips.

'Something *has* happened. I've done something to upset you. But what, *what?*'

His face went red, then white. He felt himself slipping perilously nearer the edge of that disaster which he wanted to avoid.

'Celia, please—try to understand——'

'I don't. I won't. You promised to open all the Continental Dogs' Homes with me. You wanted it terribly when we first left Monte Carlo. The project was as dear to your heart as it was to mine, if not dearer. You've *got* to explain why you've changed your mind.'

Because he felt his strength being sapped, he was suddenly brutal with her.

'If you've brought me to Grebe just to have a row, I wish I'd never come.'

She gasped and moved back as though he had hit her physically. His voice had been harsh and his face was stern. It was a hostile Geoffrey whom she had never seen before, and she felt sick with misery and astonishment.

He saw that look and at once he crumpled up. It was too much for him. He took hold of her with a grip that hurt, pulled her into his arms and kissed her on the mouth—like a man dying of thirst. He went on kissing her until she was breathless, then let her go.

'Oh, you little idiot, Celia,' he said despairingly. 'Can't you see that I'm madly in love with you and that I can't go on. I must stay away at least until I've got myself under better control than this.'

She gasped again. The pink had come back to her cheeks, the stars to her eyes. Those kisses had been so wonderful that she wondered how she could ever have imagined that what she felt for Philippe Clermont was love. This was the real thing—the wonderful, stupendous, real thing at last! And Geoffrey was the man with the power to draw as much passion and response from her as he gave.

188

As they stood staring into each other's eyes in that inarticulate rather wild way, she suddenly laughed. She laughed until the tears ran down her cheeks.

'Oh, Geoff, Geoff, *darling*, why didn't you tell me this before?'

'Because I had no right to and I've no right now. I am your father's one-time P.A., and still in your employ. How the devil do you think I can ask you to marry me?'

'Would you have asked me to marry you if I *hadn't* been Celia Frayne?'

'Of course I would,' he snapped, 'and you know it. You know that I love every hair on your head and have done since I first met you. And now I had better get my suitcase down and go straight back to the airport and catch the first plane out of this country.'

Her lips were still burning from his kisses. Her breath came and went unevenly. She said:

'Then you'll have to get two tickets for wherever you're going because I shall go with you.'

'Celia, don't make it harder for me than it already is. Our positions make it impossible. I cannot and will not marry an heiress.'

'Okay,' she said, 'then I'll give away every penny I've got, whether to Dogs' Homes or people I know. Or I'll just give it all to Aunt Tiny. But I'm not going to be told I can't marry the man I really love just because I've got more money than he has.'

'Celia—you really love *me*?' he asked incredulously.

She went close to him and put her arms around his neck.

'Yes, you darling old idiot—I do!'

His hands were on her slim, supple waist.

'I'm very much in love with you,' she went on, bluntly, clearly, eyes raised to his. 'I've been in love with you for a long time now and it's not a question of rebound so don't dare suggest it. I have had plenty of time to recover from Philippe and I've seen plenty of you. And lots of other men, too, who'd like to marry me,' she added mischievously.

'Oh, Celia,' said Geoffrey and put his cheek against her hair and shut his eyes.

'Well—are you going to the airport, and leaving me all alone for Christmas? Or are you going to stay and give me the nicest, most beautiful Christmas present in the world? Your promise to marry me just as I want to give you my promise

189

to marry *you*. Money or no money. Just you and I, for ever and always!'

He knew then that he could not argue any more, and that he was the happiest man in the world. He held her more tightly. He whispered:

'You do at least know I'll never let you down, my darling. I never will—until I die.'

'You jolly nearly did just now,' she said with a broken laugh.

'Darling, you've got to forgive that and try to understand my position.'

'I can't be bothered to remember about it. I only want you to kiss me again.'

And after that there was a long silence.

Gigi sat on her haunches and looked up at the man and the girl, both of whom she worshipped. And she decided that human beings were exceeding strange people—yes, quite incomprehensible.

A dog never knew what they were going to do next!

**THE END**

**DENISE ROBINS**

**SECOND BEST**

When Barry Elderton came back from Ceylon to marry Virginia Brame, it was to find her the wife of the wealthy Sir Ian Kingleigh. So Barry turned to Virginia's cousin Joan for consolation.

But Joan, loving Barry as much as he loved Virginia, knew that for him she could only be 'second best'.

'Few, if any, women writers can equal the remarkable popularity of Denise Robins'
*Daily Mirror*

'Rarely has any writer of our times delved so deeply into the secret places of a woman's heart'
*Taylor Caldwell*

**CORONET BOOKS**

## ALSO BY DENISE ROBINS
## IN CORONET BOOKS